ALIGHT

LEGACY OF FLAMES
BOOK ONE

EMMA L. ADAMS

PROLOGUE

The world ended on a cloudy Tuesday afternoon when Cori and I were haggling with a witch over the price of hair dye. If there'd been any precursors to the apocalypse whatsoever, neither of us noticed. We were too busy trying to convince Magic Avenue's stingiest merchant to sell us enough dye to compensate for the fact that my bright-red curls were poking at the roots.

"C'mon, Twill, don't be a dick," I said to the sour-faced merchant. "You know for a fact that this was half the price two months ago."

My sister and fellow dragon shifter, Coriander, propped her elbow up on the counter. "I remember, too. And the witch around the corner is offering it for a third less than that."

Twill scowled. "You got proof of that, runt?"

"*What* did you just call my sister?"

I might have got out my claws to make him back down fast, but that would be unwise. Sure, most people in Magic Avenue knew we weren't regular old shifters, but that didn't mean I needed to break the most basic rule of being one of us: *don't flaunt your power if you don't want to end up dead in an alley.*

Besides, there was someone else in the shop, too. A man I was pretty sure I'd never seen before, maybe early twenties like me, from what I could see of his face. Tousled chestnut hair, clean-shaven, and hovering near the door with his hands in his pockets in a way that should have struck me as casual but somehow didn't. The long coat he wore was an odd choice for a day as warm as this, but some of us were more cautious than others. Strangers showed up in Magic Avenue often enough, which was one reason Rhea didn't like us coming here, but she'd given up the argument when I'd pointed out that it was one of the few places in London we could mingle in the open and stretch our wings. Metaphorically, not literally… yet.

Twill ground his teeth, yanking my attention back to my sister. She wasn't amused at the term of endearment either.

"Yeah, I'll take an extra ten percent off for that comment, thanks. Oh, and I'd like a healing spell for free."

The merchant scoffed. "You have some cheek, runt. Why don't you and your sister piss off and go bother someone else?"

"Language," Cori said in a singsong voice, which caused him to unleash a further stream of expletives in response. I might have laughed—our ongoing joke was the result of a failed attempt to keep a swear jar in the kitchen, much to Rhea's exasperation—but honestly, who the hell talked to a fourteen-year-old like that?

"You gonna walk back that comment, or would you like us to give you a reason to need a healing spell for yourself?" I said. "It's hair dye, Twill, not the elixir of life. Be reasonable."

Twill's jaw set. "Pay full price or walk out with nothing. Final offer."

It was then that I noticed the stranger was walking towards us. As was habit, I tried to pin down his supernatural type. Shifters were typically taller, bulkier, and he was an inch or so taller than I was, if that. The coat he wore wasn't the fancy sort the mages favoured, and they never came here, besides. Neither did the necromancers. Witch, then, and not a bad-looking one either. My dragon side stirred with interest.

"Is there a problem here?" He fixed Twill with an unblinking stare that actually made the merchant back off a little. Normally I preferred to fight my own battles, but the stranger added a third to our number, and Twill apparently decided it wasn't worth pursuing the issue.

"A third off," he said, "and that's my final offer."

"Deal." Cori dug in her pocket for the cash while I surveyed the stranger out of the corner of my eye. He'd turned away, seemingly absorbed in the contents of the shelves.

"What're you looking for?" I peered over his shoulder and read the label. "Gargoyle scale rot?"

He swivelled to me, confirming that he'd been paying zero attention to what he'd been looking at. "Is that often a problem?"

"You'd be surprised." In a few words he'd confirmed he was no shifter, but I'd suspected as much already. Might be for the best. Most cat or wolf shifters were wary of us, as something primitive in their nature reacted to being too close to a larger predator. As for gargoyles, Rhea was one of few I'd met who wasn't a territorial nuisance.

Did he know what I was? Doubtful. At a glance, neither Cori nor I carried a trace of the reptilian beasts we'd one day be able to transform into whenever we wanted. Our auburn hair was more candle than furnace, and our eyes were grey. My claws would come out when I was angry or scared, but that was a rarity. I'd spent the last year in anticipation of my first shift, though Rhea had made it clear that we were supposed to stay hidden, not crave open spaces to spread our wings and rain terror down on unsuspecting humans. Okay, that last part's a joke. Modern dragons don't spread destruction and fire. We're too civilised for that.

Twill was still giving us the evil eye, so I beckoned to my sister to follow me. Cori slid the extra spell into her bag and shot me a wink, gauging the level of interest between myself and our would-be rescuer. She could be annoying sometimes, but I was happy to deal with her teenage antics if it meant getting to leave the house for something that wasn't my minimum-wage bar job. Even at twenty-one, Rhea still watched me almost as closely as she did Cori. I understood why, given how many people would happily hunt down a dragon to put their head on the wall as a trophy, but sometimes I wished I could just have a day to myself, a moment to breathe freely. This was the closest I got, so I let Cori overtake us and fell into step with the stranger as we approached the shop's exit.

"You didn't need to intervene," I said to him, "but thanks."

He opened the door to let Cori through first. "I don't much like people who bully young girls."

"I hope you meant my sister."

"Obviously." His gaze raked over me, and heat stirred inside me as my dragon side took notice. All shifters experienced that strange duality in which the animal took over our human mind when our primal instincts were engaged, and mine had latched onto this guy. Probably because it'd been a long while since I'd got any action. "You're here all day?"

"I could be." *Whoa there, dragon, settle down.* "Though I've gotta drop off my sister at home first."

"Like hell," Cori said. "I'll go torment Twill some more while you two 'talk.'" She made quote marks with her fingers.

Heat rushed to my cheeks. I didn't get too many chances for casual hook-ups, and this was a screaming example of why. "You certainly won't."

"Then I'll walk you both home," he said easily, falling into pace with us as we followed the winding street.

"No, we live too far." And I'd utterly lost control of the situation. "Tell you what, you go and buy whatever it is you were looking for at Twill's place while you wait for me."

"We won't tell anyone if it's something embarrassing," Cori said, ever the helpful wingman. Or woman. "Like a spell to cure genital warts."

Why, Cori? I suppressed a groan.

His lips twitched in apparent amusement. "No, but given how that guy was acting, maybe that's *his* problem."

"Don't make me think about Twill's balls, thanks," I muttered.

"Is that something you think about regularly?" said Cori, and I gave her a warning look.

"Ignore her," I said. "My sister is every stereotype you've heard about younger siblings. Do you have them yourself?"

"No… it's just me." He looked mildly discomfited for a moment, as if he hadn't intended to answer. Kept his cards close to his chest, this one. "I'll wait at Argyle's." He named the pub at Magic Avenue's entrance.

"You can finish talking about Twill's—ow," said Cori, as I poked her in the arm. "Hey! Rhea said not to go off alone with strangers."

"She told *you* that, not me." Though she had a point. I didn't know his name, nor what kind of supernatural he was, either. "We don't have to be strangers. I'm Ember. You?"

"Astor." Again, a moment of hesitation preceded his reply, as if chatting up someone in the street wasn't something he did on a regular basis. A good sign, if anything. "I'll wait."

"Won't miss it." I all but dragged Cori away before she

could embarrass me any further. "Seriously? Did you have to?"

"Yes." Cori grinned, skipping ahead to the boundary of Magic Avenue and the shimmering wards that separated us from the regular humans on the other side. "I'm going to treasure the mental image of the look on your face for the rest of my life."

"It'll be five minutes long, at this rate." I stepped through the wards first and emerged onto the busy London street near Charing Cross, experiencing the mild disorientation of walking straight into a throng of tourists with no clue that another world lay a few feet away.

I didn't notice the strange light in the sky until several people pointed upward or stopped in their tracks to stare up at a sky that now burned an angry red like the inside of a flame.

Next to me, Cori came to a bewildered halt. "Red sky at two in the afternoon... is that a thing now?"

The redness slipped away, leaving the sky the same slate-grey colour it had been before. I blinked a couple of times. "You saw that, too, right?"

I turned back to Magic Avenue in case the light had come from there, but I didn't see any unusual bright flashes or hear any signs that someone had screwed up a spell. The wards were as inscrutable as ever, and ordinary humans would only see a blank wall between a Thai restaurant and a shop selling souvenirs plastered with the Union Jack.

Right. We're going home. I nodded to Cori. "Better go, before we attract trouble."

"Trouble other than Twill's balls?"

"Oi." I nudged her in the side. "Seriously, though. Someone has a death wish. That light was too bright to be anything but magical."

And I didn't want to be in the vicinity of the person responsible if I could help it.

As we joined the heaving crowd heading out of Trafalgar Square, my gaze snagged on a black-clad figure weaving amid the ordinary tourists and shoppers. *Shit. A hunter.*

It was by no means unusual to see a member of the Orion League walking out in broad daylight, but not near Magic Avenue. Not here. A trickle of fear ran down the back of my neck, and my heart began to beat faster as two more hunters joined the first, making their way purposefully through the crowd of ordinary humans. Cori and I didn't stand out by any means, but their presence coupled with the strange red light set my nerves on edge.

Something's wrong. I took Cori's hand, as if we were little kids again, and she tugged herself free indignantly.

"Ember, for god's sake. I'm not five."

"The hunters don't assemble like that unless they have a target." I spoke in an undertone as we continued through the busy street, my heart jackhammering against my ribs. Maybe Rhea's paranoia was rubbing off on me, but it was hard-earned. The hunters were highly trained in one task: killing any supernatural who crossed their path. With a reputation matched only by their body count, the methods they used were effective enough that no supernatural, not even the mages, dared to challenge them openly.

"Yeah, whoever just caused that fireworks display." She waved a hand at the sky. "Not us."

True. Whatever fool had used that spell had painted a beacon on their heads that would draw every hunter for a mile around.

"Poor fuckers," I murmured.

"Language."

I didn't manage a smile. I'd only ever seen hunters alone

or in pairs, and never this close. Certainly, I'd never had cause to find out if the rumours that they carried guns loaded with bullets that could kill even a dragon shifter in a single shot were true. Rhea said so, and I generally believed her, but her warnings could be a tad overblown sometimes. So could her training methods. I still had bruises all over my arms from our sparring session that morning, but she'd prepared us both the best she could to fight against an enemy that no shifter had ever bested.

Cori and I had trained for nearly a decade, ever since we'd first arrived in London with nothing but a note leading us to Rhea's address. There hadn't been much else to go on, as whoever had sent us here had also wiped our memories clean. They hadn't said why, but we'd always assumed that it was a precaution, so that our enemies would never—no matter what level of torture they employed—be able to force us to lead them to our home.

The home of the dragon shifters.

I wasn't sure I believed such a place even existed. Since the best efforts of a dozen witches had been unable to break the spell clouding my early memories, I'd been forced to concede defeat and accept that I'd find out when I was ready. According to Rhea, that moment would come when I'd fully shifted into a dragon and not a minute sooner. She'd flat-out refused to let us even start searching for the other dragons until then, but a cynical voice in the back of my head told me she was just trying to placate us. That she didn't believe any other dragons existed either.

Some people would prefer it that way, I thought as I watched the last black-clad figure disappear around a corner. Nobody else gave them a second glance. The hunters were almost as accomplished at hiding themselves as the supernaturals they hunted. London, with its tall buildings, tangled streets, and communities old and new rubbing shoulders against one another, was the perfect cover. Hence our rule. Don't flaunt your power, and don't draw their attention. Simple.

Until that day.

As Cori and I emerged from the side street, reddish light split the sky in vibrant streaks, and ribbons of lightning arced over the rooftops in a mesmerising dance that made me momentarily forget that supernaturals weren't the only ones who could see it. For a heartbeat, Cori and I stared, suspended, as though if neither of us moved, time would rewind and everything would make sense again.

Then came the screaming. A chorus rose from the heart of the city, the sound of nightmares. The crowd began to panic in unison, a crush of bodies surrounding us on all sides.

"Shit." I seized Cori's wrist again, and this time she didn't shake me off as I dragged her through the tide of terrified humans. "All right—back to Magic Avenue."

I didn't know where else to go, and Magic Avenue was at least a known element. We'd find allies there. An explanation, maybe.

A familiar scent caught my nostrils, distinct amid the general stench of human panic. My heart lifted as I recognised Rhea, her broad-shouldered frame easily parting the crowd, her stern face set. She must have followed us here, and for once I didn't mind her overprotective nature. I also owed her for all the times she'd insisted upon Cori and me each carrying an emergency pack with enough supplies to last us a few days every time we left the house, because it meant we already had what we needed to make a run for it.

Problem: all our usual escape routes were via the Underground, and none of our escape strategies had accounted for a public display of magic that would have the whole city in a frenzy.

"What the hell is going on?" Cori asked Rhea. "What's with the light display? Has a mage or witch gone rogue?"

"No, but it's not the supernaturals we have to worry about," Rhea said. "The Orion League will believe this is a sign of their prophesied war."

"That was just their bullshit propaganda. It wasn't *real*." Cori gave me a pleading look as if she thought Rhea had a screw loose. "It's not true. Is it?"

"No way." I didn't believe any of the ridiculous stories the hunters spread about us, including the more outlandish claim that they were destined to come out on top in some kind of Ragnarök-style all-out battle against the best of our kind. I mean, the hunters had to find some reason to justify their attempts to exterminate us. But we hadn't caused this madness.

Someone did. A screeching cry drew my gaze upward, and my stomach lurched. The rainbow-bright streaks in the sky didn't look like ribbons any longer, but cracks splitting the world at the seams.

And out of the cracks came… monsters.

The cry rang out again, and a winged shape the size of a small car descended over the rooftops. Formed like a cross between a person and a twisted mockery of a bird, it had a coating of reddish-black feathers, batlike wings, and a beaked face like a crow or raven.

"The fuck is that?" Cori's hand gripped mine, nails digging in. "Ember, tell me you're seeing what I am."

"I wish I wasn't." A second winged shape joined the first, then another, until the air was thick with beating wings and cries that set my nerves afire.

It had a worse effect on the crowd. As we tried to shove our way forward, the fleeing humans went chillingly silent and stopped mid-run, their attention fixed on the descending monsters.

"What's wrong with them?" Cori reached out and shook the arm of a young human who stared at the sky with the rest. "Snap out of it!"

"Whatever magic those creatures are using, we must be immune," Rhea hissed. "We need to run."

My stomach twisted, seeing those poor humans frozen into statues as nightmares descended upon them, but those claws were sharp enough to tear one of us apart as surely as a regular human. Adrenaline surging, I pulled Cori after me through the inert crowd. The sky above continued to darken, both with the beating wings of the monsters' descent and with a peculiar fog that accompanied them, seeping downward until it seemed like the clouds were touching the rooftops.

The familiar *O* sign pointed me towards an Underground station, but the stairs had collapsed into rubble and a mass of humans tried to climb over one another to reach the surface. As they did so, tremors shook the pavement underneath our feet and cracks spread outward, wide enough to swallow a person whole.

A giant head emerged from within, shaking off shards of tarmac, followed by a pair of boulder-like fists. Shuddering quakes rattled my teeth as it pulled itself out, its body easily twice the size of a gargoyle's and stark naked to boot.

"Motherfucker," Cori squeaked. "That's a sight I didn't need to see."

"Cori." I tugged at her hand, felt her sag against me as if her legs were in danger of giving out beneath her. "Come on."

The giant looked blearily around, then its huge saucer-like eyes fixed on the dark haze of the sky. With a bellowing cry, it ran forward, cracks splitting the tarmac with every pounding step and its huge fists swinging at its sides. Each swing caught an unlucky human in its path, and the sickening crack of broken bones reached my sharp ears beneath the general clamour.

My gaze wrenched from the giant as Rhea grabbed my arm and dragged Cori and me down a side street. Then she pushed open a manhole cover and all but shoved me inside.

I fell, too startled to scream, but my feet hit the ground an instant later, and my sturdy shifter body easily absorbed the impact. When Cori came tumbling down, I caught her in my arms. Rhea descended to join us, landing softly and tugging the manhole cover back our heads.

"We can't stay in here long," she whispered. "Just enough to work out our next move."

"I thought," Cori gasped, clutching a stitch in her side, "you said to worry about the hunters. Not whatever *that* is."

"Giants are fae." And as far as I knew, none existed in this realm. Something had gone very, very wrong. "And I don't know what the hell those birds were."

"If the faeries have attacked this realm, it's worse than anything we planned for," Rhea said in a low voice.

"No shit." My mouth went dry. "We can't use any of our escape routes if we can't access the Underground, can we? We're screwed."

Above, the manhole lid trembled. My senses flared with a warning.

"I can get us to safety," Rhea said. "Ready?"

I nodded, my throat as dry as tarmac in a heatwave, my palms curled into damp fists around my knives. My claws pressed against my fingertips, ready to burst out if anything threatened my sister or my mentor.

"Ready," croaked Cori.

Rhea opened the lid, and we all leapt out into the alleyway. The grey haze had descended even lower in the short time since we'd ducked for cover, and within the fog, I made out human-like figures, faint and indistinct.

"Ghosts," whispered Rhea. "The dead are restless. Be careful."

"They can't harm the living, can they?" Cori let out a yell as a cold, solid hand swiped at us both, his icy fingers snagging at my coat.

I slapped his hand away, swearing. The man was undoubtedly dead, but he'd *touched* me, and the chill that swept up my arm was as cold as the grave.

"The faeries' arrival has even disturbed the dead," Rhea said grimly. "Climb on my back, both of you."

Both of us stared at her. "What?"

"This isn't the time for secrecy," said Rhea. "Faerie's attacking this realm. We're at war."

For once in my life, I did not think she was exaggerating. As Rhea shifted into her stone gargoyle form, she grew to seven feet tall, leathery wings sprouted from her shoulders and curved claws planted on the ground as she stooped down to let us climb onto her back. I helped Cori up first and then seated myself behind her. Rhea's feathered wings spread wide, launching into flight.

I'd never even flown in a plane before, but a sense of familiarity seized me when the buildings and roads dropped away and a sense of rightness settled over me that momentarily dispelled my terror.

Until Cori screamed. Above, the sky was thick with black horses, fearsome beasts whose riders were wreathed in shadow. Encircling them were countless giant black hounds that cast a dense shadow that blanketed the rooftops.

Okay, escaping via the sky is impossible, too. I hung on with one hand and gripped Cori's jacket with the other as Rhea dropped into a dive. My sister had buried her head in Rhea's feathers, whimpering in terror. I'd never heard that sound from her before, and it set my protective instincts ablaze.

We landed on the road, Rhea's clawed feet tearing at the

tarmac. She'd landed next to another Underground station with a collapsed roof. While everyone else gave the area a wide berth, we ran straight for the entrance. The glass doors had shattered, but we climbed through the ruin and continued past the broken-down cafes and shops.

Rhea shifted back into her human form and came to a halt. A group of figures waited near the entrance to the Underground. All wore black, their faces were masked, and each was armed with an identical gleaming black gun. Hunters.

Rhea and I both snatched Cori's arms and pulled her out of their line of sight, behind a collapsed roof beam. They hadn't seen us, but it'd been a close call. Did the hunters know the supernaturals were trying to escape through the tunnels? Why the hell were they fighting *us,* and not the monsters out in the streets?

The first bullet whistled past, striking another gargoyle shifter who'd tried to make a run for the ticket barriers square in the chest. The shifter crumpled in an instant, and the utter stillness that followed made Cori shrink against me, her body shaking with silent sobs.

I stared, numb. The rumours were true. A single bullet could bring down a shifter no matter where it struck, and if every one of them carried the same guns, we'd never make it into the tunnels. We had to turn back.

Another bullet pierced through a pile of debris nearby, and three wolf shifters ran out of hiding. My stomach lurched. Two of the wolves were far smaller than the other. Children.

"Stop!" Cori's cry was muffled when Rhea pressed a clawed hand over her mouth, and the third wolf—the mother —roared at the others to run.

Twin shots rang out, followed by a sickening thud as two small, furred bodies fell to the ground. A second roar echoed from the mother, cut off in a choked sound as she fell, too.

The hunters moved forward, fanning out as if they'd rehearsed the formation a thousand times. Locking onto their next opponent.

Us.

Rhea seized my shoulder, hissed in my ear. "Get Cori into the tunnel. Run."

Before her words sank in, she'd thrown herself out of hiding and launched into flight, shifting into her gargoyle form again. Her talons lashed out at the hunters, breaking their formation, ripping through flesh and bone.

One of them pointed a gun straight at Cori and me. I shoved her to the ground, throwing myself over her body. Protective rage exploded inside me; red scales spread from my elbows to my wrists, ending in curved claws sharp enough to rip out a hunter's throat.

I lifted my head in time to see Rhea fall, the echo of bullets resounding in the empty station, and her last word reverberating in my head: *run.*

"Bastards!" Cori screamed and lunged forward, but I grabbed the back of her jacket, my claws snagging in the fabric.

"No. We have to run—we're outnumbered."

Tears tracked down my face as I pulled Cori through the gap Rhea had created when she'd drawn the hunters away from the Underground entrance. She'd died to give us a fighting chance, but the thunder of footsteps on the tunnel floor told me that the hunters wouldn't easily give up the chase. When I reached the stairs down to the platforms, I lifted Cori in my arms and *leapt.* My legs absorbed the impact, and I placed Cori's feet on the ground and launched into a run. The hunters might be trained to fight us, but they weren't superhuman themselves.

We just had to make it to the hidden panel in the wall.

I rounded a corner, pushing down the scream building in my chest like a fireball intent on being unleashed. My breath burned my lungs. My legs screamed.

That was when a lone hunter appeared ahead of us. I skidded to a halt, snatching at the back of Cori's jacket. Too late. He'd seen us—and unlike his buddies upstairs, he wasn't wearing a mask over his face.

"You," I whispered. It was the guy from the market. Astor. He'd shed the long coat he'd been wearing, revealing a uniform that matched the rest.

"Me." His reply was emotionless, his hand reaching for the weapon at his waist.

Shock and revulsion froze me to the spot. *He's a hunter. He was hunting us all along.*

I moved in front of Cori as he lifted the gun. At least my death would win her a few seconds to escape.

Or not. The pounding footsteps in the tunnel halted, warning me that the other hunters had caught up. Trapped on both sides.

Time slowed. My ears picked up the snap of a bullet firing as the fireball building in my chest exploded. Wings burst into life behind my shoulder blades, and my body extended, scales rising to the surface of my skin as the bullet harmlessly skimmed beneath my wing.

A torrent of fire roared from my mouth, and the hunters fled in its wake. Flames licked at the walls, scorching hot, lapping at their heels. A second bullet snapped behind me, made me whip around to face the man who'd deceived me, but he'd vanished along with the rest.

Bastard. I screamed, a wordless howl of pure anger and grief, but the space was too tight to fly in pursuit. Damn if I didn't try. My wings spread from wall to wall, a stream of flame erupting from my lungs as if I breathed hard enough,

I'd catch any hunters who remained and reduce them to cinders.

A scream hit me like a slap. "Ember!"

Cori. She crouched behind my scaled legs, eyes wide with horror, ashes clinging to her face. Remnants of the hunters I'd killed.

My claws collapsed into human legs which gave way beneath me, and the fire inside me died to ashes.

1

"Ember!" Cori called out. "This is our place."

"You sure this isn't another false alarm?" I climbed over the garden wall to join her, and my feet sank into a giant claw-shaped footprint. "Shit. I see your point."

I gingerly climbed out of the print, which easily encompassed both my feet. If anyone still lived in the dilapidated house in front of us, I didn't see them through the curtained window, and I figured anyone would gladly let us onto their property to catch whichever creature had been roaming around the front garden. Deep gouges marked the already battered lawn, churning the rain-damp mud into prints that were as close to a dragon's as I'd ever seen.

I sniffed at the ground. "Can't catch the scent. Rain's washed it away."

"Hasn't washed away the prints, though." Cori leaned over to see, her bright hair a splash of colour against the grey dampness blanketing everything else. I hadn't wanted to bring my baby sister on the mission, but she still had the uncanny younger sibling talent of persuading me to let her tag along, and besides, there was a fair chance she'd have followed us anyway. She hated being stuck at home alone.

I held my hand up and imagined it shifting into a claw, mentally gauging the similarity to the claw-shaped print. I stopped short of an actual shift, though. We were too exposed, and dragons, even post-faerie apocalypse, were a rare sight.

That day, two years ago, I'd thought things couldn't get worse. The universe stamped out that notion pretty quickly. We were far from the only ones to end up destitute—the bar I'd worked at had gone up in smoke along with our home and most of our possessions—but supernaturals the world over had lost the secrecy we'd cherished for thousands of years, and shifters had been an easy target for the regular humans to point the finger of blame at. While the mages had claimed authority, we'd been forever associated with the monsters who'd wiped out half the city.

The one job they *did* need our help with? Dealing with said monsters. Hence why we'd ended up here in some unknown corner of London following an anonymous tip. Will, the source of that tip, perched on a rooftop, watching the sky. As a gargoyle shifter, he often took the role of look-out, and anyone who glanced up might mistake him for a statue. Stone grey, six feet tall, and equipped with wings and long claws that rivalled a dragon shifter's, he'd have struck an intimidating impression if not for the top hat perched on his head. Since most gargoyles looked near identical, we'd devised signals to recognise him from afar. Some of the other local gargoyles weren't friendly.

I spotted Becks's sleek wildcat form climbing over the wall before shifting into a woman in her mid-twenties. Her dark tanned skin suggested Middle Eastern heritage—like us, she was an orphaned shifter who didn't know much of her own background—but in human form, the only sign of her ability to transform into a cat was the slight ombre effect on her hair, which faded from dark brown on top to light brown at the roots. Shifting forms didn't mean losing our clothes, luckily. Don't ask me why. Unfortunately for Becks, she'd been in human form when she'd lost her glasses two years ago during the invasion and had never been able to replace them. She made up for her short-sightedness by punching twice as hard.

"Damn," she said. "That's not a fire imp."

"Unless they've grown a lot bigger than we're used to." I crouched, peering under the bushes. "It's got to be some kind of fae. No shifter gets that big."

Present company excepted. Becks and Will knew Cori and I were dragon shifters, but I'd got a lot choosier about sharing that information in the past couple of years. We'd bonded with Becks after we'd dug her out of the ruins of one of our old hideouts a day or two after the faeries had arrived, and Will had offered us shelter under his roof as a favour for helping drive a bunch of territorial gargoyles off the street. If anything, the invasion had proven that we stood a better chance of survival together than apart, and the four of us made a damn good team.

Becks flashed me a grin. "The bigger the monster, the bigger the payment."

"There's that." Will had clearly been thinking along those lines when he'd taken the job. "If it's a shapeshifter fae, it might've hidden with glamour. We'll need to lure it out into the open."

"Unless it smelled us coming and legged it," Cori added.

"If it had, it'd have left more prints." The placement of the claw marks suggested it'd trekked across the garden and then either hopped the fence or evaporated into thin air. I reached the fence and stood on tiptoe to peer into the rain-washed alley on the other side. "Must've climbed over."

"Would a monster of that size fit in here?" Becks sprang over the fence herself, landing in a catlike crouch in the alleyway. "I think someone might've been screwing with us."

"Will seemed certain." Even if this was a false alarm, there was always the chance it'd turn out to be a lone shifter who'd been seen by the wrong humans. Twice in the past month, I'd accidentally caught a shifter who'd been mistaken for one of the faeries, and my conscience had urged me to let them go, forfeiting a potential payment. We all held to our old rule: no betraying our own kind. Personally, I blamed the hunters' propaganda for perpetuating the shifters' bad reputation even among other supernaturals, some of whom thought shitting on us would win favour with the regular humans.

"He's always certain." Cori trod closer, doubt creasing her forehead. "If this is some kind of fae we haven't seen before…"

"We'll handle it."

My sister was a lot more careful than she'd been pre-invasion, and I'd be lying if I said it didn't break my heart a little. Once, she'd been afraid of nothing at all, but the trauma of losing her home and guardian had taken their toll, and the weeks we'd spent on the run had only further whittled away at her sense of security. The final straw had been a second unpleasant encounter with the hunters a couple of weeks after the invasion in which we'd narrowly escaped captivity.

On the plus side, those events had led us to form our team with Will and Becks, but that the Orion League had survived had been a shit cherry on the top of a sundae of crap, as Cori had charmingly put it. It hardly helped that the humans had decided to lump all shifters in with the invading fae and blamed us for the ongoing apocalypse. While the Mage Lords had swiftly seized authority and even the hunters weren't fool enough to mount a direct challenge, the mages were a tad preoccupied with rebuilding civilisation after the fae had torn it to shreds. Or hiding behind their money and prestige and leaving the rest of us to deal with the fallout.

I climbed over the fence myself and landed beside Becks in the alleyway, reaching for one of the knives at my waist. I didn't like fighting with weapons—my claws itched to come out—but I preferred to pretend to be human up until the last possible moment. While I didn't see any signs of giant beasts, I *did* see a metal lid a few feet away from us, positioned in such a way that any escaping monster might easily have climbed in.

"I think we found our hiding place." Becks trod closer to the lid, sniffing at the metal edge. "It smells familiar."

"In what way?" A faint sharpness tickled my nostrils, like smoke lingering after a fire, and a growl rumbled in my chest. My shifter instincts recognised the scent, but I couldn't put a name to it. "Let's see."

I lifted the lid, revealing a dark hole in the ground.

"What's that, a secret tunnel?" Cori's tone echoed my own curiosity. "Not one of ours?"

"Nah, we're too far from the Underground." We still used our trusty methods of getting around the city, but it had never been quite the same since the invasion, and my dragon's brain was hard-wired for open skies and vast spaces, not stifling air and darkness. If there was a frightened shifter stuck down there in the dark, we needed to get them out, but the dim light made it hard to tell if anyone was in the hole, friendly or otherwise.

But that smell… why was it so familiar to me?

Cori reached for the lid. "Smells nice, actually. Kinda like a bonfire."

"Doesn't smell like that to me," Becks commented. "More like… I dunno, some kind of herb."

"Which does it smell like to you, Ember?" Cori looked questioningly at me.

"A bonfire, I think." Deeply buried suspicions reared within me as my dragon's instincts stirred. Rationally, I knew the dragon wasn't a different person—just a more impulsive side to my own personality—but I so rarely tapped into those instincts that they felt almost alien to me. Most other shifters slipped between forms like changing outfits, but dragons were unusual enough to be a security risk even in normal circumstances. Or a fire hazard, at least.

Still, I could always trust when my dragon side told me we were in danger. As Cori crouched down at the edge, I thrust my arm into the way. "Wait. Becks, can you grab a rock or something?"

"Huh?" Becks looked at me in bafflement. "All right."

She reached and picked up a loose stone, tossing it to me. I extended a hand and dropped the stone into the hole. An echoing clatter ensued, followed almost immediately by a metallic *snap* as if a large door had slammed somewhere under the alley.

The door to a cage, its gleaming metal bars visible in the sunlight streaming from above the alleyway.

Cori gasped. "Damn. Good job we didn't climb in."

"That smell." Recognition flared. "Remember when Rhea showed us moonbeam leaves at the market that one time? They call it shifter catnip, because it changes scent depending on which kind of shifter we are."

Becks's eyes rounded. "It's bait."

"For us." Cori sprang to her feet, her hands curling into fists. "We're the targets. Not the monster."

If Cori had climbed in… I cut off the thought as white-hot anger coursed through me. I turned my back on the hole, and my first glimpse of a black-clad figure at the alley's entrance sent me scrambling back several steps.

"Cori," I whispered. "It's the hunters."

Panic flashed in her eyes as the same realisation hit both of us. If the hunters had set up the trap, how the hell had they known we were coming here?

Becks shifted into cat form, and the three of us backed down the alleyway on soft feet. If we stayed quiet, the hunters might think we'd fallen into the trap, but that would only last until they realised the cage was empty. Fire rumbled in my chest as my nerves flared with a deep-seated dread. The hunters couldn't possibly know that they'd cornered more than a regular group of wolf or cat shifters when they'd set the bait. I hadn't fully shifted since that awful day two years ago and Cori had never done so at all, but any hunter who brought back the head of a dragon would be showered with riches for the rest of their life.

I took one careful step after another, assessing the odds of escaping into the back garden. The fence was too high to see if there were more hunters hiding within, but there was a park at the alley's end, and while it might be crawling with fae, I'd take a nest of goblins over the Orion League.

A second group of hunters ran around the corner, blocking the route out of the alleyway.

2

As Cori and I skidded to a halt, Becks leapt onto the garden fence, drawing the eyes of the hunters at the alley's back end. Perhaps she'd hoped to lure them away from Cori, but while one of them moved into the garden to meet her on the other side, the other pair kept advancing towards us.

Will took flight with a gargoyle's ear-splitting screech, and the hunters halted their advance, enabling me to grab Cori and lift her bodily over the fence. As I climbed after her, there came the heart-stopping crack of a gun being fired.

Those fucking bullets. That the hunters had access to their most powerful weapons while the rest of the world had gone to shit was further proof that nobody was looking out for us at all, but I'd never heard of them setting up sophisticated traps like this.

Another bullet cracked over the rooftop and narrowly missed Will. The average gargoyle was a fearsome sight to behold—six feet or more tall with leathery wings, a curved beak and claws designed to tear at flesh—but the bullets the hunters used were as deadly to him as they were to a dragon.

I jumped over the fence behind Cori and sprinted across the garden. Becks had already vanished into the park that backed onto the rear, and I hoped the local faeries would see the hunters as a more appealing target than us. The trouble was, those bullets were just as effective on a gnome or troll as a shifter, and the fae were unpredictable on a good day.

As we neared the back fence, a gate swung open and two more hunters ran in. I didn't slow, positioning myself so that I covered Cori's back. Images of wings flashed through my head, and fire stirred inside my chest. I pushed it down. My dragon would only get to fight as a last resort.

With our escape route cut off, I made for the fence adjoining this garden to the one next door. Adrenaline coursed through my veins, and paranoid theories ricocheted around my head. How long had the hunters been following us? What if they'd figured out the route to our shelter?

We can't lead them home. We were too far from any heavily populated areas, which torched the idea of losing them in a crowd. The League was still gun-shy about creating a public spectacle somewhere that might be seen by the authorities, just in case the Mage Lords realised how much of a threat they presented, but this corner of London was practically off-grid. That was one reason we'd taken to using the nearby shelter as a base while on missions. If any monsters followed us home, at least they wouldn't get to our main hideout.

As Cori and I cut across the garden, the hunters closed in. I met them, slashing out with my knife. The blade wasn't as sharp as my claws, but blood sprayed out, and the female hunter I'd targeted lost her grip on the gun. I kicked it aside and then slammed my heel into the second, male hunter, aiming for the ankle. My heavy combat boot coupled with my shifter strength knocked him onto his back, and Cori moved in and kicked him, too. I shot her a warning look telling her to run, but she ignored me and delivered a wicked uppercut to the female hunter's chin that caused her to stagger back, still bleeding from the arm.

As a third hunter ran in to join them—this one also female—Becks reappeared in a tabby streak across the top of the fence. With a flying leap, she landed on the newcomer's head. The hunter swore and hit out, trying to dislodge her sharp claws. Seeing the second hunter trying to rise, I slammed my foot down on his face. His nose gave way beneath my heavy combat boot, but he didn't make a sound other than a faint grunt as he twisted to the side and tried to raise his gun hand.

I stomped on his wrist then pried the weapon loose. My hands were shaking too hard to pull the trigger, but I didn't need to apply much pressure to crush the gun into a useless lump of metal. Tossing it aside, I kicked its owner in the ribs. That had to hurt like hell, but he didn't make any more noise than his buddy had. Hunters were known to have a freakishly high pain tolerance. Rumour said that one of their initiation ceremonies involved walking on hot coals in the dark.

"What the hell is your problem?" I went for the female hunter who'd grabbed her gun again and struck her weapon hand with the end of my knife. When the gun slid free, Cori stamped on it.

With both hunters disarmed, we ran to help Becks. She'd made her own attacker drop her gun, and I disposed of the weapon with a well-placed kick.

"Shifter scum," she growled as I kicked again, this time aiming at her shins. She lost her balance and went down, Becks's claws still slashing at her face.

The two disarmed hunters ran at Cori and me. I ripped off a fence post that had been knocked askew and swung it, baseball-bat-style, at the nearest, who dropped like a stone.

Cori's scream brought my gaze to the second hunter. Unseen, he'd pulled a knife on her, and she'd blocked the slash with the side of her hand. The sight of my little sister's blood sent my dragon instincts into a frenzy. I yelled, tackling him to the ground, my sharp claws digging into his chest. He let out a gargled choking sound and went limp.

I whipped my claws free and heard a harsh shout. "Those claws! Look, she's—"

"Shut the fuck up." Cori, still bleeding from her leg, limped towards the hunter who'd called out from near the gate. Two more stood behind, and now they'd seen my claws, we couldn't leave any of them alive.

Becks leapt onto a hunter's head and dug her claws in until the gun slid to the ground. A bullet flew wide across the garden, warning me the newcomers were still armed, and I ran at the shooter first. Sweeping low to avoid another bullet, I brought my claw into his leg, pierced through to the bone. As the hunter fell, I kicked away his weapon, my heart racing. *How many are there?* I'd seen at least two at the front of the house, and if they'd brought backup, we were far outnumbered.

Another hunter fell to Becks's claws. We'd taken out the ones in the garden, but a glance through the open gate confirmed my fears. They'd filled the area at the back, blocking our route to the park.

Bloodlust rang through me, a primal instinct calling back to the generations of dragon shifters who'd fought daily to survive, but I couldn't run straight into the fray without getting hit—or worse, losing Cori.

Time to escape, then. I resumed my sprint towards the neighbouring garden and let Cori overtake me. As she climbed the fence, hands grabbed her from the other side. Hunters, at least five, crouched in the garden, seizing Cori's wrists and pulling her into their midst.

"Stop!" I roared, cleared the fence in a flying leap, and tackled one of the hunters to the ground. An instant later, a dazzling flash lit the air and billowing smoke filled the garden. I glimpsed Will flying over the rooftops, wings outlined against the cloudy sky and another flash-bang spell in his extended hand.

As he'd no doubt hoped, the hunters began shooting at Will instead of us, but the two who held Cori refused to relinquish their grip. Will couldn't aim at them without risking Cori being caught in the blast.

I tackled one of the hunters from behind, my claws piercing his gun hand and forcing him to drop the weapon. In a swift lunge, I grabbed the gun and turned it on the hunters holding Cori.

"Let her go!" My voice came out in a low growl more animal than human, but their guns were pointed at the back of Cori's head, and any move I made might spell her end. "Or I'll shoot you both."

"Those bullets won't kill us," one of the hunters said. "Unlike you."

Damn. My claws clenched hard enough to snap the weapon in two. I let the twisted pieces of metal slide out of my grip, my gaze fixed on Cori.

"Give up, shifter," the hunter said. "Or the little one dies."

Why hold her hostage at all? They didn't normally spare any shifter's life, and their hesitation made no sense unless they knew…

They knew she was like me. A dragon shifter, too young to have shifted yet.

I reached for the fire building deep within me, ready to be unleashed. The snap of a bullet drove me to the ground, arms over my head. A second explosion went off, and smoke flooded the garden in clouds. As the hunters' guns misfired, I ran into their midst, my claws tearing into flesh and bone.

"Cori!" I screamed.

"Ember!" Her hoarse response hit my ear from further

away than it should have. I ran that way, tripping headlong over a fallen hunter. Becks's cat form appeared amid the smoke, her claws tearing at another hunter's face, and I shoved the hunter off me and ran forward through the smoke Will's spell had conjured.

Sudden pain seared my thigh. I yelled, kicking at the hunter on the ground who'd leaned up and stuck a knife deep into my leg. Icy shock blurred my vision as blood fountained out of the wound, but I stomped on the hunter's head with my other foot and reached the fence bordering the park.

Cori. I tried to climb, but my leg was a dead weight, and I lost my grip twice before my hands found purchase. The impact of landing on the other side made my knees buckle and pain threaten to steal my consciousnesses, but I forced myself upright, to scan the untamed jungle that had once been a park. The hunters' scent remained, but they'd vanished amid the greenery.

And so had Cori.

My clawed hands curled into fists as a sob lodged in my chest. *Cori.* Had the hunters run through the park itself, risking an encounter with wild fae, or had they found another way out? This area was a rabbit's warren of streets, old houses juxtaposed with modern ones, and the Orion League knew the city better even than the taxi drivers did.

A growl from inside the thicket told me that the wild fae had smelled the blood. I swore, limping alongside the fence in search of the most likely escape route the hunters had used. Becks caught me up at the alleyway and shifted into a human again. Blood plastered her hair to her face, and stark horror filled her eyes. "They took Cori? Where?"

"I don't know."

A screech from the sky caused me to look up as Will descended in more of a fall than a glide, collapsing into human form nearby. Clumps of blond hair were matted to his forehead with blood, and more crimson streaks ran down his side.

"Will." I ran to him. "Are you okay? They didn't shoot you?" They couldn't have, or he'd be a goner.

"No, they didn't, but one of the bastards threw a dagger straight through my wing when I tried to fly after Cori."

A gasp caught in my throat. "Which way? Did you see?"

He pointed vaguely eastward where the road was bisected by another. "They went north of here, but that's all I saw before I fell."

I ran, pushing my bleeding leg to its limits. Fury seared my veins, masking the pain, while a single notion rose to the forefront of my mind. *Kill them.*

Fire seared my chest and scales crept higher up my arms as Cori's disappearance lifted the lid on the emotions that I normally kept caged. I hadn't dared fully shift into a dragon since that day two years ago, in case it brought the hunters back, but now it didn't matter.

They'd taken my sister. This was war.

I emerged from behind the row of houses and ran straight into a black-clad assassin, tackling him to the ground. My claws smacked off the tarmac, inches from his neck, and ripped his mask loose.

A pair of green eyes glared into mine.

Oh fuck, I thought. *Not him.*

Tousled chestnut hair, longer and more tangled than last time, framed his narrow face. Pure anger suffused his expression. We both moved at the same time; as my claws sliced at his face, he brought up his knee into my injured thigh. Pain exploded up my leg, and my own swipe missed. He dodged my second swing, rocking to the side to try to buck me off. Had I been a normal human, I'd have hit the ground, but I dug my claws into the tarmac, keeping him pinned down.

"You," he growled, an echo of the last word I'd spoken to him two years ago.

"Nice to see you, too," I said, and drove my claws at his throat.

He drove his knee into my injured leg again. My claw's momentum continued, blood spurting from his jaw, but I'd missed hitting anything vital. As my leg gave way, he rolled free and sprang to his feet.

"No you fucking don't." I grabbed his collar from behind, my claws digging into his jacket. "You owe me an explanation."

And my sister. I'd thought—hoped—he'd been killed in the invasion, so I didn't have to think about what I might do if we were to run into one another again.

"I don't owe you a thing." He twisted, fighting against my grip with more tenacity than I'd expect from a human. Shifters were supposed to be stronger, but blood soaked my jeans where I'd been stabbed, and spots danced at the corners of my vision. I gritted my teeth. If I lost consciousness now, he'd pull out his gun, and that would be it for me.

"Ember!" Will's shout was followed by Becks leaping over the fence at the hunter. When she landed on his head, his jacket slid free of my claws. The spots enclosing my vision merged into one dark blur.

"No!" I screamed. "Don't let him get away. He owes me."

At least, I think that's what I said. That was the point where I passed out, and blackness descended like a sweeping wing.

3

My mind replayed the day Cori and I had come to London. How we'd run through Euston Station at rush hour, my hand gripping Cori's hard to avoid losing her in the crowd. I remembered the hum of an escalator underneath our feet and the cool air of a huge industrial fan, five-year-old Cori running alongside me as I led her through the noisy confusion of the Underground. Reaching the ticket barrier, fumbling in my pocket, and finding two tickets I didn't remember being given. Nor did they say where we'd come from. Someone had ripped that information away, leaving only our destination: Camden, London. With them had been a note with Rhea's address.

Otherwise, our memories were wreathed in fog as dense as the cloudy London sky on the day of our arrival. Hundreds of trains reached Euston station every day, from all parts of the UK. We'd never found out where we came from. Not even in the notebook I'd found in the rucksack someone had placed on my back. Part of the book was written in a foreign script we'd never been able to figure out how to read, and the other was a warning.

That was how I'd learned—or relearned—that I was a dragon shifter and that the Orion League wanted us dead.

————

CONSCIOUSNESS RETURNED PIECE BY PIECE, calling me away from memories and into a realm of bruises and dizzying pain. My whole body ached, like I'd fallen from a ten-story drop. A fragrant smell filled my nostrils. Healing spell. Weren't they for emergencies only?

Oh god. Cori.

My eyes snapped open, a gasp on my lips. Thoughts slid through my mind in quick succession. The hunters. The fight. My sister—

They'd taken her alive. I had to get her back.

I sat up and gripped the bed in both hands as the world spun, my vision wavering again. The healing spell had taken care of the stab wound, but not the blood loss. Crimson plastered my jeans to my leg, but no pain seared my upper thigh when I gingerly pushed off the bed. The others must have brought me back to the shelter, and from the sunset painting the street outside in pink streaks, I'd been out for a few hours at least.

I grabbed some clean clothes and limped to the bathroom, stripping off my bloodstained T-shirt and jeans to assess the damage. Bruises purpled the skin across my chest and back, but the wound on my thigh had healed to a faint mark. Will must have used one of our stronger healing spells.

I showered quickly, going through the motions as I tried to figure out what the hell to do. The hunters operated all over the city, and they might have taken Cori anywhere. Capturing shifters alive was not their standard mode of operation, but there'd been one stark exception. Two weeks after the invasion, when Cori and I had first met Will, he'd been trapped in the middle of a standoff between the hunters and the local gargoyle clans as a result of the hunters kidnapping their children. I'd thought, initially, that there was no chance we'd find the kids alive, but I'd been wrong. The hunters had been rounding up shifter children to transport elsewhere, and…

I clenched my fists and squeezed my eyes shut, a few tears escaping and mingling with the water on my face. I drew in a shuddering breath, trying to pull myself together. My baby sister needed me. I'd bring her back and rain hell down on the hunters who'd taken her from me.

I tugged my clothes into place and left the bathroom, experiencing a fresh pang of despair when I saw Cori's bed was still unmade, covers tangled from where she'd tossed and turned last night before crawling into bed beside me like we were kids again. She'd had bad dreams every night since the invasion.

She'd be spending tonight in a cell. Or worse.

Quick breaths rushed from my chest. I braced my hands on my knees. *Calm, Ember. You can't do anything now.* Night would fall in a short while, and walking out after dark would make me a target for monsters that could give the League a run for their money. Besides, running after the hunters without a plan might end in worse than a knife in my leg.

They took her alive. They won't have killed her.

"Ember?" Becks called from outside the bedroom. "You awake?"

"Yeah." I pushed open the door and joined her on the narrow landing.

This shelter had once belonged to a friend of Rhea's, and since its original owner had never come back after the invasion, we'd claimed it as our north London base when we weren't staying at Will's house on Magic Avenue. Since we took jobs from all over the city and travel aboveground was hazardous on a good day, we used the tunnels to navigate between shelters depending on where we were needed.

"She's awake?" Will bounded upstairs to join us. As a human, he was tall, lanky, with floppy blond hair and a surprising lack of coordination compared to his gargoyle form. Seeing him wearing such a serious expression added a new gravity to the situation. "Damn, I thought you were a goner. I've never seen someone jump over a fence while bleeding from a major artery before."

A new wave of dizziness passed over me as if to prove his point. "Was I?"

"Yes, and you were out cold for at least three hours." Will peered at my face. "You're not a zombie, are you?"

"No." My thoughts moved sluggishly. "You... the hunters..."

"Ah." Becks fixed Will with an accusing stare. "He doesn't know how the League knew we were coming. Claims all his contacts are airtight."

"They're *witches*," Will said indignantly. "No self-respecting witch would give a League member the time of day."

I followed the others downstairs to the living room, my mind roiling. Thinking of a fellow supernatural turning traitor was hard to accept, but how had the hunters found us if not through our contacts? That trap they'd set up had been too sophisticated to be pure chance—and if someone had told tales on us, every single shifter we'd worked with might be a target by association.

Unless, of course, the person responsible was a hunter who'd already known my name.

I took in a breath, steadying myself. "Guys, I think it's my fault. That last hunter I fought... I met him before. He knew me."

"What?" Becks's eyes rounded. "Oh, is that why you asked us to bring him here?"

"Huh?" I looked quizzically at Will. "She doesn't mean you actually brought him here, does she?"

Becks and Will exchanged glances.

"Well, yeah," said Will. "Before you passed out, you said, 'Don't let him get away.' Right?"

"I did." I'd also said *he owes me.* "What did you do to him?"

"Tied him up and put him in the basement," Will said. "It was a massive nuisance, too, considering you were unconscious as well."

I gaped at him. "A hunter knows where our hideout is?"

"We stuck a blindfold on him. He didn't like that. Oh yeah, and we stole his phone and took his weapons away, don't worry." Will sounded absurdly pleased with himself.

Honestly. Will's penchant for adapting to any given situation had saved our lives more than once, but what in hell were we meant to do with an imprisoned member of the Orion League? Even if he hadn't seen our hideout from the outside, there was still the chance his companions might come back for him.

"Right. Next time I'm on the brink of losing consciousness, ignore everything I say."

Becks's forehead wrinkled. "I thought he might know what his League buddies are planning to do with Cori. That's why I figured you wanted to bring him in."

She was right. He *might* know what they'd done with Cori. Whatever history the pair of us had, I couldn't let a potential asset slip through our grasp, not with my sister's life at stake.

"The other hunters didn't follow us," added Becks. "They'd already cleared off when we took him. He must've been the last straggler."

"Yes, and you also said *he owes me*," Will recalled, frowning. "Which is kind of an odd thing to say about a hunter."

Ack. I'd never told them. Not only had I hoped Astor was long dead, but it was fucking *embarrassing* to admit I'd been duped by a pretty face and the gallant-white-knight bullshit he'd pulled with Twill. Just thinking of that day sent a fresh wave of anger coursing through my veins. My fists clenched, threatening to become claws.

"What on earth did he do to you?" Becks noticed my reaction. "Shit, was he the one who shot—"

"Rhea? No." I unclenched my hands and willed them to stop shaking. "He shot at *me,* though, back when I first shifted. Which means he's seen my dragon form."

A tense silence ensued for a few short moments as the implications sank in.

"Damn." Becks sucked in a breath. "Okay. If he can't help us, we'll kill him."

Will's expression was conflicted. While he generally objected to cold-blooded murder, claiming it made us no better than the scum who wanted us dead, this guy was a *hunter.* Not one of us. "I agree. If he knows your face and what you are, he'll sell us all to the highest bidder if he gets out of here."

"Yeah." Inexplicably, the idea of killing him there in the basement where he couldn't fight back repelled me, even though I'd have fought him to the death earlier if I hadn't lost consciousness. "Best see what our prisoner has to say first."

Becks nodded. "We tied his hands, but you know what those hunters are like. Be careful."

Careful. I should have taken that advice from the outset. Instead, I'd let him slip behind my defences then point a gun at my heart.

I took a deep breath. "All right. I'm going in."

4

I grabbed a knife before I climbed down the narrow stairway to the basement. It was a converted bunker from an earlier world war, one of the reasons this had been a prized shelter among shifters, and the space was wide enough to accommodate ten or more of us, at least in human form.

The hunter sat alone in the empty space, his back to the wall. Ropes bound his hands, and someone had pulled off his jacket, revealing dark tattoos circling his arms from wrist to shoulder. Otherwise, he looked just as I remembered. Lean, but not starved, like a lot of humans I saw these days. The low ceiling light glinted off my knife, reflected in his open eye. The other was swollen shut. Someone had worked him over while I'd been unconscious, or else he'd taken more hits in our fight than I'd thought. I didn't remember. I'd been caught in a frenzy of pain and rage.

His open eye watched me, but he didn't speak a word. Not even when the end of my blade touched his throat, drawing out a thin stream of blood. How easy it would be to plunge the knife in, to put an end to the matter for good. And yet.

"Get on with it." His voice scraped like tyres on gravel. A chill raced down my spine, a reminder that this man was a cold-blooded killer. My sister's kidnapper.

The only person within reach who might know what they'd done with her.

Dammit.

I lowered the knife. "Tell me what you did to Cori."

"I did nothing."

"Don't lie." I grabbed the scruff of his neck with my free hand and pulled his face up to a level with mine. "Didn't you have the sense to leave me the hell alone after I vaporised your buddies? Or is this supposed to be your revenge?"

It was the first time I'd acknowledged our history aloud in more than a year. I hadn't even discussed the subject with Cori except in the briefest of details. There was too much trauma tangled up in that whole day to revisit our trip to Magic Avenue before our world had fallen apart.

His open eye narrowed. "Whatever ideas you've got in your head about me, you're wrong."

"I seriously doubt it." I fought to get a grip on my scattered thoughts. Leaning closer to him, I bared my teeth. "Right now, the only reason you're alive is because of my little sister. Any funny business, any escape attempts, you're dead."

"Noted." He stared right back at me, not at all deterred by my closeness and the grip I had on his torn shirt. One heartbeat and my claws could easily skewer him on the spot. He must know that, and yet he might as well have been cast in stone for all the emotion he showed.

I'd seen all manner of horrors in the past two years, but I'd never met anything like this man. The hunters' unconventional induction methods were the subject of legend, but I had the horrible suspicion that I might inflict any torture on him and he'd never talk.

Though he'd sure been willing to talk that day at Magic Avenue. As the thought crossed my mind, the merest flicker of a smile tugged at his mouth, as if the same notion had occurred to him.

I released him with a shove.

He caught himself against the wall, and his smile widened. "If you wanted me dead, you'd have killed me before. Back in the Underground."

"I thought I did. *Hoped* I did." I had to regain control. Someone tied up and unarmed should not be able to rattle me that easily. "As it is, you're going to stay down here until you can tell me exactly where your people took Cori."

A shrewd expression crossed his face. One I didn't like at all. "I had nothing to do with your sister's kidnapping."

"Bullshit." Granted, I hadn't seen him arrive with the hunters who'd taken her, but there was no way I'd trust a word he said.

The trouble was, if he was content to stay silent indefinitely, we ran the risk that keeping him here for too long would draw his buddies right to our doorstep. I'd bet he knew that, if the way he was smirking was any indication. My hand clenched. His eyes—well, the one that was open— dared me to come closer and finish him off.

Screw it. Lifting the knife, I pressed the blade to his neck again.

"But I do know where they took her."

"What?" My knife hand wavered, and a thin line of blood ran down his neck where I'd broken the skin.

"I listened in on their conversation," he added. "The ones who took your sister."

I lowered my hand. "Really."

He's lying, I thought, but who knew, maybe he didn't have a death wish after all.

"Yes." His mouth tilted into another half-smile. "I have nothing to lose."

"Except your life."

The air tightened between us as he met my stare steadily. The dragon side of me might have admired him for it, had he been anyone else, anywhere else. His tongue darted out over his lips, red as the blood streaking his neck where I'd cut him. His voice was a low purr. "I'd like to think I can persuade you otherwise, little dragon."

I jerked back. "That's not my name."

"I know." A gleam of satisfaction entered his eyes, as if he got a kick out of rattling me. "It's Ember. Appropriate choice on your parents' part."

His words brought a further surge of anger. I didn't even *remember* my parents, and the League was entirely to blame. Sure, this guy wasn't old enough to have joined up before I'd come to London, but his fellow hunters had hunted my ancestors to extinction.

"Astor." I remembered *his* name. Unfortunately. "Now the friendly reunion part is over, tell me where the League took Cori."

"At a guess?" He shrugged one narrow shoulder. "One of their prisons. I don't know which, but I used to work as security at one of those very places."

"You'd better not be lying."

An amused look passed over his face. "I'd say it's in your interests to believe me. That is, if you want to see your scaly little sister again."

My hands gripped the knife hard. "Was it you who ratted us out? You told the others what we were and where to find us?"

A guarded expression entered his eyes. "No, I didn't tip anyone off. I didn't know where you lived."

"Huh." I didn't believe him. I couldn't afford to. But neither would I let him die without wringing as much information on Cori's whereabouts out of him as possible. If his claims turned out to be worthless, I'd enact the consequences on him with my bare hands. Or claws, as it were.

In the meantime? Whatever personal history I had with him, I might not get the chance to capture one of them alive again. "Then tell me where they're holding Cori and how to get in."

"You're asking for the impossible. I can tell you where to go, but after that, you're on your own."

That figured. "Why did they take her alive?" I had my suspicions, but I wanted to hear the truth from his own mouth.

In answer, he coughed, blood foaming his lips. My eyes tracked the tense way he held himself, and the blood seeping down his sleeve and soaking into his torn shirt.

"I was hit by three bullets," he said in explanation. "I'll be dead in a day if I don't cut them out. Unless you'd like to do the honours." He bared bloody teeth at me. Ugh.

"What, you were just going to sit here and die?" I sure as hell didn't trust him with a weapon, which meant my only option was to get the bullets out myself. If I wanted him to live.

I didn't. I did. Dammit.

I sucked air through my teeth. "If I get those bullets out of you and you attack me, I'll stick the knife somewhere you won't recover from."

He gave me another bloody smile, which I returned with a frosty glare. He held out his arm—the best he could with his hands tied—to show me where the bullet had pierced the flesh. It looked like at least one rumour about the hunters was true. There was more tattoo than skin, and an ugly red mess pointed to where the bullet had struck.

I held my breath, having to aim the knife by guesswork. If I'd been in his position, I'd have screamed when the point of the blade pierced the skin, but he merely looked down at the knife with a detached expression. A flicker of admiration stirred, which I squashed down. His reaction wasn't normal, wasn't human.

With the first bullet out, I searched for the others, my gaze skimming the tattoos visible through the tears in his shirt. Some supernaturals said the tattoos weren't ink, but the blood of murdered shifters. I didn't really believe it—the tattoos looked like ordinary black ink to me—but the sharp tally marks across his collarbone made my blood freeze. What did they mean—the number of shifters he'd murdered?

"Take your time, little dragon," he said lazily.

"I told you not to call me that, you creep." I found the two bullets embedded in his shoulder. It was a wonder he could lift his arm. "Why'd they shoot you?"

"I got in the way."

"Careless of you."

"I've been known to make unwise decisions."

"Major fucking understatement." The knife cut deeper than I'd planned, and his breath hissed out. Finally a reaction. I'd been starting to wonder if he was made of stone. "Were you playing me from the moment we met back in the Avenue? That was all a distraction because you knew your hunter buddies were outside waiting to come in and shoot us all dead?"

Little knowing, I assumed, that the faeries were about to blow the whole world sky-high and render our feud a mere footnote in the apocalyptic fallout of their attack.

He let out an indistinct noise that might have signalled

frustration. "That… look, just get the bullet out. I can't think straight."

"Good." My knife found the third bullet almost by accident, and when it fell to the floor, he sank to his knees.

In a blur, his hand locked around my wrist, grabbing for the knife's handle. He'd somehow freed himself from the rope. *Of course he did.*

I kicked him in the still-bleeding bullet wound in his arm. Another kick connected with his side, and his grip loosened enough for me to yank my hand free. I kicked him again to make sure he stayed down. The knife was slippery with blood, but if I'd got the bullets all out, he'd live. Unfortunately.

"What did I tell you about escape attempts?" I extended the knife in warning. "If you make me regret getting those bullets out of you, I'll redo the work myself. And I'll enjoy it."

And with that, I retreated upstairs, his coughing laugh following me from the room.

5

The blood loss caught up me when I reached the top of the stairs. I slumped against the wall, my head spinning almost as much as the thoughts inside.

"Whoa." Becks looked at my bloodstained hands and the knife in alarm. "You killed him?"

I shook my head. "He got shot earlier. Had to get the bullets out or he'd have died without telling me where Cori is."

"And did he?" she pressed.

"Kind of." I should have asked for specifics, but I'd been too freaked out, and now I was in too much danger of passing out again to risk going back down into the basement. I gripped the wall, sucked in a breath. "He claims he used to work as security for one of the League's prisons."

"He's lying," she said immediately.

"Might be." I thought back to our last encounter with one of the League's prisons and suppressed a shudder. "He said he'd tell us where to go, so I'll go back for specifics later."

"Really." She pursed her lips. "He's a villain. He'd sell you misleading information just to save his own skin."

"Maybe he would, but his life's in our hands." I made my way towards the kitchen, from which the smell of baking drifted. "Is Will seriously baking cookies at a time like this?"

"You lost a shit-ton of blood," said Becks. "You need a blood sugar hit or you'll be no use to any of us."

"Right." What I needed was my *sister*. But she was right. I needed to regroup and then wrangle more information out of our prisoner when I had my head back together. "He undid the ropes around his wrists, by the way."

"I'll lock the door to the basement." She moved to do so while I entered the kitchen, angry with myself for letting someone who ought to have been utterly at my mercy get into my head.

Then again, the League made torture into a training exercise. For all I knew, asking a dragon out on a date before stabbing her in the back had been some kind of assignment. The hunters' twisted idea of a joke.

I might come to regret leaving him alive, let alone bargaining with him, but I'd only be doing him a favour by doubting myself now.

"There." Will deposited a plate on the table containing a pile of what looked like a cross between cookies and scones. "I might've substituted some of the ingredients with magical ones. Otherwise, dinner is three pies of dubious origin."

"Meaning you grabbed them from the market."

"The vendor insisted there's actual meat in there this time."

"I'm more worried about which animal it came from," I muttered, grabbing a cookie. Will was a damn good cook, but even he couldn't work miracles. The cookie tasted like sawdust and was as hard as a rock, but I probably needed the fuel, so I took two more. "And we never did get our payment for the mystery monster."

"I spent three hours on the phone trying to find who sold

us out." Will removed a second tray from the oven and tipped the pies onto a plate, too. "Nobody's talking. They all claimed ignorance."

"Nobody offered to help us get Cori back?"

"I didn't tell them they took her." He moved the plate to the table and sat down, his expression uncharacteristically dark. "Call me paranoid, but if someone ratted us out, we don't need them to find out their plan worked. I implied we were moving to a new shelter and starting over. They don't have this address anyway, but still."

"They might if someone comes after that guy." Becks picked up one of the pies, bit into it, and choked. "What is this, pigeon?"

"Seriously?" I groaned.

"You don't mind eating them when you're in the form of a cat," Will retorted. "And you, Ember, are a *dragon*. You're supposed to fly around terrorising the local bird population anyway, when you aren't raiding farmers' livestock."

"Where'd you get that one?" My dragon side reminded me that food was food, so I reluctantly grabbed one and took a bite. The post-collapse world wasn't exactly overflowing with culinary options, and we'd been close to starvation too many times in the past to be picky.

But my appetite wasn't there, despite the blood loss. I'd let my baby sister get kidnapped right in front of me. I'd failed in the most fundamental way possible. For a shifter, nothing mattered more than family, blood or chosen or both.

They took her alive. That knowledge was my sole anchor to sanity, but I was no closer to knowing precisely why they'd taken her—and where.

"He mentioned a prison, right?" Becks asked, bringing my attention back to the present. "We already know where one of their jails is."

"Didn't Will set it on fire?"

"Partly," Will acknowledged, "but that was a while ago, and they might've rebuilt. Also,

I didn't know they were in the habit of incarcerating us rather than shooting us dead."

"Neither did I, but remember they wanted those kids." When we'd run into the hunters' turf war with the gargoyles, we'd rescued a bunch of shifter children from the back of a truck they'd been using to transport them to what Cori had heard referred to as a *lab*. I could draw several conclusions from that, each more horrifying than the last.

Even post-faerie invasion, the League operated in secrecy, not strutting around publicly proclaiming themselves as the big bad dragon slayers. They worked in the shadows via a chain of command that even most hunters weren't privy to, and the sheer volume of outlandish rumours circling them made it near impossible for me to know whereabouts this recent group had come from, much less the location of the prison where they'd taken Cori. My plan to find out was entirely too reliant on taking our prisoner at his word. He'd have access to some information just by being a member of the League, but convincing him to share was another matter entirely.

"We can start by going back there," Becks suggested. "It's not far from Magic Avenue."

"What if it's back in full operating order and she isn't there?" Will chewed a mouthful, shuddering a little. "We need to know for sure where they took her before we consider anything else. And I wouldn't mention that place to our little friend downstairs. He might encourage us to pursue a false lead."

"I still think we should have killed him," Becks said. "He's trained to resist torture. Nothing we do will make him talk if he doesn't feel like it."

"I know." I wanted to believe him, but wasn't that exactly how he'd fooled me in the first place?

"We can still leverage him for information," Will said. "The other hunters clearly don't value him that highly if they shot him three times."

"He said he got in the way." I wiped my greasy fingers on my jeans. "If it's true, there's less chance the hunters will bother to send anyone to pick him up. We have that going for us."

"I still think we should move out in the morning," said Becks. "Head back to one of our other shelters and avoid this one for a bit."

"Yeah." Will drummed his fingers on the table. "None of it adds up, I can say that much. The hunters aren't supposed to have access to our networks. They're supposed to hate us too much to form alliances with any supernatural, shifter or otherwise."

"They hate everyone, including each other," I said. "From what Rhea used to say, they're loyal to the cause, and that's about it. Half of them die during the initiation process, and they make a spectacle out of executing traitors. It's positively medieval."

Becks pulled a face. "You'd think sticking together for their own survival would be more logical."

"They used to hunt dragons." I pushed my half-eaten dinner aside. "That says it all. If you're a plain old human, you have to be out of your fucking mind even to consider going head-to-head with a dragon."

Yet they'd developed those bullets to take us down anyway. Given how tough shifters were, they must have needed to test them first, and I had a sickening suspicion that capturing shifters alive would have been part of their strategy.

And now they had Cori. They might not have assumed

her to be a dragon shifter right off, but our prisoner would certainly have told them about seeing me shift the first time around, and we looked enough alike for anyone to guess we were related.

Over my dead body would my sister pay the price for my mistake.

An inexplicable grin crept across Will's face. "Yeah, they're batshit. I think we can use that against them. I have a plan."

"Good, because I'm all out." Short of shaking our captive until he spilled all his secrets, that is. "It doesn't involve an explosion, does it?"

"All the best plans do."

———

I woke to the sound of shouting and a frantic knock at my bedroom door. I shot to my feet, alarm blaring through me, and grabbed my emergency pack. We'd been turfed out of so many hideouts in our first months after the invasion that we all held onto old habits. Sleep in clothes, keep a rucksack stocked with basic supplies within reach, and never go to bed without a plan for a quick exit.

"Hunters!" screamed Becks. "They're out the front!"

Had they come for their friend after all? I shoved my feet into my combat boots—which I'd also left laced up by the bedside—and ran out into the landing. My ears picked up on a peculiar scraping sound from outside, followed by the crack of a bullet. My heart plummeted, and I pelted downstairs to find a wild-eyed Becks in the hallway.

"The prisoner got out," she said. "The lock's broken. Told you we should've killed him."

"Shit." That was what I got for showing mercy to a trained killer. "Sorry."

"It's not your fault. Will thinks they found our address via the same person who sold us out."

The front door buckled as something heavy slammed into it. I swore and retreated down the hallway, hoping the hunters had left the back door alone. "Where is he?"

"Outside giving them trouble, as usual."

With a tremendous crash, the door flew off its hinges, and I caught a glimpse of what looked like a mechanical arm over my shoulder as I ran through the kitchen to the back door.

What the hell was that? I cringed at the metallic scraping noise from the hallway but didn't stop to look back. Becks ran past in cat form, climbing nimbly over the fences as I walked out into the overgrown garden.

The hunters must have revised their usual tactic of not causing a public disturbance, because that racket was loud enough to be heard the other side of the Thames. I crossed the garden, spiny plants and nettles snagging at my jogging trousers, and swore softly. All the fences were topped with barbed wire in a neighbourhood effort to keep the fae from getting into any of the houses, and I hadn't a hope of removing them before the rampaging monster caught up to me.

A mewing sound drew my attention to a thick-branched tree overlooking the back fence. I gave Becks a thumbs-up and ran to follow her. The tree looked sturdy, so I shimmied up the trunk and pulled myself onto a low branch. It creaked alarmingly under my weight.

Then a hand grabbed my ankle and pulled me out of the tree. I crashed down into the bushes, kicking out at whoever had grabbed me, and heard a sharp exhale as my claws burst out.

Releasing me, Astor shook droplets of blood from his hands. "That hurt."

"What the hell are you doing lurking down here?" I scrambled upright, disentangling my claw from the thicket.

"Running for my life."

"Very funny. If you ratted me out to your people—"

"I didn't tell a soul, but the automaton will crush the lot of us into paste if we don't get the hell out of here."

"The *what?*"

"Automaton," he said. "A prototype they've been building. Clearly, they think you're worth bringing out the big guns."

"Crap." I didn't believe for a minute that he hadn't told tales, but I'd never seen anything like that giant mechanical monster before. "And you pulled me out of the tree… why?"

"You were about to fall on top of me anyway. I thought I'd speed up the process."

An ungodly racket echoed from back in the house, somewhere between a car crash and a giant rampaging through a brick wall. That mechanical hand I'd seen had been bigger than my head, and self-preservation outweighed my desire to skewer him on the spot. Instead, I grabbed the scruff of Astor's neck and hauled him out the bush.

"Let go of me."

"I'm not letting you go running back to your friends. You're sticking with me until we lose their trail, or you die."

Problem: we still needed a way out. Since climbing over the back fence was out of the question, I made for the neighbouring garden instead and found a spot where the wire was thinner. Astor showed suspiciously little resistance and scrambled over without protest, moving with the lithe quietness of someone who'd spent a lot of time climbing up walls and across the rooftops. A second later, a resounding crash shook the air.

"They just knocked your door down," said Astor.

"Bastards." I felt bad for the people in the other houses— the two which were inhabited—but shouting a warning would be a death sentence for all of us. "Not bothered about causing a stir with the human authorities, are they?"

"By the time anyone gets here, they'll be gone." He tugged himself free of me but continued to move in the same direction, heading for the next fence along. "The automatons are pre-programmed, so the hunters don't have to be here in person to use them. They also can't tell friend from foe."

"Oh, so that's why you're afraid they'll trample you." I reached the fence at the end of the row of houses and climbed over into a green expanse that hadn't existed until two years ago. London has always had its green spots, but the faeries preferred wilder spaces, so they made their own, whether we humans liked it or not. Tarmac was buried beneath the startlingly bright grass, glowing with Summer magic even in early March. Bright flowers which had never existed in this realm before bloomed everywhere, the trees were evergreen, and the ponds sparkled with iridescent water. With the faeries, beauty meant danger, but I'd take the local fae over mechanical monsters and the hunters that used them.

I'd taken two steps before it registered that Astor hadn't followed me. I turned back to the fence to see him facing the house, and I climbed back over, catching his arm. "Nice try."

"I'm not walking through the middle of the faeries' territory."

"Tough shit. It's that or the—automatons? Since when did the hunters employ giant robots?" I grabbed him by the scruff of his neck in an attempt to drag him after me, but he resisted, and his torn shirt ripped even further, exposing more tattoo marks on his upper back and neck.

"I had no idea you were so keen to take my clothes off, little dragon. Your timing might be better."

"Oh, go fuck yourself." My claws pressed against my fingertips, itching to end him, but I resisted. "Come on."

"You're icy cold, for a fire-breather," he said. "What do you plan to do when you've drawn the faeries after you as well as the hunters, exactly?"

"Find my friends." Both moved faster than me in animal form, but Will would have had to lie low until Becks and I caught up to him. Gargoyles were just too conspicuous. "This part of the faeries' territory's harmless." If you knew where you were going, which I did.

He scowled as I shoved him towards the fence, prompting him to climb over. As I led the way around a large pond, a flock of nixies surfaced, giggling and pointing at him. They looked like petite women with blue skin, gills, and seaweed-coloured hair, and none wore a stitch of clothing.

"Pretty human. Want to come and swim with us?"

Astor made a rude gesture and stormed past without answering.

"You know, I take it back." I hurried alongside him, with a wary glance at the nixies. "This *is* a death trap if you decide to insult every faerie you come across. I forgot people who follow a brainwashing cult don't have any common sense."

"Who's brainwashed?"

A loud splash echoed behind us, and out of the corner of my eye, I watched as the pond water rose upward over the outstretched hands of the now furious nixies. Their pleasant faces had turned grotesque, with sharklike teeth and finger-nails sharp as knives. Astor and I ran for a swathe of trees, but not before the wave slammed down on our heads.

It shouldn't be any surprise that dragons didn't like water, especially unexpected showers. I swore bloody murder, trip-ping over thick tree roots with every step, wet hair smacking me in the face and impeding my vision. Astor had taken the lead, and I caught up with him as he reached for the nearest low-hanging branch.

I grabbed him first, my hand locking around his wrist.

"Don't. I know you're used to climbing on roofs when things get hairy, but the trees here don't play nice."

A pair of bright-green eyes stared out from the trunk, and he let go of the branch abruptly as it moved, snake-like, reaching for his throat.

I fumbled in my pocket for a short knife, glad I had at least some iron on hand, and the dryad ceased its advance when I gave a warning swipe at its trunk. The trouble was, a whole snarl of trees stood between us and the way out, and there was no telling how many might conceal a living being. A single knife wouldn't be able to hack through all of them.

He shot me a furious look. "Any better ideas, genius?"

"Excuse me? If you hadn't insulted those nixies, we'd have been able to run that way instead of being soaked." I pushed aside a curtain of sopping-wet red hair and scanned the area. The trees covered all possible escape routes, leaving us with no way of avoiding them. Which might have bothered me less if I trusted him not to get us both impaled by angering the dryads, too. "Got any iron?"

"I did, but someone confiscated all my weapons."

"Pity for you." I reached into my rucksack and pulled out a second knife, but I didn't hand it to him. "All right, stick behind me and try not to antagonise anyone."

"Except you?" He took one step and halted, head lifted with the sort of still alertness I associated with a shifter who'd scented a predator. "Do you hear that?"

"Hear what?" Wait. The noise of automatons demolishing the house had noticeably faded, which meant either they'd retreated, or they'd found another target. "Don't tell me they're coming here."

Sure enough, the silence was broken by the sudden splintering of branches on the other side of the swathe of trees, followed by a metallic crunch.

I looked at Astor in disbelief. "No way. Even the League

ought to know better than to piss off the faeries. Do they *want* to be transformed into a herd of deer?"

"At a guess, the hunters have gone and left the automaton to do its work alone." He took a step back as a branch whipped out at him. It looked like the dryads hadn't taken kindly to being grabbed, and while I might have been content to watch him struggle, the automatons would reach us both within moments. I needed to get the hell out.

I held a knife in each hand and cut left and right, sending blood-coloured sap spurting from the branches and causing the dryad to cease its attack on Astor. Ducking under its branch, I grabbed Astor and pulled him after me. He snarled when the knife I held in the same hand cut the back of his neck, but the metallic crashes on the other side of the trees were proof that this was the only way out, and the sheer volume made it hard for me to tell which direction the automaton was in.

I sniffed, inhaling an unappealing stench akin to a blocked drain. A troll's nest. An idea forming, I dragged Astor through the tangle of branches until we fetched up against a deep trench.

"Was this your plan?" He tilted his head back, his shirt still caught in my fist. "Walk us into a troll's nest?"

"No." There *was* a way around the pit, but the path was narrow and I didn't have Becks's catlike balance. Dragons were better at trampling the door down than performing acrobatics. This would be risky. "Walk *around* the troll's nest so our mechanical beastie blunders straight in."

Astor pulled himself free of my grip and skirted the edge with a level of balance I'd thought only a supernatural could attain. Teeth gritted, I trod after him, but I didn't dare pick up speed in case I fell. "What did they have you do in training, walk on tightropes over broken glass?"

"Something like that." He sounded amused, as if this was

nothing but a joke to him. "Can't you turn into a dragon and fly out of here instead? Seems like it'd be a field advantage."

"In a city?" Did he think I'd been shifting on a weekly basis since the incident two years ago? *I wish.* Old habits were too ingrained, and the League was as big a threat as ever. As well he knew. "Do you even know where you're going?"

As he reached the pit's far side, a horrific splintering noise hit my ears as the trees just behind us split apart in a mechanical crunch. The automaton had bulldozed them flat, and now I got a good look at it, I realised how screwed we truly were. The mechanical beast was vaguely human shaped, but boxy and covered in armoured plating which made it impossible to see what made it tick. Being made of metal, it'd be more than a match for any fae it encountered and would likely be immune to most faeries' defensive spells, too. Even a troll might not stand a chance of besting it.

I picked up speed, my feet skirting perilously close to the pit's edge, and caught up with Astor near the carcass of a collapsed office block. I'd almost forgotten that before the invasion, there'd been buildings where the trees were now, as the plants growing up its height were fuelled by the over-flowing surge of faerie magic that had erupted in the inva-sion. Walking into an enclosed space on the heels of an assassin went against my instincts, but with a giant robot on our tail, I didn't have much choice.

I followed Astor, hoping I wasn't making a huge mistake.

6

I raised an eyebrow when Astor began to climb the wall in front of us. "The automaton will see us."

"They can't see," he said. "They sense movement, that's all, and there's a nest of trolls between them and us."

"Until they've finished demolishing the forest." I glared across at the fallen trees left in the mechanical beast's wake. I wasn't much of a fan of dryads, but permanently destroying their homes with iron feet seemed unnecessarily cruel. In other words, right on par for the Orion League.

Cursing under my breath, I followed him up the rickety skeleton of the collapsed building. Thick plants had gouged holes in the windows, some studded with sharp thorns, but Astor avoided them expertly. He climbed up to the first-floor level then slid through a window whose glass had long since shattered. The empty room inside was almost unrecognisable as the open office it had once been. Nature had well and truly taken root, spreading its arms over every wall and surface and curtaining each doorway in ivy.

"Are you sure there aren't faeries in here?" I hissed at Astor.

"There's too much iron," he returned. "And anyone else in here will have hidden or run like hell when they heard that mechanical racket outside."

I might have argued, but said mechanical racket sounded closer with each passing moment and we didn't have time to debate. Once we found another shattered window, he climbed out again.

"Isn't there a downstairs exit?" I whispered. "Wouldn't it be quicker to use the stairs?"

"All the doors are blocked. Didn't you look before you climbed up?"

"I was more concerned with the giant monster on our heels." Apparently, in the time it'd taken to get around the troll pit, he'd scanned the building and memorised all the possible exits. Shouldn't surprise me, given his profession. Letting him take the lead had not been my plan, but the bastard was at home when climbing in high places. This was his domain, not mine.

Metallic crashes accompanied our descent. I hoped they meant the automaton had fallen headlong into the troll's pit, but the subsequent crack of branches told me that it must have changed direction and cut back through the forest. Whatever pre-programming had been built into it was way more sophisticated than should have been possible for anything made by humans. What the hell had the League been doing in the past two years following the invasion?

The sound of branches grew more high-pitched until it sounded like screaming, and a wave of anger rose inside me. Demolishing the faeries' territory would have everyone in the area suffering the consequences for weeks. As per usual, the regular people would take the brunt of the backlash, and as he'd rightly pointed out, the human authorities wouldn't show up for hours yet. As for the magical ones? Forget it.

"Bastards," I muttered as I climbed. "Killing off dryads will get you cursed by the Seelie Court for life."

"The faeries invaded our realm and killed millions of people."

"The Sidhe did. The dryads were already here. But I guess you guys didn't pay too much attention to supernaturals except the ones on your kill list."

I dropped the last couple of feet to the ground and landed in a jog. He was already ahead of me, briskly walking across the street without looking back.

"Hey!" I picked up speed, catching him up. "Where do you think you're going?"

"What?" He glanced sideways at me. "I thought we had an understanding. We're out of the park. You go your own way, I go mine."

"You're going nowhere until I say so."

I halted when three figures flew down to land in front of us, all sporting wings and pointed ears that marked them as half-faeries. Their green eyes glimmered with the magic of Summer fae. At a guess, they'd seen us come out of the park and assumed we had a hand in destroying it.

I raised my knife in warning. "We didn't destroy your territory, but the people who did are right behind us. You need to run."

In an impossibly quick movement, Astor snatched my knife from my hand and flung it at one of the winged half-fae. He went down in a cry of pain as the blade embedded itself in his shoulder.

"You—" I cut off as the half-faeries flew at us, the injured one trailing behind the others, and Astor ran to meet them. Lifting my second knife, I shouted, "We don't have time to fight. If we stay here, we'll be trampled."

The mechanical crashes grew louder, as if to prove my point. Rampaging through faerie territory had hardly slowed it down, and once the giant monster had reached the edge of the trees, there was nothing to stop it from making directly for us.

"You destroyed our park," said the injured half-blood, attempting to pull the knife out of his shoulder.

"Believe me, if that was us, you'd be dead." The noise grew louder, and Astor tackled the half-faerie around the waist, yanking the knife free in a fountain of blood.

The third of their number, a skinny girl scarcely older than Cori, took flight, hovering above the road with a decidedly nervous expression on her face. They clearly hadn't realised they'd end up against an assassin trained to kill supernaturals like them. *They're kids.* They didn't deserve to die because Astor had no concept of how to avoid a fight.

The first girl aimed a clumsy punch at me. I ducked and retaliated with a hit to the jaw, not quite hard enough to knock her out. As she crumpled, her hovering companion dived at me. I punched her full in the face with my non-weapon hand, and she fell, whimpering, blood gushing from her nose. As I'd held my claws back, she'd live.

"That enough of a lesson for you? Astor, come *on.*" I grabbed his wrist, preventing him from dealing a killing blow to the bleeding half-faerie. "What's more important, winning a fight or not getting trampled to death?"

I tugged, hard, and as he finally relented, there came the wooden scrape of a fence collapsing. The automaton had reached the road, and with that, all three half-faeries fled, trailing blood in their wake.

I shot Astor an exasperated look. "There. Faerie blood. You've given this entire neighbourhood a redcap problem for the next month." As if the rampant destruction wasn't enough on its own.

Astor yanked his hand free. "I don't let enemies get away alive."

"You and our mechanical friend have that in common." I broke into a run, and as we rounded the street corner, I aimed for the nearest place we used as an aboveground shelter. The old coffee shop was boarded up and closed, like most of the other shops on the street, but when I pushed on the door handle, my foot brushed against the portable iron barrier spell Will had hidden beneath the door frame. A semi-transparent grey barrier shimmered into existence, which Astor regarded with narrowed eyes. "Why are you going into an empty coffee shop?"

"Why else?" I beckoned, and as the mechanical racket reached the corner, he crossed the threshold behind me. I closed the door, hoping that the automaton would assume the place abandoned and wouldn't look too closely.

Astor's dark clothes blended into the shadows as he trod after me towards the back. "This won't fool the automaton for long, you know."

"I'm waiting for my friends. Then we're going to rescue Cori."

"Just like that." He gave a soft laugh. "You don't have a plan at all, do you?"

"Sure I do." I bared my teeth at him in a smile. "You're at the centre of it. Firstly, you're going to tell me where exactly the hunters took her."

"I don't recall giving you that information."

"You didn't need to." He might have claimed not to know, but everyone the League had sent after us would have been briefed prior to the mission. "And I'm more than happy to shove you into the path of that monster if you don't talk, so start talking."

Astor, naturally, didn't say a word.

I sighed inwardly and seized on the brief moment of peace to check on my supplies. My rucksack had taken a few hits during our escape, but it looked like the contents were intact, which was good news, because our house would be a pulverised mess by now. As if our finances hadn't been in a dire enough state already. I grabbed an energy bar for fuel and shoved half of it in my mouth while I waited for Astor to speak.

No such luck. Astor stood next to the counter, as still and impassive as ever. A twitch in his jaw betrayed impatience, but otherwise he remained as motionless as a gargoyle in tourist season.

Maybe I needed a new approach. A peace offering. I took out a second energy bar and offered it to him. "Here."

He didn't take it. "Poisoning me is a quick way to be rid of me."

"Why would I stock my supply bag with poisoned snacks?" Assassin logic. I shook my head and made to close the bag, but he snatched the bar from my hand. With the other, he grabbed a water bottle from over my shoulder. Bastard moved quickly when he wasn't impersonating a statue.

"You didn't say please."

"Since you already have such a low opinion of me, it didn't seem worth the effort."

I didn't even know where to begin with that, so I shoved the rest of the snack bar into my mouth and kept an eye out for Becks and Will. Becks moved quicker but might not know I'd left the park, while Will would have had to turn into a human to avoid drawing the beast on his heels. A monster of that size would even give a gargoyle trouble in close quarters.

"What did you plan to do if your friends never show up?" Astor tossed aside the energy bar wrapper, his sharp eyes scanning the coffee shop. "Or the hunters come back?"

"You think *your* friends will rescue you?" I said. "The same ones who filled you with bullet holes?"

He stiffened. "They were never my friends. Don't you get it? I'm not part of the League. You kidnapped the wrong guy."

A moment passed. "You expect me to believe that? Really?"

"I haven't been part of the League since the invasion."

I let out a humourless laugh. "And that uniform is just a fashion statement, is it?"

The plain black gear he wore was too well-tailored to belong to anyone but the League. As for the tattoos, nobody in their right mind would go through that much pain and walk away, surely.

He gave me a look that said plainly, *are you dense?* "Obviously, I needed the uniform to get close to them."

"And why exactly would you want to do that?" Nope, I wasn't buying it. For one thing, if you left the League, you died. The stories varied about exactly how the hunters executed traitors, but everyone agreed that the only person who wanted to be near the League less than a shifter was a betrayer. "I thought your initiation ceremony involved novices beating a traitor to the point of death and then throwing them into a pit of hunting dogs."

He smirked. "Not quite. They use wolves instead."

"What?" Did he think the whole matter was a hilarious joke? "You're fucked in the head."

His smirk grew more pronounced at my reaction, but his words were flat. "I'm telling the truth. I haven't worked for the hunters since the day I met you."

"Sorry I disrupted your peaceful life, then."

He laughed shortly. "You've no idea."

What was with the accusatory tone? "You know, I have the distinct recollection of you pointing a gun at my head, unprovoked."

An unreadable expression passed over his face, like a

pebble skimming the surface of a pond. It transformed his features from impassive to dangerous, in a way that alerted my dragon side to a potential threat. My spine straightened, my claws pressing against my fingertips.

"You were about to attack me." His tone was flat. "I was acting in my own defence."

"I was running for my life." What the hell kind of twisted logic had led him to that conclusion? "A half dozen of your hunters tried to kill my sister and me. Instead of, you know, shooting the actual monsters who were rampaging across the city, slaughtering the human population."

"Remind me who shifted into a monster herself?"

The bloody cheek of it. "You have your own weapons. I have mine." I displayed my hands, letting my claws flicker to the surface. "The faeries didn't treat us with any more mercy than you did. And for the record, I've spent the past two years hoping I vaporised you."

"I had no idea I got into your head so much."

Shit. Why had I told him that? "Don't flatter yourself. If you really aren't with the League anymore, you're useless to me."

"Really." His voice dropped to a low purr. "I didn't get that impression when you grabbed me and tried to rip my clothes off."

Something in his tone brought the memory of our first encounter to the forefront—specifically, my dragon side's interest in him—and my skin warmed. "Stop doing that."

"I'm not doing anything, little dragon." He edged closer in a manner somewhere between casual and carefully deliberate. I lifted a hand as the skin rippled and became scales, and the point of one claw rested inches from his neck.

"Are you really going to kill me?" His flat, empty eyes contrasted with the easy smile curling his lip. This was all a game to him, and while he was deluding himself if he thought a human stood a chance against a dragon, I still had far too many questions to let my instincts take over.

"Not yet." I lowered my hand. "Unlike you, I still have something resembling a conscience, and you're unarmed."

He laughed. "If your conscience bothers you about the likes of me, you won't have the strength to go ahead with this ridiculous rescue mission. You sister's life was over the second they put their hands on her, little dragon."

Anger roared through my veins, and my claws flickered into life again. "I never said I wouldn't cut you down if necessary. So don't get any ideas in your head about what I'm willing to do to get her back."

"I think I have some idea." He eyed my claws. "And I never said I knew nothing at all about the League's current operations. For instance, I know that all high-priority prisoners are transferred to a facility outside of London, a place known only to the Elites."

"Elites?"

"Top-ranked hunters."

"Like you."

He inclined his head. "We know it as the Orion Stronghold."

The name rang a bell somewhere in the recesses of my mind. A rumour I'd heard a long time ago, that I'd never paid much credence to. When the hunters shot any shifter they ran into, what need would they have of a prison?

"And you think that's where she is?"

"I think it'll be their eventual destination. Once they're out of the city."

My skin prickled. I knew better than to take his word for it, but I did know that at least one facility existed, and that this wasn't the first time they'd captured shifters alive.

I might have asked any of a dozen questions, but the one that came out first was "Why *did* you quit?"

For most hunters, the League was their whole life, and after the invasion, they finally had their chance to openly destroy supernaturals without any concern for the regular humans. Why would anyone back out at this point?

"Because everything they told us was a lie." His tone was flat, his expression unreadable as a blank slate.

"You mean when they claimed your mission was to fight a prophesied war against an army of supernaturals?" I queried. "I figured they'd have found a way to claim the invasion was precisely that. Even though, you know, the Sidhe screwed over all the other supernaturals as well as humans."

"No." He spoke quietly. "They claimed nothing at all. The leader of our ranks vanished underground and left the rest of us to suffer the aftermath of the invasion alongside the regular humans. When the Mage Lords took power and the League made no effort to stop them, I quit while I had the chance."

"Really." His claims made sense, but so did a dozen other explanations, most far less benign. "How do you know the eventual plan wasn't to topple the Mage Lords from their position once the Sidhe left?"

"Would you fight a war against an enemy no humans can defeat?" His eyes scanned my face as if he genuinely wanted to know. "Maybe our leader was right to flee, but fighting for a lost cause isn't my style."

His openness disarmed me. If I didn't know him to be a liar, I might have fallen for the act.

I opened my mouth to speak, and the front of the shop burst apart in a shower of glass. A mechanical whirring followed, and Becks's cat-form came sprinting ahead of her giant pursuer.

"Oh," I said, "bugger."

7

The automaton ripped its way into the coffee shop, its thick metal feet tearing up the floor while its swinging arms propelled fists hard enough to bash someone's skull in. The beast was clumsy as hell but made up for its lack of speed with brutality alone.

Another hideout bites the dust.

I ducked into the back room, with Astor behind me. Figuring he'd guessed there was no other way out that didn't involve running straight past our mechanical adversary, I followed Becks through the fire door at the back. The alley behind the shop led to another street lined with shops and cafes, most abandoned. On the pavement lay the broken halves of a red sign indicating an Underground station. The entrance appeared to be hidden behind rubble at first glance, but I moved a few loose stones aside and exposed the path down the stairs.

Astor trod softly behind me. "You're going into the Underground?"

Becks halted, one paw on the top step, and gave a short

meow that I translated as *Do you really want to let the enemy into our main shelter?*

The answer would usually be 'no way in hell', but I'd already broken several significant unwritten rules that morning, such as 'don't share your snacks with a demented assassin' and 'don't run directly at a troll's nest'. And while his claim not to be working for the League might be bullshit, he was the only source of information I had on this supposed Orion Stronghold.

I replied to Becks with a brief nod and we descended into the station, a single intermittently flickering light guiding the way to the tunnel. The smooth wall panels were smeared with blood and other less pleasant substances, but while the wards that had once entirely hidden the area were absent, nobody aside from shifters had ever found the concealed door. Since the trains were cancelled until further notice—or rather, until the Mage Lords managed to get rid of the faeries and undead currently infesting the tunnels and stations—we had free run of the Underground. Good news for us, because the shifters' network had operated down here almost as long as the trains had, and you could walk from one side of London to another without going aboveground. If you knew where to go.

Reaching the blank wall between two platforms, I rested my hand against a smooth white panel and pushed. The panel and its neighbours slid aside with an echoing groan which carried down the stairs into the darkness of the old station. Becks's cat-form sprang ahead, and I beckoned Astor to follow. When the three of us were in the dark tunnel, the panels clanked shut behind us, leaving us in near darkness. I released a shaky breath. "That was a close one."

"Damn, that thing was persistent." Becks turned back into a human, regarding Astor with a distrustful expression.

"What the hell *was* that mechanical monster? I've never seen anything like it before."

"Automaton." I nodded to my companion. "Some kind of pre-programmed robot made by the Orion League."

Becks made a disbelieving noise. "Now they're mad scientists as well as depraved killers? Has he told you anything useful?"

"Yes." I hoped Astor himself would speak up, but he did not oblige. "Haven't verified the information yet, mind. Where's Will?"

"Already waiting for us, I hope. He's the one who drew the hunters away by flying around making a racket."

"That's why they left their monster behind," I guessed. "Damn thing trampled the dryads' forest, so all the local half-fae will be out for our blood, if we ever go back."

"Ah, shit," she said. "Well, if the hunters want the Seelie Court to transform them into a herd of deer, that's their problem, not ours."

She took off into the tunnel. I made to follow, but when Astor didn't move, I backtracked to his side. "You do realise that if you run off now, you'll be fair game for that monster."

"Strangely, I like my chances better out there than involved in whatever absurd scheme your friends come up with," he said. "Also, not all of us can see in the dark."

"Way ahead of you." I reached into my pocket for a light spell. Will made them in the shape of bracelets with a simple activation switch that cast a torch-like glow over the walls when I extended my hand. "There used to be lights all along here before the undead showed up."

"And you're willingly walking into a tunnel infested with them?"

"We'll smell them a mile off if they're here, but I like *my* chances better with a few harmless zombies than out there with your people."

"How many times do I have to tell you they're not my people? They know I'm a deserter. We're even lower than supernaturals, in their eyes." He gave me a knowing smile. "So you're in good company."

I didn't find anything funny about it. Even if he did turn out to be telling the truth, who was to say he wouldn't hand us over regardless? Who knew, maybe the hunters would happily let him back into their ranks if he gave them a dragon shifter.

"What?" Becks, who'd also backed up a few steps when she realised we weren't following her, lifted a brow at me. "Is there something I'm missing?"

"Apparently, he dropped out of the League after the invasion. When he found out they lied and didn't have a plan. Not because he didn't want to carry on killing us. That's giving him too much credit."

Astor made a soft noise of irritation. "You know, I really don't have to put up with this crap from you."

A resonant scraping noise from somewhere above made my body tense all over. "The automaton won't try to follow us down here, will it?"

"It might." Astor's mouth dug into a thin line. "Or the hunters themselves might come back."

"Shit." Becks resumed walking, cursing under her breath. "C'mon. Will's going to be pissed off. Also, Ember, why's your hair wet?"

"Our ingenious friend here decided to insult some nixies in the park," I replied. "That as well as starting a fight with some half-faeries while there was an automaton right behind us."

"Seriously? Remind me why we're letting him tag along?"

"Because we're not like those sadistic animals?" The reply slipped out before I could reconsider. For one, I hadn't initially brought him along out of any desire to keep him alive. Not beyond how I might use him for my own goals. And while my shifter side saw the world in black and white, with each person designated an ally or enemy, my human side was more conflicted.

"Sadistic animals?" he said in a low voice as we walked on. "Your people kill one another for fun, or so I hear."

"I really wouldn't," I said, as Becks growled. "Will and I might forgive you for taking jabs at shifters. Becks won't."

And we made our way through the winding tunnel in silence. As tempting as it might be to ask more questions, every noise echoed to such a degree that it immediately became apparent when the sound of footsteps entered the tunnel behind us. Human footsteps, undoubtedly, but that automaton would never have fit in here anymore than my dragon form would.

"How the hell did they find the entrance?" I gave Astor a sideways look, suspicion prickling between my shoulder blades. "Did you tell them?"

"How would I do that? You people took my phone. I'm not psychic."

"Oh, heaven forbid I imply you have magical powers."

"I didn't think there was such a thing as a mind-reading spell," he said. "Unless the rumours about one of the Mage Lords are true."

"What rumours?" Did the hunters have their own lore concerning supernaturals, like the stories that shifters shared about the League? "Is that why the League has never openly challenged the mages? They're afraid?"

"Hardly." A mocking note entered his voice. "The League never challenged the mages because the leader views them as no real threat."

I scoffed, disbelieving. "If that's true, the hunters are seriously overestimating their own prowess."

Yes, the Mage Lords thought of shifters as little more

than a public nuisance and wouldn't go to the trouble of taking on the League for our sakes, but that didn't mean they had no awareness that the hunters existed. They were bound to have taken precautions in the event of a direct challenge.

"Guys," Becks hissed. "We can't go back now, but it they keep following us…"

"I know." Leading the hunters to our shelter was out of the question, so we'd have to find another route. Luckily, there was no shortage of hidden passageways and dead ends amid the tunnels that had been added over the decades it had taken past supernaturals to carve out our territory under the city. "We'll try the tunnel near Trafalgar."

"Doesn't that have a troll living in it?"

"We know that, but they don't." Trolls were notoriously territorial, and it was anyone's guess as to whether it would take our presence as a threat, too, but at the very least, we'd give the hunters a hell of a distraction.

Becks swore under her breath, but she transformed into cat form and made her lithe way down the tunnel until we came to another hidden panel. The distinct smell of troll emanated from within, like a sewer crossed with a slaughterhouse.

Astor peered into the narrow space. "I'm not going in there."

"Then don't." If the hunters mowed him down, it shouldn't have been my problem. The slight issue was that our shelter was close enough that if Astor was remotely familiar with this part of London, he must know our destination was Magic Avenue. I couldn't take the risk.

The echoing footsteps prompted me to move. Impulsively, I grabbed Astor's arm and yanked him after me through the tunnel opening.

Astor swore in a low voice when I closed the panel behind us. "You're going to get us all killed."

"What makes you think I haven't done this before?" Not with a hunter in tow, admittedly, and his constant objections were seriously grating on my nerves. Yet again I found myself questioning whether it was worth the effort of trying to keep him alive. "It's this or wait out there for them to fill you with bullet holes. Got any better ideas?"

"I would have if you hadn't disarmed me."

"Cry me a river." My light spell flickered and died. Dammit. "Come on before they catch up to us."

I'd left the panel half askew, and our footsteps echoed loudly enough that the hunters were bound to follow, but walking in darkness was too slow for my liking. I wished I'd brought a spare light spell. At least my night vision was half decent while Becks's was better, even short-sighted as she was. As for Astor, I didn't hear him stumble, not once.

"Do they routinely have you walk around blindfolded?" I whispered, more to distract myself from my own apprehension than anything else.

"Actually, yes." A note of amusement entered his voice. "I believe one of our initial tests involved crossing a hallway lined with armed hunters. The more bullets we dodged on the way, the higher we scored."

"You're fucked in the head, did I mention that?"

"At least once."

There came the scraping sound of someone opening the panel on the wall. Then footsteps. I quickened my pace, the best I could in the dark, but Becks's scent was masked by the foul stench of the creature that made its home here in the dark.

My feet splashed in dampness, telling me we'd reached the right place. So did the eye-watering stench, which was more potent to a shifter than to a human, but foul enough for any sane person to run the other way.

"Where are we going?" Astor hissed in my ear. "You can't

pretend even your shifter senses can find your way in this stench."

"Becks and I know these tunnels, don't worry," I said. "We won't fall in a plague pit."

"A what?"

"Don't you know your local history? They say that when the Underground system was put in, they dug up old pits where plague victims were buried. That's one reason there are so many ghosts lurking down here."

"Very funny."

"No, really," said Becks. "Don't you know that's why the trains are out of order? There aren't enough necromancers in the city to get rid of the screaming dead."

"And at this rate, we'll be joining them." Astor swore under his breath as we continued to splash through the darkness. I had to admit part of me drew some satisfaction from knowing that he wasn't as unruffled as he pretended to be, though the question of what to do with him when we reached the end of this unwanted partnership remained in doubt.

More splashing behind us. I listened harder, straining my ears, and picked out three distinct sets of footsteps. Three too many.

If the hunters thought they could infiltrate our tunnels, I'd show them the real monsters lurking in the darkness.

My steps halted as the ground dropped away before us into a pit filled with faintly glowing lights. The gleam of treasure within was hard for my dragon side to resist. I crouched down, my fingers snagging an emerald necklace draped over the side.

"Is this the time for you to be trying on jewellery?" Astor said disbelievingly.

"Watch and learn." I dropped the necklace at the pit's

edge, the clinking echo reverberating through the tunnel before the splash and thud of footsteps overtook it.

"In here." Becks gestured to a gap in the wall just big enough to fit two people in. Or two people and one cat, as you were.

"You've got to be kidding me," Astor muttered.

"Maybe you fancy a swim in a troll's treasure trove, but I don't." I edged into the hole after Becks and regretted it instantly when Astor squeezed in, too. Two people couldn't stand side by side, so I nudged my way in front of him, trying to ignore the press of his body against mine.

"You know," Astor whispered, "if you wanted to get this close to me, I can think of several more appealing places than this."

"Screw you."

"While your friend is right there? No thanks."

I'd walked headfirst into that one. And, as he'd rightly pointed out, Becks could hear every word. *Wonderful.*

The loud splash of approaching hunters spared me from having to think of a reply. I tensed, and Astor went completely still. He might as well have not even been breathing.

"What is this place?" rasped a masculine voice. "They're baiting us. This is a faerie's lair."

Damn right it is. I hid a grin, listening for the inevitable clunk of one of the hunters crouching to pick up the necklace I'd dropped.

Then came the rumble of stone feet echoing in the tunnel, followed by the clatter of the necklace being dropped. A bellowing voice drowned out everything else. "Thieves!"

Have fun with that. I braced myself as the wall gave a tremble, the troll's heavy footsteps shaking the entire tunnel.

A gunshot sounded, and the troll roared in anger. Hoping the hunter had missed, I listened to the discordant splashes and shouts, punctuated by the wall-shaking thuds of the troll's pursuit. Then came a scream and the crunch of broken bone.

"One down," I murmured, listening hard. "Two to go."

"And you call *me* fucked in the head," Astor said.

"Would you like to join them?" I stiffened at the sound of a second bang, followed by a rumbling howl of pain. Ah, shit. One of the bullets had reached its mark. The troll was a goner, and based on the direction of the shouts outside our hiding place, two of the hunters were still alive.

Okay, change of plans. My fingers itched, claws pressing against my skin. My heart pounded as blood rushed through my veins. Tilting my head, I whispered to Becks, "Ready?"

A meow of agreement. Then Becks and I moved at the same time, leaping out of the hole in the wall. The faint glow from the troll's nest showed me the way to my quarry, and a strangled yell escaped the hunter as the momentum of my jump sent us crashing into the filthy water.

Beside me, Becks crashed into the other surviving hunter in a flurry of cat claws and fury. My opponent twisted to the side, kicking at my knees to unbalance me, but I dug my claws into his chest until he went limp.

A furious yowling warned that the third hunter had dislodged Becks, but in the process, he'd unintentionally backed right up to the edge of the troll's pit. I readied myself to strike. Astor got there first. He appeared in a blur, and the hunter went flying over the pit's edge. There came a distinct thud, then silence.

Becks watched the pit, her yellow cat-eyes wide. Then she turned human again, shaking herself like a cat after an unexpected downpour. "That is bloody disgusting."

"It is." I was soaked in filthy water, too, and to top it all off I'd lost my sole light spell, which meant we had to find our way back in the dark. There'd better not be any more hunters on the other side of the door. "Better get back to Will. He'll think we're dead."

We made our way back up the tunnel, pausing every so often to check no other unfriendly ambushes were waiting. Astor didn't offer any commentary, nor an explanation as to why he'd decided to step in. Maybe he'd wanted to prove, unequivocally, that he was on our side.

Then again, no hunters had escaped alive to tell tales, and all League members were known for looking out for themselves and nobody else. Not even each other.

We emerged from behind the panel to a tunnel blessedly free of more intruders. I trod ahead, dripping filthy water with every step, and felt a shudder of relief when I spied a flickering light ahead. We were close, enough for my doubts to come surging back. Turning to Astor—or what I could see of him—I whispered, "This goes without saying, but if you tell a soul about the shelter on the other side of this tunnel, you'll regret it."

"Now you're making threats again?" He tilted his head. "I think it's a bit too late. I've seen enough."

"Yes, but I thought I'd give you a reminder." My warning lacked any real heat, but now our shelter was around the corner, my very nature reacted against the notion of bringing him into the closest I'd had to a home since the invasion.

"Why are we arguing in the dark?" asked a new voice from up ahead.

Astor called out, "Who's there?"

"Knock, knock," came the reply.

"Will," I breathed. "You made it?"

"Yes, and I've been waiting for you lot forever."

Rounding the corner, we emerged from the dark into a stretch of tunnel illuminated by witch spells affixed to the walls. Will stood waiting for us, arms folded over his chest. He goggled at Astor. "You brought the assassin with you?"

"He claims he can help us," I said. "And that he doesn't work for the League any longer."

Will wore a sceptical look, but he shrugged. "Come inside."

The tunnel led into a basement smaller than the one at our other shelter but much more practical, with proper lighting and defensive spells built into the tunnel door to warn us if anyone else got close to the entrance. A short ladder led into a narrow hallway that ran behind the shop in the front and the living quarters in the back.

"You're in luck," I told Astor. "This is our VIP shelter. First things first: I really need a shower."

8

Magic Avenue. Home of our main base—and where Astor and I had first met.

Now I knew the truth of him, I was kind of surprised he'd willingly walked into a witch's shop back then. The trapdoor sat directly in front of the door leading into Will's spell shop, and Astor's expression when he set eyes on the glimmering handmade spells that filled the shelves behind the shuttered windows suggested he expected a cackling witch to rise from behind a shelf and put a hex on him. I half-expected him to start making the sign of the cross and douse everything in holy water.

"Don't go outside," Will told him. "There are hunters sniffing around out there."

My heart sank in my chest. "Looking for us?"

"Nah, they're hassling the local witches, same as usual."

I scowled. Even the Orion League found it near-impossible to navigate the current state of the world without aid from the witches, at least in some capacity. Unlike the mages, who'd been able to fall back on the centuries of resources they'd amassed, witches had been forced to improvise with what little they could find, and there was a reason this was one of the few parts of the city with reliable running water and electricity after the faeries had brought down critical infrastructure. You could get anything on Magic Avenue, from fae-proof wards to herbal remedies, and while the hunters flat-out refused to touch anything created by actual magic, that didn't stop them from haranguing our local spell-makers for other supplies.

Will had slipped their notice mostly by turning his own storefront into something more ordinary like a bakery or flower shop whenever the hunters came to this end of the street, which wasn't all that often. Otherwise, the local witches were too reliant on one another to have anything to gain from telling tales on us to the League. Witches these days usually traded in favours and spell supplies rather than cash. Hence why we spent our spare hours hunting mystery monsters to stay afloat.

"Did you ever find out where that tip-off came from?" I called to Will, who'd opened the door to the living quarters on the hallway's other end. "You know, the one that sent us into the hunters' trap?"

"Nope," he called back. "Don't come in here. I'm not having you shedding sewage all over my carpets."

"It's troll water, not sewage."

"Somehow that makes it worse."

He wasn't wrong. "Becks, you shower first. I'll stay with Astor."

Will reappeared, opening a small cupboard underneath the staircase. The fragrant smell of herbs wafted out, and my eyes followed Astor's retreat with some amusement.

"The herbs don't bite," I told him. "Except the mandrake."

"Never been in a witch's shop before, have you?" asked Will, giving Astor a dazzling smile. "We aren't all that bad."

"There are hunters outside," I reminded Astor, seeing him

scanning the corridor for a way out. The shop door was bolted against entry, but even Will's strongest wards wouldn't hold up to an automaton. "Will, are you absolutely sure they aren't the same hunters who set the automaton on us?"

"No. I flew for ten minutes over the Thames before I lost them, then I had to *walk* back." He emerged out of the cupboard with an armful of spell ingredients. "My blisters have blisters. We'd better find where those pricks are keeping Cori soon. Weren't you going to tell us?" he added to Astor.

"No," he said.

"Friendly," said Will. "Why didn't we kidnap a nice one?"

Astor offered an eye-roll in response. "I can't tell you where the hunters are holding your friend because I wouldn't know. That said, there's a prison used by the League not ten minutes from here. Since there are already hunters in the area, it's not too big a leap to assume they're keeping her there."

Will returned to the living quarters, saying over his shoulder, "If you're deceiving us, I'll turn you into a coat rack."

"There *is* a prison not far from here." I didn't elaborate, still in two minds as to whether Astor needed to know the details of our last close-up encounter with the League. From the assessing look on his face, he'd already begun to wonder, but luckily, Becks returned from the shower before Astor could ask any questions.

I showered as quickly as possible and changed into fresh clothes, glad to be thoroughly clean of swamp water and the general stench of the troll's lair. Mercifully, everything in my supply bag had also survived the soaking, including my most valuable possession, if not the most useful. Namely, the notebook that I'd been given by whoever had sent Cori and me to London. Perhaps it was unwise, carrying written proof of being a dragon shifter around with me, but it held sentimental value and I'd always hoped that at some point I'd figure out the meaning behind the handful of sentences at the front written in a language neither Cori nor I could read. I skimmed them again out of habit before replacing the notebook in my rucksack and returning downstairs.

Astor stood where I'd left him in the hallway, one eye on the shop, the other on the stairs, as if watching for a potential ambush.

"Shower's free." I pointed upstairs. "If you try to escape out the window, there's a trapping spell up there to catch pigeons. Fair warning."

"Pigeons?"

"They're much tastier than rats," Will called out from the living quarters. "Come back to join the land of the living, have you, Ember? You looked like a zombie and smelled worse."

"That's what swimming in a troll's nest will get you," said Becks, who lounged on the sofa in human form. "I'm never doing that again."

"I feel bad for the troll," Will said. "The hunters shot it?"

"Yeah." I grimaced. "I didn't know what else to do to drive them off. I just hope they didn't tell everyone else about the tunnels. Those bastards outside better not be connected."

"They don't have the faintest idea our tunnels exist." Will backed out of the kitchen, accompanied by a cloud of billowing green smoke. "Anyway, while you lot were crawling around a troll's nest, I was working on our plan."

"The one we discussed last night?" The only viable idea we'd come up with was to find wherever the hunters were holding Cori and either go with the stealthy approach or the all-guns-blazing one, depending on how many hunters were present. "Yeah, Astor said there's a prison in the area, and I bet I know which he meant."

"That place?" Becks pulled a face. "We can't know for sure that Cori's in there, though. Don't forget the hunters who survived the incident two years ago won't make the same mistake again."

"I bet they didn't want to let the facility go that easily." The prison had once belonged to regular humans, and evidently, the hunters had convinced the local authorities to hand over the keys in the aftermath of the faerie invasion.

"Maybe not." Becks yawned, stretching in a cat-like manner. "If the place is back in working order, I doubt we'll be able to convince a pack of gargoyles to help break the doors down again."

"No, which is why I'm opting for stealth first," Will said. "Seems to me that we have two options: disguise ourselves as League members or use one of my prototype cloaking spells."

"Didn't the last prototype we tried blow up in our faces?"

"The first option is riskier," he said. "For one thing, the hunters will see through our disguises if they check IDs on the door. And that's if I get the uniform right."

"That won't work."

Astor had entered the room with his usual silent steps. His black eye had healed, the blood was gone from his face and hair, and he'd changed into clean clothes that must have belonged to Will, since he didn't have any spare ones of his own. With his tattoos hidden by the long sleeves of a flannel shirt, he looked almost... normal. Like the day we'd met. I couldn't help but stare a little.

I gave myself a mental shake as Becks said, "What do you mean by that?"

"I mean that a simple disguise will never fool the League," he said. "If your sister *is* at that facility, they'll be expecting you."

"Will they now?" I gave him a challenging stare. "I think you're underestimating how effective illusion spells can be.

Will's been making them for years so shifters can go about their business without anti-supernatural zealots shooting them on sight. I wouldn't underestimate him."

Without waiting for an answer, I crossed the room to the kitchen, more to get out of his line of sight than anything else.

Will looked at me from where he was enthusiastically beating at a bunch of herbs inside a bowl. "What's up with you?"

"Did you give him one of your healing spells?" I asked.

"Well, yeah. He was bleeding everywhere."

"He didn't tell me."

"Assassins. Guess they're trained to not make a sound even if you decapitate them."

"Then they'd be dead, Will." Shaking my head, I went to make a sandwich. I was starving, and the burst of adrenaline which had carried me all morning had long since depleted. "Are you sure this prototype of yours won't explode on us this time around?"

Most witches were part of a coven, but Will had been self-taught for the most part and rarely did more than flick through the spellbook his mother had left him after she'd died. That meant he tended to think outside the box—or, occasionally, blow that box wide open. It made for a hair-raising time, that was for sure.

"No explosions this time, don't you worry."

"What was that?" Becks came into the kitchen and peered into the bowl Will was stirring. "What're you concocting, Will?"

"A potion that gets rid of nosy cats." Will scattered a handful of leaves into the bowl and began stirring. "It's a surprise."

"If you say so." Becks sprang over to the fridge and opened it. "Hey, you stocked up."

"Keira owed me for a half-dozen spells I gave her last week," Will said. "She must've stopped by at the bakery."

"She's my new best friend." I opened the cupboard and inhaled the smell of freshly baked bread. "I'm making a sandwich. Want one, Will?"

"Sure."

"Becks?"

"Hell, yes." She glanced over at the doorway, where Astor had moved into view, eyeing Will's concoction as though he expected it to come to life and eat him. "And… Astor, right?"

"No," he said coldly, and stalked back into the living room.

Will looked up. "What's his issue?"

"He thinks we're trying to poison him," I guessed.

"Poison?" Will frowned after him. "I'm a pacifist."

"He hates witchcraft. He might not be a hunter anymore, but he still thinks we're abominations who eat human children."

"Ah." He shook his head. "Pity. He's a looker."

"Don't get any ideas."

"I was going to say the same to you, given that you brought him here."

I ducked my head into the fridge. "I think he's a filthy monster, and the feeling's mutual."

Part of me hoped he'd heard me. And that he'd avoid so much as alluding to the day we'd met. I did not need to explain that mess to my friends, certainly not while he was still present.

I finished making a plate of sandwiches and took it into the living room. Placing the plate on the coffee table, I scooped up a chicken sandwich and sat down in the armchair nearest to Astor. "This isn't poisoned, you know. We wouldn't have wasted a healing spell on you if we planned to kill you."

"I'd sooner you let me leave."

"With the hunters roaming around outside?" I took a bite. "You know, I don't think you ever told me *why* you were following them in the first place. Seems an odd hobby for someone who left their ranks."

He said nothing. Nor did he meet my eyes. We were back to stubborn silence again, apparently.

"Come on," I said. "It'll go easier for all of us if we get along."

"I don't know, most partnerships don't begin with one party tied up in the basement. Unless you're into that sort of thing."

Heat crept up my cheeks, but I threw out a flippant reply. "Oh, all the time."

"I gathered." He looked entirely too amused by my reaction. Worse, from the way Becks was watching the pair of us, it would be impossible to hide the real history between us for much longer. My friends were too sharp for their own good.

I returned my attention to my sandwich and then grabbed a second one. "Seriously, they aren't poisoned."

"Fine." He reached for one, running a hand over his newly healed black eye with the other hand.

"Not a fan of witch spells?" I guessed. "You hunters seem to like magic just fine when the plumbing isn't working."

Astor scowled. "Do I need to repeat myself? I'm not with the League. If you can't get that into your head, I won't help you."

"Because you were already being so accommodating." I chewed another mouthful. "How much security would you typically expect at one of these smaller jails? What do they normally do, hold shifters there until trial? Or whatever passes for justice according to the League?"

"Something like that." His gaze skimmed over my face as if gauging how much to tell me. "There are bases all over the city, but once the higher-ups learn they have their hands on a dragon shifter, they'll take her straight to the Orion Stronghold."

"The what?" Becks put down her own sandwich. "The name rings a bell."

"Supposedly, it's their main base," I explained. "Outside of London, he says."

"I don't have the address, before you ask," Astor said. "I've never been. The hunters who work there are sworn to secrecy."

"And they'll keep her there until they figure out what she is?" Assuming they didn't already know.

"No, they'll keep her there until they're able to send a message to the boss," he replied. "Whoever hands her over will get a bonus big enough they'll never have to do grunt work again."

I choked on a mouthful of bread. Swallowing, I tried to regain my composure. The short time I'd spent in the hunters' local jail had not been a fun experience, but I'd been lucky. The League's higher-ups had presumably still been hiding underground at the time, if I believed Astor's claim, and had never found out they'd briefly held two dragon shifters in captivity.

I finished eating and went out into the shop to peer through the shutters. No hunters lurked on the other side, but I didn't dare believe their presence here was mere coincidence. Half our contacts were on this very street, and if one of them had tipped off the League in the first place…

"I thought your friend was a gargoyle, not a witch." Astor stepped out into the shop behind me, careful to avoid treading too close to any of the shelves. The latest trend in witch spells was to make them look like colourful accessories, so half the shelves were lined with what looked like bangles and necklaces and the rest occupied by sealed bottles and jars more typical of a witch's establishment. From Astor's expression, Satan himself might as well have been perched on the counter.

"He's both. A hybrid. He's harmless compared to me and Becks, but watch you don't touch anything in here."

Will didn't know much about his gargoyle father, who'd died when he was a baby, but he'd been closer to his mother, and her shop meant enough to him that we hadn't vacated Magic Avenue even when it might have been safer to relocate elsewhere.

"I wasn't planning to," he said, with a distrusting look at the shelves. "But if the League realises you're hiding here, they'll pulverise this place. No ward can keep out an automaton."

"I wasn't aware you knew anything about wards," I said. "Is that what the League's doing here, buying up witch wards?"

Or buying information? a voice whispered in the back of my head. Someone had tipped off the hunters, but few of Will's contacts knew the truth about Cori and me. Rather, the one person who'd seen me transform, who'd known there were dragon shifters in London—was right here.

That was why we couldn't afford to let him go. And that was why I couldn't let myself be relieved that he was staying.

"No, of course not," he said in answer to my question. "You know, the League won't ignore those three hunters who disappeared in the tunnel forever. They'll send others to investigate, if they haven't already."

"And are you going to explain *how* they found their way in?"

He cut me a sharp look. "I didn't tell them. I couldn't have. I've never been inside one of your tunnels before."

You almost did. When you shot at me.

His eyes narrowed, as if he'd caught the general train of my thoughts.

Aloud, I said, "Well, someone did. So even if we took your advice and left Cori at their mercy, they'd still come back for the rest of us."

"I never claimed they wouldn't."

My eye twitched. "What's the point in you belittling every idea I come up with, then? If I wanted to listen to someone whine all day, I'd go hang out at Twill's place."

"He's still alive?"

"Unfortunately." For some reason, his acknowledgement that he remembered the grumpy old witch took me off guard. Maybe because it was a moment that connected the pair of us—and Cori—in a way that didn't involve any friction. We both thought Twill was a dick. "He's proof there's no justice in the world, if you ask me."

He grunted, and our brief moment of connection slipped away as my questions returned. "Why were you there? Two years ago? I mean, this place was completely hidden from human eyes. The League shouldn't have known about it."

"They guessed after seeing so many supernaturals in the area," he said, without looking at me. "Then they sent in people to find a way around the wards."

"Like you." Bitterness filled my voice despite my best efforts to keep my emotions in check. "If not for the faeries showing up when they did, you'd have run in here and killed us all. Was that the idea?"

Another moment of silence. "I don't know what you want me to say."

"An apology would be a start."

"A start," he repeated. "If you can't get past that, there seems little point in pursuing the matter further."

"You captured and killed my kind. There's no *getting past* that."

"I've never killed a dragon. And you've killed plenty of humans."

"In my own defence," I retaliated, "I never claimed otherwise. But I'm still as much a person as the average human is."

Will stepped into the shop. "It's a fifty-fifty split. Half monster, half human, all awesome. What are you two doing lurking in here, anyway?"

"Making sure the hunters aren't going to storm in." My voice sounded as hollow as I felt inside. "We'll have to go through the tunnels to reach the jail."

"That was the plan," he said. "Are you coming?"

"Yeah." As he went through the door to the living quarters, I swivelled to Astor. "I'll tell you what's better than an apology. Helping me get my sister back from the League."

A heartbeat passed before he answered. "They'll break you if they catch you."

"No, they won't." I wouldn't break. Nor would I surrender. I'd get my sister back or die trying.

No other option was acceptable.

9

I returned to the back room to find Will proudly holding up an illusion spell that was shaped to resemble one of the black masks the hunters wore.

"I've made three," he said. "They'll make us appear to be League members, at least from a distance."

"Nice," said Becks. "Then we fuck them up, right?"

"You've got it. I have a half-dozen new illusion spells to take for a drive."

Only Astor was unimpressed. "It won't work. Most hunters have at least some experience with illusions."

"Oh, trust me," said Will. "They won't have seen this one before. It's state of the art."

And it won't blow up in our faces? I refrained from asking the question aloud, mostly because I didn't need to give Astor any more reasons to question our strategy. Since Will had made three masks, only the three of us would be able to approach the prison directly, but I hadn't really expected Astor to accompany us that far. He'd killed one of his fellow hunters in close quarters, yes, but he'd done so discreetly. Walking into a prison full of them was a different level of risk—and might also make it harder for him to resist turning us in, to get that coveted bonus for handing the League a second dragon shifter.

"I'll check the tunnels," Becks said. "Will, you watch the skies. And Ember…"

"I'll scope out the jail from the outside. Find out how many people they have on duty, that sort of thing."

"Best wait until I've checked the tunnel first." Becks fished her phone out of her pocket and sighed. "Signal's down."

"Is it ever up?" Will said. "Don't worry, I won't need to give you a signal to let you know I have them distracted. Everyone in London will be able to hear."

"Will, *what* exactly are you planning?" I asked warily.

"Something spectacular." He peered out into the shop. "I'll meet you on the other side. Becks, check the tunnels and then give Ember the go-ahead to follow."

"Got it," she said.

Unfortunately, that left me alone with Astor, who'd reverted to impersonating a statue almost as efficiently as a gargoyle. Which only added to my general twitchiness. To take my mind off the dangers my friends might have run into, I asked, "So, you mentioned you've been on security duty before?"

"Not at the place you're thinking of," he replied. "That facility only came into use after the invasion and was shut down for a while."

"That's our fault. We set it on fire."

"Why am I not surprised?" He studied me, a knowing glint in his eyes. "I thought you'd avoided shifting since the first time."

How in hell had he figured that one out? "Not with that kind of fire. And I don't. Avoid shifting, I mean."

"You didn't shift when you fought the hunters."

"I use my claws all the time. And you might have noticed there's not a whole lot of space for a dragon in the tunnels."

I had an inkling he meant when we'd fought out in the open, though, and he was right. I *had* held back, in the hopes that they'd take me for a human.

Perhaps that same hesitation had got Cori captured.

My hands fisted, and I turned my eyes away from his face, not wanting to look at his knowing expression. "Dragons aren't like other shifters, besides."

I didn't want to get into the details, in part because I'd had to work a lot of them out through experience rather than instruction. While the book that I'd found in my rucksack on the train to London had told me the basics—dragons shifted later in life than most shifters, and we could attain a partial shift where few others could manage it—that was the extent of it. Cori and I hadn't had an elder to look up to, like the other shifters did.

I'd done my best to fulfil that role for Cori, but she was too young to fully turn into a dragon. While the first shift sometimes happened in a moment of panic, the most that might happen was that her claws might make an appearance. Otherwise, there was a chance, however small, that she might be able to get away with pretending to be something other than a dragon shifter. At least for a short while.

Hang in there, Cori. We're on our way.

I turned back to Astor, who still watched me in that unnerving manner. "Did they teach you to stare creepily at people in hunter training, or do you come by it naturally?"

"You think I'm creepy?" He seemed to find that amusing. "You stare at people, too. Also, your eyes sometimes glow."

"They what?" Yes, my eyes glowed when my dragon side was particularly close to the surface. Such as when I was angry, or frustrated, or... turned on. Oh, no. Had they been glowing when we first met? That was all I needed. "Yeah, it's a dragon thing. Didn't the League teach you that, too?"

"No." He did not elaborate. I knew that continuing to prod at the subject of how he'd been trained to exterminate all supernaturals would not remotely help my bid to keep the peace, but more and more questions arose by the minute. I knew very little of what the League actually taught, only the bare details, but I did know that they recruited their members young, to let their brainwashing take hold.

"How old were you when you joined, anyway?"

"Twelve."

I stared for a moment. I hadn't expected him to reply in such a straightforward manner—nor the number to be quite that low. "Seriously?"

He flashed me a humourless smile. "Why do you think? They want recruits to obey them without question, so they seek out orphans of shifter attacks or other magical accidents. As you can imagine, recruits are even easier to come by now than they were before the invasion."

"Shifter attacks." My heart began to beat faster. "Is that what happened to you?"

"In a manner of speaking."

If shifters had killed his family, of course he'd have jumped on board with the first people who offered him a chance at vengeance. Who was to say I wouldn't have done the exact same, in his place? Especially in the pre-invasion world, where the average person would have next to no knowledge of anything remotely close to the truth concerning supernaturals.

Forgiveness wasn't an option, but Astor *had* seemingly renounced the League, and whether I'd played a role in that or not didn't matter. Starting afresh might be a viable option.

If he hadn't taken me for a fool.

The rattle of a trapdoor announced Becks's return. Clambering out of the trapdoor in human form, she grinned at me. "Will has all the hunters on the run. I've never seen them move that fast."

"What's he done?"

"He unleashed a plague of ants in Trafalgar Square. An illusion, obviously, but every hunter on Magic Avenue took off to see what was going on."

"Amazing." I glanced at Astor, but he was as impassive as ever. "Did you check out the jail, Becks?"

"Two guards outside. They use keycards to get in." She held up Will's bespelled masks. "Hang onto those. Will is going to meet us on the other side. Your friend doesn't have one of his own?"

Astor's eyes narrowed. "No, and I still think you're going to get yourselves killed."

"He means this is all going to go wonderfully," I cut in. "And if not, he's welcome to leave."

I hadn't intended to say those words, but once they were out, I couldn't take them back. Besides, we had to part ways eventually, and this wasn't the worst note to end on. Once we were in the jail, our own knowledge and skills were all we needed to get to Cori.

Astor himself gave no indication one way or another, but he climbed through the trapdoor without speaking and followed me through the door into the tunnels at the back. Becks shifted into cat form and ran into the lead, this time taking a right turn in the opposite direction from which we'd come.

Towards the place where I'd first shifted.

The tunnel felt much tighter, more confining, than it had during our last visit. With each step, half-formed memories returned, memories of being dragged through the darkness, consciousness returning in fits and starts. Hearing my sister sobbing my name yet being unable to answer her. The shift had banished my human side and left an animal in her place, someone incapable of any rational thought. Rage and grief had consumed me utterly, and it shamed me even now to think about how I'd lost myself and nearly lost Cori, too. I'd scared the shit out of her, and it was that reality alone that had held me back from embracing my dragon side fully since that day.

Astor couldn't possibly understand. His opinion was irrelevant. And yet I couldn't help wondering how *he* recalled those last moments in the Underground. Doubtless his perspective was that he'd stared death in the face and fired the gun in self-defence. I didn't want to believe he'd shot me on purpose, but wasn't that very naivety responsible for me ending up tangled with him in the first place?

Astor finally spoke. "You're growling."

"I'm not." Shit. I was. "I was thinking about what I'm going to do to the pricks who have Cori."

"Do you routinely daydream of inflicting violence on people?"

"Oh, yeah, it's my favourite hobby," I said absently. "Aside from, you know, flying around the countryside and terrorising farmers."

He shot me an amused look. "You don't strike me as the terrorising sort."

Why was he so chatty all of a sudden? Perhaps he, too, was unnerved by our proximity to the site of our first clash. "You need to work on your compliments. Not terrorising farmers is a low bar."

"For a dragon?" he said. "I suppose 'not destroying public property' is too high."

"Oh, I plan to do plenty of that."

Becks chose that moment to interrupt by letting out a piteous meow that had me thoroughly confused until I caught the rotting stench drifting from ahead of us. Great. Undead.

I flexed my claws and ran past Becks to confront the corpse that lumbered down the tunnel of its own accord. Becks feared the dead almost as much as she did the hunters, which I didn't quite get, but the invasion had brought out fear and paranoia in all of us, and everyone had their own horde of personal demons to deal with.

I swiped out, sending the zombie's head tumbling to the ground, where it rolled to a stop at Astor's feet. Fumbling in my pocket for a jar of salt—one of many essential post-faerie supplies—I tossed some at the fallen zombie and heard the sizzle of its reanimated flesh dissolving.

"You're welcome." I stepped around the now inert corpse. "What?"

Astor had halted, his gaze fixed on the tunnel behind us. "There might be others."

"I think it came alone." Wandering undead were by no means an unusual sight, post-invasion, but my nerves jangled even more as we stepped over its corpse and into the wreckage of the station.

Fallen debris littered the way upstairs. No traces remained of the hunters I'd turned to ashes all those years ago, and Astor wisely didn't offer any commentary. Nor did I look too closely at the faint burn marks on the walls, the sole remnants of my first shift.

My nerves rattled so much that when Astor halted at the top of the stairs, I walked straight into him.

"Ow." My feet stumbled, threatening to tip over the edge, but Astor's hand shot out and caught my arm to steady me. "What did you stop for?"

"Nothing." His hand lingered on my arm for a heartbeat and then let go.

"Sure you didn't just want to get your hands on me?" I quipped, then regretted the comment when an inviting smirk appeared on his face. "You never gave me an answer. As to whether you're leaving now, that is."

"No." He studied my face, his eyes probing. "Last chance to back out."

"Back out?" I forced a laugh. "You really think I'm going to die."

"I think you'll do your best to avoid it, but those bullets don't give anyone a second chance."

"Except for you." My heartbeat drummed against my ribs. I knew the risks. But they'd taken Cori alive for a reason, and if her dragon shifter status was at the core, they'd want to refrain from inflicting a fatal blow on the sole other dragon in the city.

We emerged from the station into a street lined with broken-down shops and ringing with the shouts of a disturbance from somewhere close by. *That's Will's diversion.* I reached into my bag for the masks and followed Becks's cat form through the ruin that had once been a busy tourist district.

The jail had always been exactly that: a regular human prison repurposed by the hunters post-invasion. For that reason, it was easy to spot its red-brick walls set apart from the neighbouring buildings and circled by overgrown car parks littered with broken-down vehicles.

Becks shifted into human form and took one of the masks from me. "Will's having way too much fun over there. I think he's forgotten we're meant to go in through the front."

Astor made a low noise of annoyance. "Those masks will only work until you reach the doors anyway."

"I'm aware." Becks held up an arm and tapped the wrist-band she wore, another of Will's illusion spells. "This will get us in, if you stop bitching long enough not to give us away."

Will came swooping down from the rooftop, trans-forming into a human with a cackle of laughter. "Oh, that was priceless. I can see the headlines. An ant swarm in Trafalgar Square, and two hunters fell into the fountain to top it off."

"Excellent." I nudged Astor, hoping for a reaction, but his eyes were on the prison. "All right, here are the masks. Ready?"

I handed Will the last one and prepared to turn on the illusion. At a flick of a switch, black uniforms overlaid our regular clothes, and every real part of us—down to my bright-red hair—was smothered in a shimmering haze. I had to admit it kind of creeped me out to see my friends' faces replaced by featureless masks.

I glanced at Astor. "Last chance to back out."

At his own words, echoed back to him, he stiffened. But he didn't follow us across the car park, and when I next looked at him, he'd gone.

Go time.

The guards at the door spotted us instantly. My dragon side growled a warning despite the knowledge that my true face was hidden, and I reached for the knife concealed at my waist.

"Get them, Becks," I whispered, and all hell broke loose.

An explosion of light dazzled my eyes, and a burst of colour filled the air, like someone had set off a box of fire-works. As the guards outside shielded their eyes, Becks's cat form streaked past and climbed up the right-hand guard's trouser leg, claws digging in tight. By the time I reached the doors, she had a white keycard between her teeth and tossed it in my direction. I caught it in an outstretched hand and drove my knife into the second guard's thigh.

Blood fountained, and he slumped to his knees into a puddle of crimson. I stepped around him and slammed the keycard onto the gleaming pad on the front doors. Then I was in.

Fireworks accompanied my entrance, courtesy of another of Will's spells, but I didn't slow down to check if they'd hit their mark. My last visit here had been two weeks post-faerie invasion, and it was momentarily disarming to find myself in a pristine entryway and not a chaotic ruin filled with brawling gargoyles and disorganised hunters trying to keep a grip on an operation already sliding out of their control. Not a sign remained of the damage inflicted by Will's explosive spells during our escape.

Becks crossed the polished floor and leapt at a hunter who ran out of another pair of keycard-operated doors. As he reached for a weapon, I punched him in the throat and kicked at the shins of a second hunter directly behind. My other hand slammed the keycard into the door—which, if memory served me right, led to the cells where Cori and I had both briefly been held captive.

Last time I'd escaped by myself to find that Cori had been shoved into the back of a truck to be transferred elsewhere alongside several other shifter kids, mostly gargoyles. At the time, I'd been too relieved at our escape to probe any deeper into why the hunters had specifically wanted children… and where, exactly, they'd been taking their captives.

Shouts of "Stop that cat!" pursued Becks and me through the doors into a long corridor lined with cells. I slammed the door in the hunters' faces and took off at a sprint. *I'm coming, Cori.*

Skidding around a corner, I reached the first cell. The door was closed, but I didn't see anyone through the small barred window at the top. Empty. The second was the same. Becks trod ahead of me, sniffing at the ground, and briefly shifted to human form.

"I smell her, but she isn't here." She turned into a cat again at the sound of footsteps somewhere ahead.

Dread trickled down my spine. Had they moved all the prisoners, like the last time? Or—the alternative didn't bear thinking about. I began to move faster, and so did Becks. She ran around the corner, and a yowl and a thump sounded. I picked up the pace and reached the corner in time to see Becks leap away from Astor with a furious hiss.

"What are you doing?" I demanded of him. "Did the hunters clear the place out?"

"I wouldn't go through the back door," he warned. "The League must be transferring every prisoner elsewhere."

"Then Cori's out there." I pushed past him, spying the open doors to the rear car park, and spied the hulking outline of an automaton crouched outside. Hunters ran around, shouting orders at one another, and I glimpsed a large truck off to the side.

When its engine rumbled to life, a current of fury ran through my nerves like a live wire. *Cori.*

The mechanical beast swivelled towards the exit. I hurled my knife point-first at it. The blade glanced off its forehead as though it was made of solid concrete. Worth a try. I backed up a few steps, gauging the odds of reaching the front door before the truck had gone.

"Ember." Astor beckoned me into an alcove where a pair of fire doors led to a narrow stairway. I didn't follow. Going upstairs would not bring me any closer to that truck, but maybe if I climbed out the window... *ah, that's the plan.*

As I made to follow, a gunshot rang out behind me. I swore, catching sight of a group of hunters advancing through the vacated jail. Between them and the mechanical monster, I'd take the latter, so I ducked through the back exit, skirting the wall. The automaton might be far bigger than the hunters, but at least a punch from one of those metal fists wouldn't be fatal, even if it hurt like hell. The truck was right there. *Cori.*

Then the automaton lifted a colossal arm and pointed a gun at me. *I stand corrected.*

10

I legged it. I didn't have a choice. The sole escape route was the one Astor had chosen, up the fire escape to the floor above. The hunters must all be downstairs or outside, and the corridor was deserted. At the sound of footsteps on the stairs, I ran into the nearest office. Astor was already opening the window, and Becks was first out.

I crossed the office, my gaze snagging on a desk upon which lay a closed book. A journal, maybe. Impulsively I snatched it up and shoved it into my pocket, my nose picking up on a faint scent that reminded me of Will's kitchen. "Why does this place smell like a witch's brew?"

Astor didn't answer. Pushing the window as wide as it would go, he climbed out, his feet resting on the sill. I clambered after him and reached for the drainpipe, making up for my lack of a hunter's trained balance with sheer desperation. I scrabbled up the drainpipe and hung on with both hands, swearing under my breath when I saw the truck had already departed, the automaton stomped along in its wake. The hunters had taken a risk in transporting their prisoners on the ground, given the state of the city's roads, but that mechanical monster could probably trample any average-sized obstacle with ease.

If I shifted into a dragon, I'd easily be able to catch up to the truck, but a dozen or more hunters waited below, all armed, and Will's explosive distraction was still in effect. Fireworks lit the sky over the rooftops and left sizzling holes where they struck. It'd be a fine thing to display my dragon form to the whole city only to get taken out by a sparkler.

A hunter turned back, seeing me. Suspended from the drainpipe, I had nowhere to run from the gun pointing at my head.

I let go. My body fell, too slowly, as the bullet snapped towards me—then Astor was in front, falling in a graceful dive that carried him right into the path of the bullet. A dull grunt escaped as he hit the ground. I landed behind him, ran at my attacker, and brought my claws up into the hunter's throat. Grabbing the gun from his limp hand, I crossed the car park in pursuit of the truck. If that damn automaton wasn't in the way—

Becks meowed a warning, and I spied Will's gargoyle form amid the haze of sparkling lights from the spells he'd set off. Screams rang out, the sound of humans fleeing from the mechanical atrocity making its way through the centre of London without a care for how much damage it left in its path.

As I ran in pursuit, the automaton ceased its advance. Its mechanical arm swung around, once again pointing its gun in my direction.

I flung myself flat as a bang shook the world, and something far too large to be a bullet ripped overhead. Smoke billowed across my vision, making me cough. I rolled over and saw that the former prison had caught ablaze, as the automaton had fired something akin to a small missile directly through the open window.

"Holy fuck!" I coughed again, my eyes stinging. Pushing to my feet, I blinked the haze from my eyes as I ran like hell.

When the automaton and hunters alike were out of sight, I spied Will descending over the Underground station and caught up to him at the stairs. He turned back into human form, clutching his ribs, blood seeping between his fingers.

"It wasn't a bullet, don't worry," he said breathlessly. "I got careless. Is that their gun?"

I looked down at my hand, shuddering inwardly. "Grabbed it by instinct. I also stole a book from their office."

"Read it later. We need to move."

"Cori." Damn. The truck had left, the monstrous automaton stomping in its wake, but descending the stairs still felt like giving up.

Becks nudged my ankle on the way past, prompting me to follow. The stairs were zombie-free this time around, and we made our way through to the Underground without resistance.

Only when we reached the tunnel's entrance did I realise that Astor was gone.

"Ember?" Will beckoned me through. "What is it?"

"Astor must have left."

"Was he any help back there?"

"Believe it or not, he took a bullet for me." That got me a raised eyebrow, but the amount of blood soaking Will's side was more important than looking for our wayward assassin companion.

When we reached the back room of the shelter ten minutes later, Becks flopped in front of the sofa and turned back into a human, her expression more downcast than I'd ever seen. "That was..."

"A fucking disaster?" I finished. "Either they were prepared for us, or they always planned to move the prisoners elsewhere."

"Both, I'd say, given what they did two years ago," Will said. "I tried to follow that truck of theirs, but I'd have needed a grenade to get those doors off. I'd say they learned their lesson from last time."

Pity I couldn't say the same for myself. While Will fetched himself a healing spell, I retrieved the notebook I'd swiped from the hunters' office and flipped it open. I didn't know what I'd expected to find inside. A manifesto on capturing evil shifters and how we were the devil incarnate, perhaps.

What I found instead was somewhat more mundane. The notebook contained page after page of scribbled notes arranged in columns. One column listed dates, and another contained inexplicable arrangements of numbers that must be some kind of internal coding system. The final column was written in an illegible shorthand that was even less decipherable than the numbers, so I noted a couple of repeating patterns and pointed them out to the others. "What do you think this is, a record of prisoners?"

"Looks that way." Will read over my shoulder. "There's a few sequences of numbers that recur a lot. Might refer to the type of shifter. Arseholes."

Is there a code for dragon shifters? My skin crawled as I skimmed through the pages, noting the dates moved closer to the present. The final date was yesterday's and contained a single entry, marked only with the number one. In the final column, the scribbled words brought a gasp to my mouth.

Female. Age 14-16. Take to Malkin.

"Malkin." The name tasted bitter on my tongue, though it was unfamiliar to me. "That's where they're taking her."

"Cori?" Will reached for the book with a bloody hand. "Does it say why they decided to move all the prisoners?"

"They must have changed tactics fast," I said. "It's like they knew we were coming, but the only way that's possible is if someone around here tipped them off."

"Yeah." Will's mouth twisted. "I have a feeling this is all tied up in whoever gave us that job yesterday."

"You never did reach your contact?" I thought back to the strange smell in the hunters' office. "Because I'd bet anything it's a witch."

"A witch working with the hunters?" Becks's nose wrinkled. "Why would anyone in their right mind turn against their fellow supernaturals?"

Will had gone pale. "I don't know, but I can try brewing up a tracking spell to find that notebook's owner. If they're alive. I mean, I can track them if they're dead, too, but the first one is more useful."

"Because if they're alive and they left the base, we can find Cori." That wouldn't help us get past the automaton and the accompanying hunters, but we still had a chance.

"It'll take a while to brew." He paced to the entrance to the kitchen. "And I don't know that we can safely stay here for much longer. I drew the hunters away from the Avenue, but it won't take much for them to put the incident at the jail together with the most obvious supernatural haven in the area."

Unease coiled in the pit of my stomach. "True, but where else are we supposed to go? They already blew up one of our hideouts."

A rattle in the hallway had me on my feet and hurrying towards the trapdoor. My breath caught when Astor's head appeared, followed by a not-insignificant amount of blood.

"Whoa." I took a step back, calling to Will. "We need a healing spell in here. Where'd you go?" I directed the question at Astor.

"To confirm what I expected," he said in a low voice. "The hunters are speaking to a witch around the corner from here. You might know him."

"Fucking *Twill.*" I turned to Will as he tossed a healing spell at Astor. "I think we found our informant."

"Why would he...?" Will trailed off. "I did hear him complaining to the neighbours about how I'm supposedly stealing his best customers, but I wouldn't have thought he'd go *that* far."

"He went to the hunters instead of being nicer to his customers?" Becks scowled. "I'd say we go in there and shake an apology out of him."

"Two hunters are in his house, and more are waiting outside," Astor warned. "I wouldn't advise it."

"Why?" Will asked of nobody in particular. "The whole reason we've survived this long is by looking out for one another. Sure, the other witches have never liked us shifters, but even Twill knows the hunters won't spare him either, given the chance."

"I know."

Since the invasion, divisions had sprung up even amongst supernaturals. Half-faeries got the worst of it due to their association with the invasion, but the faeries' arrival had also brought no shortage of spaces for them to make their home in that wouldn't cause friction with the other local supernaturals. The mages also lived apart, while shifters and witches found themselves competing for space in a city where danger came from every angle. Including each other, sometimes, but telling the hunters our hiding place, knowing they were condemning us to a certain death... I'd thought no supernatural would cross that line.

"Did you not hear me?" Astor kicked open the trapdoor again. "It won't be long before they start searching every house for the missing fugitives."

"Is that what we are?" I backed into the living room, scanning for anything I didn't already have in my rucksack. The notebook I'd taken from the hunter was the obvious one, but

Will had dozens of spells scattered around the place, and I knew he was loath to leave them behind.

A commotion arose from somewhere outside. Astor vanished through the trapdoor, and I lifted my head, suddenly on alert. A faint smell tickled my nostrils, drifting in from the shop. Smoke. "Can you smell that?"

"What?" Becks ran into the hall behind me, looking through the partly open door to the shop.

"Fire." I paused then sniffed again. "Fire. Run."

If a dragon smells fire, you get the hell out. Problem: the only route of escape was an enclosed space, which would be deadly when filled with smoke.

Becks shifted into cat form while Will came hurrying into the hall with his arms overflowing with charms. "This place is warded. It should hold, but—"

"Have you ever tested it against an open flame?"

The smell grew more intense, while the slam of the neighbouring door set my nerves afire. I let Will climb down the ladder first and was about to follow when the shop door burst open and two hunters ran inside.

11

The hunters entered the shop, revealing a street awash in thick smoke. My heart gave a sickening dive. *They're burning the houses.*

Did Twill really hate us that much? Or had the situation spun even beyond his control? The thoughts slid through my mind in the long moment in which the two hunters lifted their guns to point at me.

A gunshot ripped through the air—but it was one of the hunters who fell, skewered in the forehead by a lethal shot. Becks stood in the shop doorway, holding the gun I'd taken from the jail. I must have left it lying in the living room, and she'd aimed well. Even a hunter wouldn't get up from that one.

I let my claws slide out and struck the uninjured hunter, knocking his own weapon out of his hand. As three more crowded into the shop, Becks turned into cat form and ran under their feet, clawing at ankles and knees, driving them back through the open door.

Will emerged, a glowing light in his hand. I had the presence of mind to duck as a spell went off in the hunters' midst, sending a billowing cloud of white smoke into the air.

I snatched up the gun Becks had dropped and fired it wildly at the hunters. A yell and thud told me I'd hit one of them, but the smoke coupled with the rapidly spreading haze over the street outside would make it too easy to accidentally hit my friends, so I twisted it into a knot and threw it aside. The smell of fire persisted, and below the general shouts and crackle of flame came the mechanical clank of an automaton.

I held my breath and ducked outside. Through the smoke, I spied its fearsome form making its slow but deadly advance through the winding street. Shouts and screams accompanied each movement. As the whirring grew louder, the fleeing inhabitants of Magic Avenue retreated into their houses, or if that wasn't an option, they ducked into alleyways or otherwise fled. Yet the automaton made no move to attack any of them. It continued to move at a steady pace, as if it had one target alone.

"Shit," Will said behind me. "Well, it's been nice knowing you."

Becks sprang away from a hunter's corpse as the mechanical beast rounded the final corner and lifted its vast hand, revealing the gun clenched within.

There's only one way out.

"Guys, get behind me," I told the others. "Get in the house. Into the basement if you can, but otherwise, take cover."

"What?" said Becks. "You can't shift."

"There's no other way. Trust me." They said dragonfire could burn through anything, even metal, and at worst, I'd be a human—well, dragon—shield for the others.

Becks and Will both watched me, their eyes wide with fear. Neither had seen me shift, and I was willing to bet most of the hunters present hadn't either. Already, my claws extended, and a rippling sensation passed down my spine as my dragon side sought to break free.

Tremors took hold of me, and I hissed a final warning to the others. Then the shift was on me. Scales spread down my arms first, merging with the claws where my hands had been. My shoulders were next, my body lengthening to six feet or more as my legs moved further apart and my feet became curved claws. Wings unfurled behind my spine, and a growl rumbled in my chest, building to a roar.

The fireball building deep inside me ignited, and the noise that escaped my throat was alien and terrifying even to me. A torrent of fire erupted from my mouth. I glimpsed people fleeing, heard their screams, but my eyes were on the mechanical adversary clanking towards me without fear. Even in my current state, the gleaming gun carried in its hand-like appendage flared a warning in my head.

A hail of bullets cut through the air. I let instinct take over, my wings carrying me higher at a speed that brought me on collision course with the mechanical beast. Claw scraped against metal with a jarring clank that might well have broken bones if I'd been in human form. As it was, my claws ripped into its arm, slicing deep until its gun dragged against the ground.

Its other arm rose as if to strangle me, but I launched back into flight, rage turning my vision to white heat.

Then... fire. Not like the pitiful fire the hunters had started but true magical fire which blasted through the metal beast as if it was nothing more than a mirage. My ears registered screaming from somewhere close by, the sound of human terror, but instinct was all that remained. My own human side was locked away, silent, as though the fire had taken away my voice.

The automaton had crumpled, but the anger remained,

consumed my being. I wanted to hurt the monsters who'd taken my sister and bathe my claws in blood. Strangled noises came from my throat, a mix of human and dragon, but when I tried to take flight, an unseen force pressed against my wings, holding me down.

"Ember!" shouted a male voice. "You can't fly out in the open. The whole city will see you."

"I think any pretence of keeping her a secret is long dead," said a second male voice wryly, bringing a flicker of inexplicable emotion to the forefront that stood at odds with the anger roaring inside me. "I'd say we let her run free."

"You're shitting me," said a third voice, this one female. "We don't abandon our friends. I'd be dead if Ember and Cori hadn't helped me hide during the full moon after the invasion."

Right. Once a month, at the full moon, most shifters lost their reason. Some unknown force caused them to revert into animal form during the night and turn human again in the morning with little memory of anything that had occurred under cover of darkness. The phenomenon had given rise to the werewolf legend back in the old world, and to live alongside humans, shifters had to adapt by locking themselves down at nights during the full moon or accepting the inevitable carnage. Some shifters were unaffected, like gargoyles, and I'd thought dragons were the same.

"Why isn't she turning back?" asked the first voice. "She hasn't forgotten how to, surely."

"Don't you have some kind of spell or potion?" said the second.

"I'm not a walking chemist!" Will... that was his name. Will, my friend. "And there's no spell that can turn a dragon back into a human. That I know of."

"There's one for werewolves," said the female voice.

Becks. Why was it so hard to recall my friends' names? And why couldn't I fly? My wings beat, and a rattling scream built in my chest as I fought to escape.

"I don't have any," Will said. "Damn, I bet Twill does. I'd love to give him a piece of my mind."

"Careful. He might have more hunters hiding in his house." Becks paused. "I'll go with you. Astor?"

Astor. That was his name—and it was him, I realised belatedly, who was holding the end of the net-like substance that had my wings pinned behind my back. I snarled, fighting to free myself.

"Oh, I suppose it's fine if she rips me to pieces," he said. "If I get killed—"

"You'll come back as a ghost you don't believe in and berate us, I get it," said Will.

"I never said I didn't believe in ghosts." Then, quieter, he whispered in my ear, "You must remember how to be human, surely. Turn back."

I growled in answer. How dare he keep me from taking flight? I ought to flay the skin from his bones. My eyes tracked each movement as he stepped around me, a rope held in each hand, until we looked directly at one another.

"I don't want to be here either," he said in a low, irritated voice. "Fuck, I should never have come back for you, but you got under my skin, little dragon, and that's just how it is."

Shocked disbelief flooded me. I whipped towards him, trying to speak but unable to find words. I felt the ropes loosen as my wings shrank away to nothing. My claws became hands, scales became skin, and I fell to my knees as Astor dropped the ropes, a self-satisfied smile on his face.

"You bastard," I growled between my teeth. "You threw a net on me?"

As I kicked the net aside and stalked towards him, I could

feel the shift threaten to overwhelm me. Primal violence gripped me like a fever. My claws emerged again, wanting blood, and my teeth bared in a snarl as Astor backed into the doorway to Will's shop.

Then he grabbed my shoulders and his mouth closed over mine.

12

The effect of the kiss was instantaneous. Heat bloomed along my skin, yet the instinct to shift vanished entirely. Rather, a different kind of fire leaped between the blazing path where our lips touched, and the angry growl in my throat became one of pure, primal lust. I was barely aware that I was moving until I'd grabbed his shoulders, shoved him against the wall, and kissed him hard with an abandon I'd never thought I'd feel for someone like him—someone who was supposed to be my enemy.

Reality hit me in a rush, travelling through my body like an electric jolt. I sprang away from him, glass crunching beneath my feet. We were inside the shop—thank god for that—and Astor stood in the shop doorway, his expression somewhere between shock and bemusement, his lips swollen where I'd latched onto him with a passion that I could only attribute to the aftereffects of shifting from dragon to human.

"You bastard," I gasped. "What the fuck was that?"

"I was trying to distract you, and it looks like you really wanted that distraction." His eyes glittered with amusement, and though the shop floor was littered with glass from a window I didn't remember breaking, I hadn't shifted and ripped out his throat. That impulse had disappeared the second our lips had touched.

"Never, ever do that to me again."

Not only had he risked his own life, but half the street might have seen, if they hadn't been hiding from the aftermath of my confrontation with the hunters and the automaton.

"I can't promise that," he said. "If you're going to forget how to turn back into a human every time you shift, then I'm more than happy to help."

"Fuck you." My knees gave way, and I sagged against the wall as the world danced around me. I didn't remember when the windows had shattered, unless I'd done it myself when I'd roared loudly enough to shake the rooftops. Splinters of broken glass littered the shop floor.

"I thought you claimed you didn't want that," Astor said. "I'm getting mixed messages here."

I growled in warning and tried to push upward. "If you want me *not* to burn you to a crisp, you're doing a terrible job."

"You're too easy to wind up, little dragon."

How in hell could he talk to me normally after what'd happened between us? Obviously, to him, it was just a kiss. He didn't have any beast waiting inside him, reckless and wanting and made of nothing but desire. And while my dragon side couldn't have him, the possessive need stirring inside me undoubtedly came from her, not me.

"Why do you call me that?" I asked. "Is it supposed to be a term of endearment?"

"Sure, if you like." His smirk didn't waver, and his voice dropped to a low purr. "That was hot as fuck."

The small hairs on my arms rose as the flames in my chest

stirred again. *Damn you, Astor.* He couldn't have more effectively subdued my shifter form if he'd tried.

And I didn't want it. I *couldn't* want it.

"What you said to me before," I began, and his smirk slipped away. "You said, *I never should have come back for you.* You didn't mean when you came back earlier today. Did you?"

All desire bled out of his eyes as his expression smoothed out to blankness. "Yes."

He's lying. I knew it as surely as I knew I could have killed him in dragon form had I not clung on, however loosely, to my human side. If part of me hadn't seen him as an ally.

"It has to do with why you were following the hunters," I said. "Doesn't it?"

"Yes." A tense moment passed. "I've been spying on them for a while, and I happened to be at their office when I heard the confirmation that they'd tracked down London's last dragon shifter."

My breath caught. "You knew someone tipped them off from the start?"

I was barely aware of moving until my claws were at his neck and had pinned him to the wall. His throat moved as he inhaled and exhaled, a bead of blood gathering where the tip of my claw brushed against the skin. Fire burned inside me, demanding to be released. This time, not lust, but pure rage.

A thin trail of blood ran down his collar. I could feel his pulse thrumming against my scales, hear his racing heart.

"Ember," he said. "I wanted to be straight with you, believe it or not. I didn't set you up. The League did. By the time I caught up with them, it was too late to save your sister. If you hadn't ambushed me, I might have got closer, but in the end—"

"Don't lie. You'd never have saved her. Never." My claw

could snap his neck easily, but my body was shaking so much that it was all I could do to stay upright.

"You're being irrational," he said. "As a matter of fact, I came after the hunters because I thought you were the one they'd been sent to capture."

A wild laugh escaped me. "You thought I needed a knight in shining armour to save me from the big bad, is that it? You get points for being creative, but you're full of shit."

"You want to know why?" He looked me dead in the eyes. "Because I spoke to you before you shifted. You and your sister. Even when you turned into a dragon, I saw the human in you."

"You *shot* at us."

"It was a reflex." He was almost shouting now. "I went back to the hunters after the faeries showed up because they were the only people not getting trampled to death. And for a moment, yes, I *did* wonder if the League was right and all the supernaturals had united to take us out."

I laughed again, but the fight drained out of me. I sank back to the floor, claws shifting to hands once more. "You expect me to believe that."

"You're back!" To my intense relief, Becks came running into the shop, killing the flames as surely as if they'd been doused in water. Will followed more slowly, casting a suspicious look at Astor. "You're okay, aren't you? I thought we'd come back and find you'd burned the house down."

"No danger of that happening, don't worry." I pushed shakily to my feet, averting my eyes from Astor. "We need to move."

"Not now," said Will. "You look like you're about to pass out."

"The hunters…"

"Won't be coming back anytime soon, if they have any sense." Will held a bottle in one hand, and the memory of their conversation while I'd been stuck in the form of a dragon nudged its way back into my mind again.

"You got that from Twill's place?" I asked.

A scowl appeared on his face. "Yes, and the slimy dickhead must have run off. Bet he's gone to join his hunter buddies."

"I hoped I burned him to cinders." I studied the bottle. "What's that for?"

"Dampening the aftereffects of shifting," he replied. "It's made for werewolves, but it might help you feel less lightheaded."

"Good." I took the bottle from him and twisted off the lid, sniffing at the contents. The potion smelled like a mixture of liquorice and spearmint. "Hope it doesn't have the opposite effect. Sorry I broke your window."

"Nah, that was the hunters," said Will. "Fucking vandals. I'd say our cover's blown, but it already was, thanks to Twill."

"Arsehole." I downed the potion, grimacing at the aftertaste. "Whose house did the hunters set on fire?"

"There were some other undercover shifters hiding a few doors down. I hope they escaped while the hunters were distracted by Ember."

"Me too." Guilt churned inside me as I trod through the hallway, fatigue tugging at my limbs. Reaching the living room, I sank to the floor. "I hope your concoction kicks in soon. I can't chase after the hunters like this."

"You can't chase them anyway," said Astor. "The League's drivers know the city backwards. I used to be one myself, so I know."

"What, as well as security duty?" I supposed that they must need a lot of drivers to ferry them around the city, if they wanted to avoid detection by the authorities. We, unfortunately, didn't even have a car, and even if I'd been in any state to fly in pursuit, there was no guarantee of catching up to the hunters before they reached their destination.

The sense of defeat tasted as bitter as the concoction I'd drunk. I could feel its effects slowly kicking in as my body fought the oncoming fatigue. I didn't know how bad it would be this time, but I'd been all but unconscious for a full day following my first shift, and Cori had been terrified I'd never come back to my senses. I'd woken to find myself lying in a tunnel, my sister curled up over me and the taste of ashes in my mouth.

Never again, I'd sworn, but I couldn't afford to hold back any longer. To get Cori out of the hunters' clutches, I had to unleash my dragon form to its full extent, no matter the consequences.

As my energy returned, so did my questions. "Astor—did you see any hunters in the tunnels when you came back?"

"No," he replied. "And the ones in the street will have fled, if they have any sense."

"Does that mean they went after that truck?"

"Unlikely," said Astor. "If their destination is the Orion Stronghold—and what I heard of their conversation told me that's where they're taking the prisoners—then only a small number of hunters know where it is."

"And that doesn't include you," I added.

"It does now." Astor reached into his pocket and produced a rolled-up piece of paper. "I have the address. Or *an* address, at any rate."

My heart kickstarted. "Where'd you get that? The jail's office?"

He handed me the paper in answer, which turned out to be some kind of leaflet printed in large font.

"'Sick of the supernatural scum infesting the city?'" I quoted. "'Ready to take London back?' Is this for real?"

"Look at the address," was Astor's response.

A growl slipped between my teeth as I skimmed down to the bottom of the page. There, I found a date and time—tomorrow, at noon—and an address.

"Windsor," I read. "Outside of London... is that where you think the Stronghold is?"

"They wouldn't hold a public event at the actual prison, but it's bound to be close," Astor said. "And there'll certainly be people present there who will know."

"Tomorrow at noon." Waiting just under a day seemed unacceptable, but I hadn't left London in more than a decade, let alone in its current state of destruction. Half the roads were unusable, if not more. "They're going public, are they?"

"They're trying to spread their message among the regular humans," said Astor. "That fits with the overt tactics we saw from them earlier. They don't fear being challenged."

"The mages should be paying attention now." They'd surely have heard about the giant automaton rampaging around Magic Avenue from their fancy mansions over in Kensington by the morning, but that would already be too late. "Well. We have to get into this event, then, don't we?"

Astor's mouth tightened, but he nodded. "I may know someone who can help you."

"Come again?"

"What are you two talking about?" Becks backed into the room, eyeing us suspiciously. "What's that leaflet?"

"An ad for recruiting new League members." I clenched my fist, crumpling the paper. "It's about 'taking back London' from the evil shifters."

Becks mimed vomiting. "I don't want to hear the rest, thanks."

"Also, Astor says he knows someone who can help us break into the prison."

"I said nothing of the sort," Astor retorted. "I meant the League's public event. I know someone who might help you get in without drawing suspicion, but I can't make any guarantees."

"It's also in Windsor." I unfurled the end of the leaflet again to show her. "So we'd need to get out of the city."

"Our tunnels don't go that far." Her lips compressed. "Shit, we'd need a car."

"And a driver." My gaze slid to Astor. "You know the way?"

"I do." He did not elaborate further.

"Will you drive us?" I pressed.

"I'd have more confidence if I was able to get in touch with my contact first," Astor said. "Unfortunately, someone took my phone away right before an automaton trampled their house flat."

"It might still be intact." Assuming the house hadn't been looted. "I'll ask Will."

I rose to my feet, relieved to find some of my strength returning. In the shop, I found Will in the act of boarding up the smashed window.

"Bloody hunters," he muttered. "They still owe me from the last time they caused criminal damage."

"Whereabouts did you put the phone and weapons you confiscated from Astor?" I asked him. "He needs to call someone who might be able to help us."

"And who exactly would that be?" Will put down a board with a surprising amount of force. "I know that hunter friend of yours came through for us in the end, but after Twill, I'm not feeling particularly charitable towards strangers."

"I get that, but look." I held up the leaflet. "This is grim."

Will read the hunters' manifesto, his expression darkening. "The bigoted twats are recruiting from the public now?"

"I know, but the event is open to everyone," I said. "That means we can disguise ourselves and get in without them being any the wiser."

"If we can get ourselves to Windsor." He pushed the leaflet back into my hands. "Which, given the state of the city, is only doable by flight."

"Astor can drive and says he knows all of London's back roads. But like I said, his friend might not help us if we show up unannounced."

He blew out a breath. "Well, the automaton didn't trample the entire house, as far as I saw. There's a chance the stuff we left behind is intact, but I can't say I'm that keen on going back. It'll probably be swarming with dark fae."

"I'll go." Astor himself appeared in the back doorway, watching Will as though expecting a challenge.

Will simply shrugged. "Be my guest."

"Not alone." The protest slipped out before I could think better of it. Heat rushed to my neck when all eyes turned to me. Including Astor's.

"You," he said, "were on the brink of passing out last I saw you. Unless you're that worried for me?"

"Only that you'll take off now you have the chance to." *Smooth, Ember.* I gave myself a mental shake. What in hell was wrong with me?

"I've had plenty of chances to already, haven't I?"

Becks poked her head out of the living room. "Ember, I wouldn't go out into the open. You're the one they're looking for."

That was true enough, but I had an inkling she didn't trust Astor any more than Will did. Whereas I wasn't sure I trusted *myself* around him.

"All right." I returned to the living room, trying to tell myself I was more worried that Astor would draw the hunters on his tail than that he might run into trouble. I could feel him watching me, and when I turned back to watch him open the trapdoor, I saw the glint of a gun at his waistband. He must have grabbed it from one of the hunters. "Try not to piss off any more faeries."

"I'd rather avoid that, too." He slid down the ladder with lithe grace worthy of a cat shifter and closed the trapdoor behind him.

"Intense, isn't he?" Will said in an undertone. "It's like being in the house with a live bomb."

"What do you expect from a hunter?" said Becks. "I don't like us putting our safety in his hands. I know Ember trusts him, but—"

"I don't." Or did I? "I mean, I trust him more than the dickheads who want to shoot us dead, but I'm fairly sure he's out for his own self-interest and nothing more."

"He's not the only one," Will muttered. "If Twill comes back, I hope the other witches run him out of the street."

"Yeah." I sat on the sofa and rubbed my forehead. "At least we know our next move. If the League has opened their doors to the public, we can use any disguise we like and we won't register as suspicious. Once we're in, we'll find someone who knows the Stronghold's address, and…"

"And storm in?" Becks sounded sceptical. "I don't know. Sure, we got into the other jail with no problems, but this Stronghold must be tightly guarded if even most of the hunters don't know where it is."

"Astor said only the Elites know it even exists," I recalled. "That's their top rank."

Will walked to the kitchen, yawning. "I guess I should start on those disguise spells, unless someone wants to go find a fancy dress shop."

"No thanks." I felt a little more alert than I had earlier, but my limbs were a little shaky and I didn't trust my balance.

Becks's next words woke me up as thoroughly as a bucket of water thrown onto my head.

"So, how did Astor convince you to shift into a human again?" she asked.

"He didn't. I mean. I have no idea." Damn. I was not ready for this conversation.

"And the fact that the shop smelled of werewolves in heat when I came in had nothing to do with it?"

"What?" I yelped, sitting upright. "It didn't."

"It did, and I'm not even a werewolf." Will pulled a face. "I wasn't going to say anything, but it was a little hard not to notice."

"It was a mistake." How else could I possibly explain it? "Like you said, he was trying to stop me from shifting back into a dragon."

Will burst out laughing. "That's a hell of a weird way to go about it. He gets points for creativity, though. And it worked."

"But you already knew one another," Becks said slowly. "Right?"

I turned my gaze downward. "We initially met here, on Magic Avenue, before the incident in the Underground. He was pretending that—that he belonged here." My cheeks burned, not with embarrassment but shame. What would Rhea have thought of me nearly hooking up with a hunter?

"What?" Becks's voice gained a dangerous edge. "He pretended to be one of us? To gain your trust?"

Will's expression was appalled. "He showed up *here*? Was it him who told the hunters this street existed?"

"They already knew." My hands fisted against the carpet. "It's screwed up, I get it. Obviously, he was given orders to come here, and when the faeries showed up, the hunters had to change their plan."

"That's when he claims to have renounced them?" Will guessed. "Right after he met you. I don't know whether that's romantic or deeply disturbing."

"The latter," Becks supplied. "I would never *touch* a hunter."

"Becks, didn't you date a troll once?" Will said.

"He wasn't a troll," Becks said indignantly. "He was just a really tall gargoyle."

"Most gargoyles aren't nine feet tall."

"Better than a hunter." Becks's eyes flashed towards me. "I get it, you didn't know. But I can't pretend it doesn't creep me out."

"It's nothing." It wasn't like I'd had any romantic notions whatsoever about taking off with Astor. What I'd felt had been pure misplaced lust. "Shifting back into a human has weird side effects the first couple of times. I don't feel anything for him."

"I should bloody well hope not," said Becks. "Well, I guess we're stuck with him as an ally now, for better or worse. And that contact of his." Her tone suggested just how much *she* trusted this unknown person, but I found myself curious about who'd gained Astor's trust enough that he considered them worth contacting in a situation as dicey as this one.

We discussed potential disguises for a short while before the click of the trapdoor announced that Astor was back. Conscious of the others watching me, I refrained from standing up when he entered the room.

Astor addressed Will. "Just so you know, there are faeries raiding your kitchen."

"Of course there are," Will said. "Did you at least get your phone?"

"Yes. The battery's nearly dead, but I warned my contact we're coming. I also procured us a car."

"Aren't you resourceful." Will paced into the kitchen and sighed. "I suppose I should start on our disguises now, if we have to set off at the arse-crack of dawn."

"There's no need," said Astor. "I know enough shortcuts

to get us there in a few hours. You can prepare when we're at my contact's house."

"Why should we trust you?" Becks eyed him suspiciously. "For all we know, you and this contact of yours have set another trap."

"Simmer down, Becks," Will said out of the corner of his mouth. "This weirdo's offering us a lift. You and Ember can't fly—well, Ember can't without alerting every hunter in the city—so I'd say we take it. That's one vote for and one against. What about you, Ember?"

Everyone looked at me, including Astor. "Well?" he said. "If you want to get where you're going, you'll just have to take a leap of faith."

Didn't I know it. The others' warnings were fresh in my mind, but to save Cori, there was only one option. "Then let's move."

13

O nce I'd packed for an overnight stay, I found Astor waiting in the hallway, one foot resting on the closed trapdoor.

"Who is this contact of yours?" I asked, doing my level best to sound neutral, as if nothing whatsoever had happened between us. "Another hunter?"

"I'm not a hunter," he said irritably. "How many times do I have to say it? I wouldn't have stood beside you while you shifted into a giant fire-breathing lizard if I were."

Whoa. That was a bit much. Perhaps he regretted what had happened between us, too, but having this old argument might be just what I needed to re-establish the boundaries between us. Necessary, necessary boundaries.

"I meant people who *left* the hunters," I clarified. "If you want to be pedantic. I assume you didn't get too many chances to make friends outside of their ranks."

"No, but if you say anything unwise to her, there's a fair chance she'll break your legs and kick you out on the street."

"Really?" I cocked a brow. "She's welcome to try."

"I wouldn't advise you to show your claws in front of her

either," he added. "I told her the League took your sister, but not…"

"Not that I'm a dragon." Not for the first time, I wondered whether it had been a good idea to bring someone else in on the plan, even partially. "You know, I'm placing an awful lot of faith in you not to get us killed, whether by your friend or otherwise. It's not just my life at stake here."

Becks's voice drifted from upstairs. "Will, you don't need to bring the Monopoly board."

"There's no better way to make new friends. Or mortal enemies, as it were."

"Your friends already made their decision," Astor said. "I didn't lie to you. If you want me to use my resources to help you, you'll have to choose whether to trust me or not. Time is of the essence, little dragon."

His words lingered in my mind as we descended into the basement. Will had re-set the wards on the door and set up defences in case the hunters showed up in the tunnels again, but it was hard to imagine ever returning to Magic Avenue when the whole street had seen me shift into a dragon.

Astor had parked the car he'd 'borrowed' down the street from the house the automaton had trampled, as the roads in that area would be less impassable than the ones in the busier parts of the city. As a result, we had a long walk through the tunnels along the reverse of the route we'd taken earlier that same day. No traces remained of our fight with the hunters—their bodies would be rotting in the troll's lair where we'd left them—but every echo set my nerves blazing, and the tight space seemed even more cramped than it had earlier. When we emerged from the broken-down station, a sense of unreality washed over me. Not far from here, an automaton had chased us through the street, and while Astor had vouched for the hunters' absence, every shadow drew me to lift my claws in anticipation of an attack.

Astor halted next to a parked car. "This should have enough petrol to get us where we need to go. I checked."

"And the roads?" Becks sounded sceptical. "They're messed up all over the city, I thought."

"I know all the back roads," said Astor, getting into the driver's seat. "It's required, since there's no other way to get around until they get the trains working again. Personally, I'm not willing to wait for the Mage Lords to stop regulating supernaturals and remember the rest of us exist."

"They don't even bother with us, most of the time." Since my friends didn't oblige, I got into the front next to Astor. At least I'd have a better view of where we were going. Becks and Will then climbed into the back, both with visible reluctance.

"I'm not going to drive you into a ditch and murder you," said Astor. "You're all carrying more weapons than I am."

"Don't you still have their gun?" asked Will.

"It's out of bullets. I used the last one on the fae that attacked me at your house."

"You were attacked?" I turned to him.

He shrugged. "I'd have stolen a spare, but I think you trod on them."

"Good." The fewer weapons the hunters had, the better. "Why *do* the bullets kill supernaturals and not humans?"

This might not be the best topic of conversation while trapped in a small vehicle, but when faced with the prospect of meeting another ex-hunter with dubious motives, I found my questions multiplying.

Astor was silent for a moment. "I don't have the faintest idea. I gather they're manufactured at a special facility."

"And tested on prisoners?" Contempt dripped from Becks's voice. "Is that what this Stronghold is really for?"

Astor cut her a sharp look. "I've never been there. I wouldn't know."

"But you do know more than you've told us," said Becks. "And so does your friend, I'm betting."

His hands tightened on the steering wheel. "If you can't get over my past, we aren't going to get anywhere. I'd suggest you hold onto your questions if you aren't going to like the answers. It's a long drive."

He wasn't kidding. While Astor knew the city backwards, we frequently ran into dead ends or obstacles like torn-up roads or collapsed buildings—and, in one case, a troll taking a nap in the middle of a major junction. The constant rattle of potholes stopped me from dozing off at first, but after the first hour, my exhaustion began to catch up with me despite the encroaching darkness and the monsters ready to come out of hiding.

The car engine's quiet purr was surprisingly soothing, and soon Becks had curled up cat-like in the back while Will sprawled across the seat, snoring softly. Eventually, I dozed off myself, jolting awake when the car stopped. "Are we there?"

Astor shook his head. "Traffic light."

I frowned at him. "There's nobody watching."

He shrugged. "I always assume someone is."

I rolled my eyes. "I should have figured you'd be a stickler for any kind of rules."

"I'm breaking some significant ones to bring you with me. Nobody's supposed to know about our hideout."

"Nobody was supposed to know about ours either. Now two are trashed and so are a bunch of other houses on Magic Avenue." I rubbed my sleepy eyes. "And here we are leaving the city instead of helping them."

"Didn't your neighbours turn you in?"

"One neighbour, and he's always been a dick." As Astor had seen for himself.

"I'm still surprised he'd take the risk. The hunters don't

distinguish between friend and foe when it comes to collateral damage."

"Well, no." I could tell we were treading close to a dangerous topic again, so I changed tack. "Does your friend live close to where we're going tomorrow?"

"Less than an hour away." He took us around a corner, avoiding the outline of something clawed and nasty-looking crouched in the road. "You haven't left the city since the invasion?"

"Nor before." At least, not in my own memories. Obviously, Cori and I had come from outside, but the life we'd lived before our first memories of the Underground might as well have belonged to another person. "You?"

"Not since I was young," he said. "The League has bases all over the country, but London's is the biggest, so they always need the most recruits."

"Are they still in contact with the other bases?" I didn't even know which part of the country Cori and I had originally come from. Our accents had been hard to place, back when we'd first moved to London, but Rhea had always said somewhere up north, or Scotland. Wherever the other dragon shifters were hiding—if any survived—none had ever come after us.

"I expect so," he answered, "but most League members aren't given that information."

"I bet." The words came out sounding more bitter than I'd intended. I hadn't spared many thoughts for our pre-London lives in the past couple of years, having been more focused on survival than anything else, but the League had been in the background until they'd come after my sister. If they'd been looking for us the whole time, what had become of the other dragon shifters? Did any still exist?

Astor's tense silence made me realise he'd thought my words were a jab at him.

"I was thinking about the others, I mean. The other dragon shifters."

A surprised look crossed his face. "You've never met?"

"No. Yes. It's complicated." I supposed he'd told me some of his own history, so it was only fair that I shared a small piece of mine. "I don't remember them. Someone wiped our memories, so Cori and I have no recollection of our lives before we moved to London nine years ago."

"Wiped your memories?" he said. "With magic?"

"I don't know how, exactly, but I've never been able to find another explanation." I rested my elbow against the darkened window. "Cori and I were sent here with nothing but an address of a shelter for displaced shifters. And a notebook telling us we were dragon shifters. I guess so there wouldn't be any unwelcome surprises later on."

A moment passed. "That seems extreme."

"I guess they worried the League would torture their location out of us if we got caught." I'd spoken without thinking, but if he'd reacted, the dark made it hard to tell. I clamped my mouth shut, wondering what in hell I was doing, sharing my history with a stranger. And this man *was* a stranger, in every way that mattered.

Even though he kissed me.

I shoved the thought firmly to the back of my mind.

Astor finally spoke. "After all that, I'm surprised you wanted my help at all."

"Wanted?" Had he forgotten I'd had no choice in the matter?

"Maybe 'needed' is a better word," he corrected himself. "I know you felt like I was the only hunter who might help you find your sister. And I owed you."

"Yes, you did." I wished I hadn't told him anything at all. "I wasn't thinking clearly, I'll admit that, but here we are."

"Here we are," he repeated. "Too late for any regrets."

I had plenty of those, but strangely, capturing him and demanding his help wasn't one of them. Hadn't he more or less been trying to do exactly that, in a roundabout fashion? Yes, he hadn't talked to me directly until I'd given him no choice, but I understood why, after he'd betrayed me once already.

Now he'd saved my life at least twice, including taking a bullet meant for me. Did I owe *him* now? I didn't have the faintest idea how we were supposed to tally up that kind of thing, or even if I wanted to. In a way, I'd preferred it when we'd been sworn enemies. It had certainly been more clear-cut back then.

Regrets aside, rescuing Cori was the priority. Whether Astor stuck around afterwards or vanished entirely didn't matter a bit. Assuming, of course, that we even made it through alive.

We will, I told myself. *We'll survive this, including Cori. I'll drag her from the hunters' clutches with my bare hands if I have to.*

14

S ometime later, we pulled up in a street seemingly empty of human presence. The terraced homes were dilapidated, with their doors hanging from hinges, windows busted inwards, gardens overgrown both with regular plants and with the fae variety. The road was clear, free of broken-down cars or other debris, suggesting someone had done a meticulous job of cleaning up and then vanished into thin air.

Becks woke first, stretching and yawning in a catlike way. She poked Will in the shoulder twice before he blinked awake, squinting at the flickering streetlamp outside. "What time is it?"

"Just after ten at night." Astor climbed out of the car and softly closed the door behind him.

I followed more slowly, a hand on my weapon. This was the kind of neighbourhood where wild fae preyed on the unwary, but there didn't appear to be anything untoward hiding in the shadows. In the absence of a sea of city lights, the stars shone brighter than I'd ever seen them.

Another light came on in a downstairs window, and there came the soft click of a door opening. Astor crossed the pavement from the parked car to one of the houses and met a hooded figure at the door who wore a robe-like garment that covered their body from head to toe. A woman, by the sound of her whispered voice. I didn't catch what she said to Astor, but he responded with "I told you these people need your help. We have to be at Windsor by noon tomorrow."

The woman's hood fell back. Her head was shaved, and tattoos covered the part of her neck I could see beneath the cloak. Ex-hunter tattoos. "Let them come in, but if they turn out not to be trustworthy, you're the one who'll have to get the bloodstains out of the wallpaper, not me."

"I don't like the sound of that," Will said from behind me. "Who even are you?"

"Name's Giselle. Get in here before you draw out the faeries."

She headed into a narrow hallway, walking with a distinct limp. The house smelled of must and smoke, the sort from an old gas fire, but nothing that put me in mind of the hunters. When Astor followed her, she flicked a light on, her sleeve riding up to reveal more of her tattoos. Not just tattoos. I'd know burn marks anywhere. Livid red scars covered the top of her back and shoulders, interspersed with the swirling tattoos. An icy chill went down my spine.

"Stare a little more, why don't you?"

"Sorry." I looked away. "The League took my sister." At least, I assumed it was the League who'd inflicted those wounds on her. It seemed a safe bet.

She grunted. "This is a rescue mission, is it?"

"Yes." I stood back as Will and Becks entered the house, slowly, with unconcealed suspicion.

"Astor seems to think you're trustworthy." Giselle closed the door and looked me up and down. "Can't think why.

First he disappears, then he brings three shifters here. If I didn't know better, I'd say you've corrupted him."

She knows we're shifters? I'd thought Astor hadn't given her any details at all.

"Don't look so alarmed. I'm not interested in turning any of you over to the League. Trust me, it wouldn't be worth my time if you insist on trying to infiltrate the Stronghold of your own accord. You're signing your own death sentence."

"I already told them that," added Astor, pushing open a door into a dark, wide room containing little furniture and few hints that gave away the character of the person who owned the place.

A number of mattresses and sleeping bags lay on the bare floorboards, and the only other furniture was an ancient couch with half the stuffing hanging out of it. A kitchenette was adjoined at the back, while a short corridor beyond led to what I assumed would be a small bedroom and bathroom. The low lighting gave the impression of a cave.

Giselle limped to the sofa, sprawling out as if to intentionally leave no room for anyone else to sit, and Astor prowled over to the corner. Weapons had been left in a pile: knives, axes, even a hunter's gun or two. I didn't blame Becks and Will for staying in the doorway, watching warily as if they were about to enter a troll's lair.

"Make yourselves at home," Giselle said. "Everyone else does. I went to all this trouble to get out of the city, and everyone else decided to turn my house into a holiday rental. Nobody's ever paid."

"I seem to remember you took the keys to this place out of the landlord's rotting hand after a troll tore his head off," Astor responded.

Giselle gave a harsh laugh. "I'm an opportunist, what can I say? Now, sit down, all of you. You're making me twitchy."

I sat down. Mostly because I could see the glint of

weapons underneath her robe and my dragon side recognised a fellow predator when she saw one. "Thanks for letting us stay."

"Don't thank me," she growled. Evidently, being thanked made her twitchy, too. "I do this for my own benefit. There aren't many people to talk to out here."

"Can't imagine why that is," Becks muttered.

"What was that?" Giselle lifted her head. "I suppose city-born shifters like you have never set foot outside of London."

"Did Astor tell you what we are?" He must have, but I detected a chance to learn more about who exactly Astor himself was, too.

"It wasn't hard to guess," she replied. "The League doesn't pursue any supernaturals as rabidly as they do shifters. I assume Astor told you as much."

"They're also making an overt power play in London, by the looks of things," I replied. "I've never heard of them infiltrating supernaturals' own networks to track us down, and they even set an automaton loose in central London earlier today."

Her brow arched. "They got that thing working, did they?"

"You knew they were building giant robots?"

"They were building a lot of things. Some more realistic than others. Had a *vision*, Malkin did."

That name again. "Is he… their leader?"

She gave a soft snort. "I thought Astor told you everything."

Astor knew. Inexplicably, her words brought anger welling to the surface all over again. "Everything relevant. We only found out the Stronghold existed earlier today."

"And you decided to plan a jailbreak." She gave a soft snort. "You've got nerve, that's for sure, but this brave rescue mission isn't going to end with you anywhere other than in an early grave."

"Thanks for the input," I said. "My sister's in there. I'm going to get her out whether you help us or not. Astor told us that you can give us assistance. That's why he brought us here."

"A likely story. He brought you here because he wants another favour. You're just an excuse."

My gaze cut to Astor. "What?"

"She's talking bullshit," said Astor smoothly. "We need a way into the Stronghold, nothing more."

Giselle laughed outright. "You need more firepower than the likes of me can offer. Aren't all supernaturals under the protection of the Mage Lords?"

"Protection?" This time I was the one to laugh, and not just because of the word *firepower*. We had that, in spades. "They're too busy trying to protect themselves and anyone they think matters from being killed by the fae. We're a long way down their priority list."

"Welcome to the club, sweetheart," said Giselle. "I can't help you get into the jail. Now, this public event tomorrow is more of a realistic target, but no less risky, and I certainly won't be coming with you."

"We don't expect you to." Becks eyed her with growing contempt. "I suppose you and Astor will be on their hit list, too, being deserters."

She grunted. "If I were fool enough to accompany you, I'd be put to death publicly as an example."

Astor himself didn't reply. He hadn't sat down, instead crouching beside the pile of weapons and examining each of them with a critical eye.

"You're both rays of sunshine, aren't you?" Will said. "I can see why he likes you."

Did he? The two of them had a history, no doubt, but I

hadn't detected any romantic vibes between them. Their mutual experience with the League would have been enough for them to build an understanding that even I wasn't privy to.

"I don't care if you come with us or not," I said to Giselle. "We just need the League not to recognise us, and it's safe to say the hunters who came from London will know our faces."

"What's in it for me, precisely, if I help you?" she queried.

"Our undying affection?" said Will. "Actually, we have our own plans. We don't need your help."

"And yet Astor went to the trouble of bringing you here," she mused. "You know, I can't say I like the idea of him getting killed because of a group of reckless shifters with an axe to grind."

"Wouldn't you do the same if they took one of your close family members captive?" Did she have family, or like Astor, had hers been killed by a shifter, too? "My sister isn't the only one they took. They went as far as to clear out their base in Trafalgar and shoved all the prisoners into the back of a truck bound for the Stronghold. I'd say this goes beyond a simple kidnapping."

She tilted her head on one side. "You *did* cause a stir. I wonder what makes your sister so special."

He didn't tell her, then. My gaze slid to Astor, who'd continued to inspect the weapons one by one as if he was intensely absorbed in the process. Maybe I'd been too quick to assume he'd spilled all our secrets.

"Is she part fae?" She peered at my face. "No, you don't look pretty enough to have faerie blood."

"Excuse me?" My face heated. I felt Astor's gaze turn towards me, but I refused to turn and see if he looked like he agreed with her. "What the hell does this have to do with whether you'll help us?"

"The League claims shifters and faeries are related to one another, going back a few hundred generations. Then again, most of what they said was a lie anyway, so I'm not sold on that one."

I scowled. "Yeah, that made it easy for everyone to point the finger of blame at us when the Sidhe destroyed half the world. As if the faeries didn't kill us, too."

"We all have our grievances, sweetheart."

"And we really do have our own plans," Becks said. "Will needs to use your kitchen."

"That's right." Will moved over to the kitchen counter and emptied his rucksack onto it. The smell of herbs filled the air, stinging my eyes.

Giselle twisted in her seat. "What are you doing?"

"Summoning Satan," said Will.

Astor picked up a sharp-looking knife from the pile in the corner. "These three have the bright idea of using simple hedge witch tricks to bypass the guards."

"Simple?" said Will. "Are you volunteering as a test subject?"

"Witch, are you?" Giselle watched him over the back of the sofa. "Thought you were shifters."

"Mostly." Will picked up a spell shaped like a paperclip and gave it a twist. A popping sounded, like the cork let out of a bottle, and the spell leapt into the air, spinning like a Catherine wheel. "Imagine that times a thousand and you'll have some idea of the state we left London in. Still think we can't get into the Stronghold?"

Giselle grunted and sank back into her seat. "I've no doubt you'll make a good go of it, but you need stealth, not theatrics."

"We have that, too." Will deflated the spinning wheel with another flash of a spell. "If the occasion calls for it. So, as you see, we don't need your help."

"Good, because nobody told me there'd be witchcraft involved. Who exactly are you people?"

There it is. Despite her departure from the League, one more ex-hunter knowing I was a dragon was still one too many. "Not your enemies. That's all I'll say."

Ignoring me, Giselle called to Astor, "I assume she's put some kind of witchcraft on you, too, but to be honest, I'm getting bored waiting for it to wear off. This place will smell of herbs for a week."

Astor stepped in front of the window, the moonlight casting pale shadows on his face. "I knew her already," he told Giselle. "That's why I brought her here."

Recognition flickered across her face. "You're the dragon?"

A visceral shock went through me, and I leapt to my feet, my claws sliding out without any conscious command. "Don't say another word."

I *knew* it. Of course Astor hadn't been honest with us when he'd claimed to have kept my identity to himself.

"Nice," she said, eyeing my claws. "I've always wondered how that works. Do your clothes rip when you shift?"

"None of your fucking business." Becks was on her feet, too, readied to shift into cat form. "We don't owe you any more information you can pass on to your hunter buddies."

Giselle let out a raucous laugh. "You think I'd turn you in? They've tried to work me over once before, sweetheart. It didn't take." She rearranged her legs, her robe riding up around her ankles to expose a visible bump on her lower shin, as if the bone had broken and never healed right. I'd bet I knew who was responsible, and even if she refused to help us, I'd be more than happy to make the League pay for *everyone* they hurt.

I caught Becks's eye, dipping my head to indicate that I'd

given up the argument. "They left you alive, though," I said to Giselle. "I didn't think they ever spared traitors."

"They don't. I got lucky." A guarded look entered her eyes. "I highly doubt I'll get lucky again, so if you don't mind, I'll be staying at home."

"Fine." I moved to help Will sort through the pile of ingredients, half expecting her to demand we take them outside. She merely watched as he fished a saucepan out of the cupboard and set it on the stove, tossing several ingredients in.

"Your spells might be subtle enough to fool a regular hunter, but not an Elite," she said. "They're trained to see through anything, even witch wards."

"That's not possible." My skin prickled at the memory of Astor's appearance in Magic Avenue. Had he seen through the wards? Or was just following a supernatural enough to get him past our defences? I'd never asked.

"It's true, and they're as fast as a shifter to boot."

"Not as strong."

"Don't make the mistake of underestimating them. They're vicious killers trained to have no remorse, not even for their own."

"Tell me something I don't know." There wasn't much I could do to help Will with brewing the potions, so I returned to join Becks on one of the lumpy mattresses someone had left on the floor. "If that's supposed to be advice, it's not helpful. Unless you want to tell us how you escaped them before?"

"Does it matter?" A challenge entered her voice. "I never set foot in the Stronghold, but even that was escapable during the invasion. That's the first and only time the League was taken off guard."

Oh. "You escaped when they were distracted by the faeries... so you renounced the League earlier than that?"

"Astor took longer to see sense, but he's playing a more dangerous game than I did." Her mouth quirked. "Seems a waste of time if you ask me, but some of us have long decided redemption isn't worth the price."

I blinked. *Redemption? Is that what Astor's mission is—making up for what he did as a hunter?* Was that why he'd helped me?

More to the point, how far was he willing to go?

"You know what I think is a waste of time?" Will gave the brewing potion a stir. "The League continuing to hunt supernaturals when they already lost the war."

"That's true." I swivelled back to Giselle. "Whatever their plans were back in the old world, the invasion ought to have blown them to pieces. Non-supernaturals are in the minority now. It's a new world, and the hunters are way out of their league. Pun intended."

"You still seem to have no idea what you're walking into," she said softly. "Even if you were to gain access without rousing suspicion, every torture instrument in the League's arsenal is inside that prison."

"I'm aware." A shiver ran between my shoulder blades. What else might they be concocting? Would Giselle tell us, or would she let us find out for ourselves? She might have shared more than I'd have expected, but she had her own agenda, and like Astor, she'd spent her life being taught we were monsters who needed to be eradicated.

"Yeah, I don't buy that." Will tipped some of the potion into a bottle and stoppered the lid before giving it a vigorous shake. "That automaton's the biggest weapon I've seen from them, and if they have one of those hanging around the jail, I have a hard time believing nobody's ever found the place."

"You might come to regret saying that." Giselle's mouth twitched into something resembling a grim smile. "However sophisticated your spells might be, they won't stand up to scrutiny from any Elites who might be at the event, and they *will* be there."

"We'll risk it," I said. "Like I said. Now either help us or stop hovering. We aren't interested in your commentary."

"That so." A gleam appeared in her eye. "What if I told you I could work a little magic of my own, if you're willing to accept my help? What do you say to that?"

15

Giselle watched me expectantly. Waiting for an answer. *She's offering her help after all, is she? Or was this some new trick?* I doubted that whatever she had planned involved actual magic, given her obvious displeasure at Will's concocting spells in her kitchen.

"What exactly did you have in mind?" I asked.

"Firstly, you'll have to pretend to be human."

My brow arched. "You don't think we look human?"

"No," said Astor from behind me, close enough to startle me. Bloody assassin. "The glowing eyes are a dead giveaway, and even if they weren't, your hair looks like a furnace, and you always smell faintly like burning."

"Now you're saying I smell?"

"You do," Giselle put in. "Elites have sharp senses."

"Are you sure you aren't all shifters in disguise?" I shook my head. "Fine, be my guest."

Ten minutes later, I stood headfirst over the kitchen sink with rivulets of black dye trickling from my newly dyed hair. Despite my best efforts, inky smudges had spread to my neck and my hands, too.

"You have dye on your nose," added Will.

"Dammit." I squeezed more water out of my hair. I'd clipped it to chin-length, but only an illusion could change my face, and as Giselle had pointed out at least seven times, the Elites would see right through it. "Are you sure they aren't going to check IDs at the door?"

"Not if the event's open to the public." She surveyed me with an approving eye . "Now, the Stronghold itself certainly will, and there'll likely be other security measures, too."

"Fingerprint scanners?" Will stirred one of the three pans brewing on the stove. "I *might* be able to devise a spell to get around that one, if we ambush three Elites outside and steal their IDs."

"Or we can just use the old-fashioned approach," said Becks.

"What, cutting a hunter's finger off?" I towelled off my hair. "Can't say they don't deserve it, but if they turn out to have eye-scanners, I draw the line there. I'm not carrying eyeballs in my pockets."

"Ugh." Will pulled a face. "Too messy. I'll make a few shadow-spells, too. I think I fixed the issues with the recipe."

"You mean the part where they kept turning us neon pink instead of invisible?" Beck said. "Because we don't really need that."

"Invisible?" Giselle sounded both intrigued and sceptical.

"It turns you into a shadow," I clarified. "Makes you pretty much unseeable unless you stand directly under a bright light."

"We'll test them all first," Will added. "Make sure there aren't any issues."

Giselle's unimpressed tone returned. "Did you not hear all the times I told you the Elites will see right through you?"

"The guests at the event won't," Will said confidently.

"And that's where we'll have our best shot at ambushing a group of hunters and stealing their gear."

"Or you could just borrow some of mine."

I looked questioningly at Giselle. "You have hunter uniforms? Enough for all of us?"

She gestured to the corner with the pile of weapons. Several rucksacks lay there, too, and when Astor tipped out the contents, I spied a number of garments in the monochrome style of the hunters.

"Cheery as necromancer wear, this is," said Will, picking up a black jacket with padding on the inside and several extra pockets to store weapons in. Lightweight shirts and dark trousers fitted with weapon belts accompanied the coats, all the items well-made and durable, and their trademark face-covering masks completed the ensemble. "We'll change into these after we steal the hunters' ID to access the Stronghold?"

"We'll have to, if they know all the Elites' faces at the gathering." I shook out my newly dyed hair. "I doubt any of them have inky moustaches or black smudges on their necks. This better be worth it."

"Your hair grows so fast it'll probably be red again by the week's end," said Becks.

"Yeah." There was a reason I'd stopped frequently dyeing it after the invasion, and not just due to our grumpy former supplier.

Thinking of Twill again didn't improve my mood. I wiped my face with an old towel, scrubbing the stray dye from my skin, and lowered the towel to find Astor looking at me.

"What?" I asked. "Did I miss any?"

"No, you look… different. I wouldn't recognise you."

"I hope the same is true of the hunters." I didn't know if he meant that in a good or bad way, but now wasn't the time to play guessing games. "I realise any League members who escaped us in London might have seen our faces, but they weren't Elites, right?"

"No," Giselle put in. "Elites are rare, even more so than they were before the invasion. Some of us might have had a little to do with that."

The laughing undernote to her voice prompted me to look at her. "You killed them? Or recruited them to work against the hunters?"

"Both." Her mouth twisted, as if wrestling with some emotion or other. "Of course, some had a change of heart and ended up turning themselves in, but that's to be expected."

I frowned. "Why would they do that?"

"Brainwashing," said Becks.

Giselle ignored her. "I imagine they did it for the same reasons that a group of shifters would attempt to storm the prison, even knowing you're likely to die in the attempt."

"What, to save—?" I cut myself off, seeing long-buried sadness behind her eyes. Had she known some of those hunters who'd given themselves up? Had they been trying to save others, still held within the League's thrall? I didn't dare push further, so I changed tack. "Why'd you stay so close to their base, then? There must be safer places than here, right near London."

She looked at me like I'd revealed my claws for the world to see. "Safe for us? There's nowhere. All we're good for is killing."

I didn't even know what to say to that. Her words made me wonder if not every hunter was willingly compliant, and hell, maybe some of their own people were imprisoned in there, too. I didn't know if we could help everyone. If the Stronghold was as much of an impassable fortress as she and Astor had implied, I wished we could have had help from someone who'd actually been inside. I knew next to nothing about who precisely we were going to face in there. Except a name: Malkin.

"What was that?" Giselle said when I muttered his name under my breath.

"Malkin," I repeated. "The leader. He'll be at the event?"

"It's at his estate, so he'll be the star of the show." Hate dripped from her tongue. "How I'd love to see you rip out *his* throat with those claws of yours."

"Might happen, if he's nothing more than a plain old human."

"He's anything but plain," she said. "They say he has talents that put the Elites to shame, and anyone who's tried to oust him as leader has met a grisly fate. You won't get near him."

"We'll see." I flexed my hands, imagined them shifting to claws, readied to slaughter the people who'd taken Cori. "Talented or not, no human can best a dragon."

"I beg to differ." Giselle leaned forward, her expression intent. "You really don't understand, do you? This man has made it his life's mission to exterminate every single one of you, and if you and your sister are as rare as it seems, he's been successful."

"Why would someone dedicate their life to tormenting other people who never did anything to them?"

A question I'd been asking myself as long as I could remember, without expecting an answer.

"You're asking the wrong person," Giselle said. "I'm not sure even his closest confidants know the truth, but the League was originally set up with the purpose of protecting humanity against supernatural threats. Their lessons offered compelling enough evidence that dragons have killed plenty of humans. Can you confirm otherwise?"

Of course not. I didn't even remember my own past, let

alone that of my fellow dragon shifters, but I didn't owe her that information.

I couldn't afford to have doubts now, not when we were too close to our goal.

"The League killed my parents," I said shortly. "I don't give a shit what my ancestors did, to be honest. It doesn't excuse the hunters capturing an innocent teenager for no cause."

"There's no need for that tone," said Giselle. "I'm simply asking you to consider if you have the full picture. Because if you do meet Malkin long enough for him to spare your life, he'll certainly make you ask that question."

Meet him. The person who'd seen to my family's extermination. My pulse thrummed, my blood heating with the need to kill.

Soon, I told my dragon side. Aloud, all I said was "He's welcome to try."

I'd planned to snatch a few hours of sleep, but I was too wound up to settle down. While Giselle went into the only bedroom downstairs, the rest of us were left to claim a spot in the main room. Becks curled up on a mattress, while Will turned off the stove and took his concoctions to a corner to make them into the spells we needed.

I paced among the sleeping bags and blankets, unable to rest. Since the lights were off, I didn't see when Astor crept up behind me and had to suppress a gasp.

"You startle easily, for a dragon."

"What is it?" I turned to face him. The darkness cast half his face in shadow, the other half bathed in moonlight that brought out the colour in the ink visible at his collar. Marks he'd never be able to entirely erase.

Maybe I'd never be able to forget either. There was too much history between us, too many lies and deceptions, for anything to ever be simple. Even if I wanted to give in to my shifter side, the part that reduced everything to bare instinct—the part that had kissed him with abandon, uncaring of the consequences. My lips seared with heat at the memory, and a frisson of desire shivered through my bones. *Not the time, dragon.*

"What?" I shoved my shifter side firmly into the background. "If you're about to tell us we're going to die, I don't want to hear it."

"That's not it."

"I don't get you." I hadn't intended to say so that plainly, but the words slid out before I could think better of them. "I mean, I don't get why you've spent the past two years working against the hunters only to avoid actively taking them down. Have *you* met this Malkin?"

"Every Elite has."

That's no answer. "It seems to me that you—and Giselle— are still holding back information."

"You're wrong." A note of frustration entered his voice. "You might have gathered that the League doesn't share anything they deem unnecessary, even to those of us within their topmost ranks. I *can* say that the Stronghold is likely to be within a mile of Malkin's estate, and that this is going to be your only chance to take the League by surprise."

"If we can't do it, nobody can, huh," I surmised. "You want revenge on them, right?"

That was a motive more in line with the hunter he'd once been, self-serving and ruthless. He couldn't have spent the past two years opposing them for my sake alone.

"Of course." A pause ensued, laced with tension. "And if you're so foolish as to think you can bring down the Strong-hold… then I want to be there to watch it burn."

Oh, my. I bit the inside of my cheek, willing my heart to stop racing and my eyes to refrain from glowing. "I'll do my best."

"I don't doubt that." His own expression was unreadable. "Do you understand me now, Ember?"

"Not in the slightest. I'm a shifter. Understanding humans isn't in my wheelhouse."

"We're not so different from you."

"No kidding. It's shifters who are supposed to be temperamental."

"Catch me on a day when I haven't been locked in a basement."

"You're going to hold that over my head forever, aren't you?"

His eyes glittered in the dark. His mouth was invitingly close, and heat bloomed deep inside my core. Dangerous, for my thoughts to be fogged when I needed to be sharp. Because this was for Cori. Not me.

I took a step away from him. "I'm going to try and sleep."

If he was disappointed, he didn't show it. "Then good night, little dragon."

———

ASTOR WAS GONE when we got up the next morning, having taken the car to scope out the site of the upcoming event. It was a good job he did, as he came back with the news that the event was going to be high-class.

"None of us have formal wear." I groaned. "We might as well sneak in the back way after all. Or wear the uniform and hope they don't ask too many questions."

"They will," said Giselle. "I have enough clothes upstairs that you're bound to be able to find something you can use. You're likely to be swiftly found out if you show up dressed as an Elite off the bat. At an event like that, they'll have strict instructions. Your best bet is to go as guests, then change into uniform once you've got the information you need."

"Count me out," said Becks. "I'm going in cat form. One of us needs to sneak around and listen at doors."

"I can watch from the roof, too," said Will.

"No offence, but you're almost as conspicuous in shifted form as I am," I said to him. "Unless Malkin's house is already covered in decorative gargoyles."

"You're a gargoyle *and* a witch?" Giselle asked.

"I'm one of a kind."

She snorted. "Unfortunately, that'll only make you more memorable, no matter which form you go in."

As for me, the only option was to go in as a human. I didn't get many opportunities to dress up, but I was too jittery to care about Astor's approving look as I emerged from the bathroom, wearing one of Giselle's dresses. It was a little too tight across the chest, but I was happy for people to stare at my cleavage if it kept their eyes off my face. On my wrist, I wore a spell shaped like a silver bracelet that was designed to alter my features enough to fool anyone but an Elite. I drew the line at heels, wearing black flats instead, but with makeup on and my newly dyed hair, I looked every inch the human I pretended to be. Dare I say it—I looked good. Apparently, Astor thought so too.

Astor himself had worn his usual hunter getup rather than opting for formal wear himself. He claimed to know a back way through which he could sneak in and eavesdrop on the Elites and discern the Stronghold's location while the rest of us grabbed enough ID cards for all of us to get in undetected. Becks had won the argument that she'd have an easier time sneaking around the estate in cat form, so Will and I were tasked with walking in as eager potential recruits who wanted to join the Orion League.

And I'd have to exercise extreme patience not to set the whole place alight.

"Relax," said Astor, running a hand up my back. I jumped

at the cold touch of his hand on my bare shoulder. "You look like you're going to a funeral, not a party."

"Better hope it doesn't end in all our funerals." I tugged the dress down over my thighs, feeling the caress of the silken material. At least the dress gave me enough coverage to wear a sports bra underneath and have some decency when I changed into the hunter uniform I'd squashed into a shoulder bag to carry with me. Weapons were another issue. As they'd be likely to trigger alarms, I'd have to go without. My claws would more than compensate. "I don't know that I want to leave a bunch of dead humans all over the venue. Most of them might not know what the hunters are up to."

His brow arched. "I'd have thought you'd have had less sympathy for them, considering that leaflet referred to all shifters as inhuman."

"I don't, but I believe in second chances. Sometimes." Too many humans had an issue with shifters for me to have the energy to fight all of them. The hunters were the real enemy here.

"I can see that." I wondered if he thought I was referring to him. I wasn't. Our conversation last night was as far from my thoughts as possible. I didn't have room in my head for any distractions.

The others were ready, too. Becks wore her pilfered uniform while Will had borrowed a tuxedo and looked much less scruffy than usual. He also looked less than thrilled about it.

"Hope this farce is worth it," he said, fiddling with his cuffs. "This is overkill. We only need to be inside the event for five minutes tops if we're quick about stealing the hunters' keycards."

"Not if the Elites are the only people carrying them," Becks said. "I'm expecting a fight."

So was I. The best I could hope for was that we managed

to corner our targets alone, without the other guests being any the wiser.

"Are the Elites the only people carrying ID cards?" Will called across the room to Giselle, who was trying and failing to hide her interest in the spells that Will had left piled on the bare floorboards.

"Yes, they are," said Giselle. "All prison guards carry them."

"And some of the guards will be at this ceremony," I surmised. "All right. Becks will lurk outside the house and jump any guard who walks outside."

"Or anyone who walks too close to an open window." She flashed me a grin. "Otherwise, you two will have to handle the rest."

"Don't pull out the explosives unless we're backed into a corner," I said to Will. "We should stick with the less flashy spells, at least to begin with."

"No problem." Will held up what appeared to be a stick of charcoal. "This one is subtle."

"It looks like a glorified pencil," Giselle commented.

"It can send someone to sleep for up to an hour," Will explained. "I made three. Just tap the button on the back, point and shoot. Like—" He hastily caught himself before he pointed it at his own head. "That. It'll work on a human, a shifter... anything except maybe a faerie. I've never tried."

I took the stick-shaped spell from him. "How many of these do you have?"

"You'll only have one each." He handed another to Becks. "Try to save them for the Stronghold, if you can."

"What should we do once we have the address and the ID cards?" Becks queried. "Even if we manage not to draw open attention, we'll need to get to the Stronghold without being followed by anyone at the party."

Will grinned. "Oh, I have a few ideas for that, too. Starting with my shadow spells."

"I thought they didn't work as well in direct sunlight." I gestured to the window and the unusual lack of clouds in the sky. Of all the days for it not to be raining.

"They have some other effects. Watch." He stepped in front of the light streaming in through the window and lifted a hand. Shadows swept in, masking his body and leaving what appeared to be a dark cardboard cut-out of Will standing in the room.

Giselle was unimpressed. "You turned yourself into a puppet show... why?"

"Imagine that, except with a gargoyle." Will flapped his arms in demonstration. "Right above the League's event."

"Oh, no," said Becks and I at the same time.

"That's too risky," added Becks.

Will turned off the shadow-spell. "Don't worry. I'll be safely up in the air."

"It's not safe up there," I reminded him. "The hunters will be carrying guns, remember?"

"If you saw a giant shadowy ghost, would your first instinct be to shoot it in the face?"

"Yes," said Astor and Giselle at the same time.

"Assassins. Always spoiling the fun." He shook his head at both of them. "This will work. Trust me."

"I'm not sure..." Becks hesitated. "I mean, if you want them to pay attention to you and not to the Stronghold, but you'd have a hell of a time getting away from their notice afterwards."

"That's a good point," I added. "We'll need to find some-where to change into uniform and put the masks on without anyone seeing us leave the party and putting two and two together."

"Definitely not," said Will. "No, we're better off changing inside the house and slipping out while they're distracted."

We clarified a few more points—mostly around finding somewhere to use a tracking spell to find the prison entrance if we weren't able to get specific enough details from the party—and then made sure everything else was in place.

As I checked my reflection in the hall mirror, making sure all the dye was gone from everywhere but my hair, I caught Astor watching me. "What?"

"You're ready for this? If you get caught, that's it. No second chances."

"Oh, I'm ready." I picked up my bag, which contained my stolen uniform. "They're gonna literally go down in flames. Count on it."

"Damn right they are," said Becks.

Will nodded, checking his spells were in place. "Let's crash the party in a way they'll never forget."

16

The Windsor estate was an hour's drive away from Giselle's house, and none of us spoke much during the journey except to occasionally reconfirm parts of the plan. The trouble was that any strategy we had for getting into the Stronghold itself entirely depended on whether we got through the League's public event without blowing our cover, and while we had backup plans layered upon backup plans, it didn't feel like enough.

Astor said nothing at all. He and Giselle had parted ways at the door, his fellow ex-hunter saying farewell with the words "If your new friends do achieve the impossible, I want to be the first to know."

"I'll tell you," said Astor, who was in grim assassin mode and had barely looked at me since we'd left. That was for the best, since I couldn't afford to let my attention lapse from our mission even for a moment.

"I wish we had a picture of the actual Stronghold," Will said from the back of the car. "Or a map. Think any of the Elites will be carrying one?"

"Don't be absurd." As Will had no doubt planned, Astor

couldn't resist replying to that. "Even some of the Elites at the event won't know where it is."

"You'd think they'd have guessed," said Becks. "How has nobody ever stumbled upon it before?"

"Because its owners pay vast sums of money to keep it off the map," said Astor. "It's secure enough that even the invasion didn't even touch it."

"That won't be the case for much longer," said Will. "When we're done, the whole world will know about that place."

Astor took a right turn rather more sharply than necessary. "Are none of you even willing to consider the worst-case scenario?"

"What would that be?" I swivelled to him. "That they'll capture all of us? They've done it before."

"I mean, I've never been captured by the League before," Will added. "Just saying."

"This is nothing remotely like their other prison," said Astor testily. "There won't be any escape routes, and your sister is likely to be in the most secure part of the facility."

"I'll tear the doors down if I have to." Yet doubts began to trickle in, chiefly concerning the others. There'd been no question that they'd help me rescue Cori, but I wouldn't ask Will or Becks to come face to face with the League's leader if it was avoidable. And Astor didn't have to be here at all. "I'll go in alone if necessary. The rest of you— honestly, just getting me into the prison itself is more than enough."

"No way," said Will. "We're with you. I am, anyway. Becks?"

"I'm going nowhere," she agreed. "You and Cori saved my life. We're here until the bitter end, now."

Astor said nothing, not offering a reaffirmation of his desire to take part in our plan, but I didn't expect him to. He knew that whether he was with me or not, I'd made up my mind.

A few minutes later, we pulled up on a country road beside a magnificent estate. A long driveway extended from in front of the manor house, the hedges on either side preventing us from seeing the size of the crowd queueing to get inside. The house was nice enough, comprising three storeys with balconies circling the upper floors and wide windows opened to let in the fresh spring air. *And for us to sneak in and out,* I thought, surprised that the hunters would pick a place as open as this to hold an event when hiding in the shadows was usually more their style. I supposed there was a chance there might be a torture chamber hidden in the basement, but maybe they didn't want to scare off their recruits before they even signed up.

"I'm surprised the League's boss is busy entertaining new recruits, given what's been happening in London." And the valuable prisoner he had locked up somewhere nearby.

"My guess is the event was already planned a while ago," Astor said. "Also, they lost a few members this week."

"So they did." The ones we'd killed. "I'd say this is our chance to take out a few more."

If we didn't get turned away at the door. Despite our assumption of a dress code, we looked a little *too* polished compared to some of the other individuals I could see lingering outside. Some didn't even look like they'd recently taken a bath, let alone changed into formal wear.

"Ready?" Becks asked quietly.

"Hell, yes," said Will.

"Absolutely not," Astor muttered. "I hope you know what you're doing."

"I might say the same to you," I said to him, adjusting the straps on my dress. The silky material would tear easily during a fight. Giselle had never said where she'd got it.

"Where do you want to meet after we're in? Every window is open, so we have options."

"Up there." He indicated the first-floor balconies. "Keep an eye out for me."

"You'll be hanging from the drainpipe, will you?" Will climbed out of the car, smoothing out his already rumpled suit. "Becks, do you have the diversion?"

"Ready." Becks sprang out, too, transforming into cat form.

Astor gave me a questioning look, but I wasn't sure which of many diversion spells they planned to use first. I knew Will had brewed more than he'd showed us—I'd heard him and Becks whispering earlier that morning and gathered they weren't totally sold on Astor being an ally— but I didn't know the specifics. I hoped we wouldn't need them.

As we walked closer to the crowd thronging the mansion, a chilling howl rose from somewhere nearby. The sound crawled down my spine and ignited every cell in my body in pure, blank-minded panic. My body jolted to a stop, and Becks turned human again, her eyes wide. "What in the hell was that?"

All of us looked to Astor, who'd gone pale. "I don't know."

He does know. The certainty seized me, as surely as I knew that whatever we'd heard wasn't human. Exclamations arose from the other guests, too, and a murmur of rapid conversation followed. Some looked around, as if in search of the cause, and my body tensed when a small group of well-dressed young women looked in our direction. I forced myself to resume walking again.

Behind me, Will hissed, "Becks, turn back into a cat, remember?"

As the guests' attention slid past us, Becks shrank to tabby size before taking off at a run. Astor had already pulled his own disappearing act, and Will and I were left to approach the party alone.

"Nothing to worry about," a genial voice was saying. "There was an incident at one of our other establishments, but you're all quite safe here. Our security will protect you from any unnaturals that might mean us harm."

He didn't mean us, did he? Surely not—there was no reason to assume any of us had worked out the address, much less that we'd have the nerve to walk into a public event in which the hunters' actual leader was present. Was that who the voice belonged to? Malkin?

I half expected to feel a sense of recognition when I set eyes on our host, but I didn't. He was maybe in his mid-forties, and while most of the people around him were dressed like they were attending a ball, he wore a military-style jacket adorned with badges and boots polished to a sheen. A similar aura seemed to surround his body, his skin shimmering in an odd way that put me in mind of a fae glamour.

He's not a faerie, is he? No, the fae had an ageless quality to their features even if they were part human. He looked like nothing more than a mundane man. A man who'd neverthe-less made it his life's mission to destroy me and my fellow shifters.

Conscious that he might see through our illusion, I grabbed Will's arm and pulled him into the growing crowd as they trailed after Malkin into the house.

"This is more awkward than the time I dragged a pretend girlfriend to the school dance to avoid having to come out to my mother," he said out of the corner of his mouth. "I can't say I'm a fan."

"This isn't a formal dance. Nobody cares if we're together or not," I muttered back, keeping my eyes on the floor rather than meeting anyone's eyes as we walked in.

Even with my nerves, I had to marvel at the level of wealth on display. The hall's thick carpet cushioned our steps, and the walls were lined with gilt-framed paintings. Famous hunters, perhaps. Not wanting to set off my temper, I didn't stop to get a close look at any of them on our way through to a pair of open doors. Beyond lay a wide, opulent room decorated like a cross between a ballroom and a cathedral. Pillars supported an arched ceiling from which hung several crystalline candelabras, and a dais topped with a microphone stood at the front. *Is our host going to make a speech?* It was probably too much to hope that he'd reveal the hunters' nefarious plans for us all to hear, but I could dream.

I hovered near the door, taking a couple of calming breaths. Malkin wouldn't know me, and no signs of recognition were evident among any of the guests. They congregated in groups, exchanging conversations that seemed to revolve around complaining about the general state of the country and why it was all the fault of the supernaturals. Nothing I hadn't expected.

"…enough is enough," an unshaven man wearing a hoodie and jeans was saying to a throng of hangers-on. "It's time to take back control of our government. We don't need the mages telling us what to do."

I suppressed a snort. The Mage Lords might not be willing to offer much in the way of a helping hand, but the majority of the laws they enforced were intended to stop humans getting eaten alive by the fae. The human government had been completely ineffectual.

"Rich people," said Will in a low voice. "Why do they never use their vast fortunes to solve world hunger instead of trying to exterminate people who've never done anything to hurt them?"

"Beats me." We'd all suffered through the invasion, but it made zero sense for these people to place their faith in someone who'd done no more to help them than the Mage Lords had. Less, if anything.

By the time we'd reached the thick of the crowd, I was feeling brave enough to move closer to our host. I spied Malkin making his way through his throng of admirers, exchanging pleasantries, talking all the while in that warm voice that drew up my hackles despite my best effort to suppress my shifter instincts. Maybe because he was trying so very hard to seem like a normal upper-class gentleman, not a depraved killer.

Will poked me in the arm, drawing my eyes to two figures who walked just behind Malkin. Each was dressed in formal wear that didn't quite hide the guns at their waists. *Elites?* My claws itched to make an appearance, but we needed to get one of those bastards alone first if we wanted to swipe their prison ID to access the Stronghold without anyone else knowing. I committed their faces to memory and moved on, scanning the crowd for any other hunters who might be present. Will, who was doing the same, whispered, "Either they're incognito or lurking outside."

"The former, I hope." If not, we'd have to rely on Becks and Astor sneaking up on them to get what we needed.

As the large cuckoo clock in the corner announced it was noon, Malkin ascended to the dais. The clock's announcement was swiftly drowned out by a chorus of howls from outside that turned my blood to water and set the guests into a frenzy of gasps and exclamations.

Over the general panic, Malkin spoke into the microphone. "Calm. You may be aware that there have been certain incidents in central London over the past couple of days that have led me to take precautions at this event. There is no danger to you here."

"What was that noise?" shouted a woman in a flowery dress. "Sounded like an unnatural."

One of us? My hands clenched. No way. No shifter would ever serve the League, not even under duress.

"You are quite safe," he said, neatly bypassing her comment. "I expect some of you will have heard the rumours of violent disorder in central London and an incident at one of our facilities. Rest assured that the perpetrators will be caught and punished."

I kept still, pressing my mouth together to hide my emotions and wishing I'd worn the mask Giselle had procured. Especially if my eyes started glowing. I ducked my head just in case as someone else in the crowd shouted out, "I heard some of your hunters were killed by a dragon."

Damn. How had the rumour spread this far? My public appearance had hardly been subtle, but it wasn't like there had been many direct witnesses outside of the people already on Magic Avenue.

"That is, regrettably, true," he said. "I chose to go ahead with this event to show the unnaturals that we will not be deterred out of fear. I can assure you of my utmost certainty that there will be consequences for everyone involved."

Sure there will. I was the villain of the day, was I? Bring it on.

"But the dragon is still at large," the speaker pressed on. "Isn't that concerning? The Mage Lords have said nothing at all!"

"The Mage Lords are swiftly losing relevance," said Malkin. "They took charge in the aftermath of the faerie invasion because nobody else did, but that does not make them fit to make decisions for the long term, least of all for those of us who have no desire to submit to the unnaturals poisoning our world."

I wished someone would interrupt, tell him he was a depraved torturing despot, but the crowd nodded along with every proclamation he made. I knew why. They were desperate for someone, anyone, to reassure them that they would fix the world. That they would keep everyone safe. Simple words, arranged like a warm hug, an embrace of solidarity.

Lies. Every word. Malkin would say anything he thought they wanted to hear no matter whether he meant it or not. His bold claims meant nothing at all, but the crowd lapped them up anyway, with fervour.

Will nudged me, pointing me to one of the windows on the left-hand side. There, Becks sat on the windowsill. Had she found something we could use? Since everyone's eyes were on the front or absorbed in their own conversations, Will and I didn't draw any attention as we made our careful way across the room.

Becks was no longer on the windowsill, but I spied her tabby form below the window and guessed that she wanted to meet us somewhere more private. Another door off the ballroom led into a corridor that was empty save for a single armed guard. I tensed, but the hunter's expression when he saw us was blank indifference. He couldn't have come from London.

"Bathroom?" I asked.

He pointed without a word, and Will and I followed the corridor around a corner. Two bathrooms lay at the end, but not a window was in sight, though a staircase lay some distance away.

"We'll have to go upstairs," Will muttered. "If anyone's there, we'll pretend we got confused about which bathroom he meant."

"Yeah." I didn't want to spend another minute inside this ghastly place.

Luck was with us, and nobody was in the upstairs landing. We reached a balconied window without being confronted and ducked outside to find Becks waiting for us, having had ample time to scope out the best ways in and out of the building.

She lifted a paw a fraction, revealing an ID card flecked with blood.

"Nice," I whispered. "One down. Now we need two more."

The slight issue was that she couldn't talk to us properly while shifted, and I wouldn't put it past Malkin to have installed security cameras. If they got suspicious of us for hanging around outside talking to a cat, it would be hard to put the next stage of our plan into motion.

"There are more than two guards outside?" I asked, and Becks dipped her head in the affirmative. "And Astor?"

A head-shake. She didn't know where he was. I suppressed a jolt of annoyance. He was within his rights to take off if he wanted to.

I stepped to the balcony's edge, peering out across the rolling hills beyond. The scenery was so picturesque that I couldn't picture a notorious prison being anywhere close. Doubtless that was the whole point. I focused on the house instead, picking out the outlines of guards standing beneath the other balconies. They were still too close to risk attacking them without the noise reaching the guests, and we were supposed to save the knockout spells for later. For the Stronghold itself.

A louder murmur of voices from downstairs warned me Malkin had finished his speech. Someone would find us soon. As I turned away, movement flashed in the corner of my eye. A blur of black descending the house, followed by the unmistakeable thud of a body hitting the ground.

Astor? My gaze snapped up to the balconies on the floor above. Astor crouched on the edge, recognisable even with his face covered in a mask. Had he just pushed a guy to his death? And I'd thought being a dragon shifter was the most likely thing to give us away.

Will swore softly. "If there're cameras, we're screwed."

"Not if you set off your first diversion." I'd had quite enough of stealth. "Becks, can you check the guy who fell for ID? That means we'll have two, and I'll handle the third."

Once I'd got out of this dress. The trouble was, Astor didn't seem to care that he was out in the open. He climbed expertly to the edge and leapt across to the next balcony. I'd seen half-faeries perform feats of acrobatics which would pale in comparison to the way Astor moved, as if he'd been climbing up the sides of buildings all his life. In seconds he was on the balcony directly above before he landed softly beside me.

"What are you doing?" I hissed. "Aren't there security cameras?"

"Not out here," he said, his voice a feathery whisper against my neck. "There's a problem. The prison? It's underneath this place."

"Underground?" I'd suspected it must be, but I'd never guessed that we were literally standing on top of the Stronghold right now. That would make our plan to leave the house in chaos and sneak in while Malkin was occupied trickier to pull off. "Okay. We have two IDs, so we'll grab the third and then—"

"What are you doing out there?" A guard had spotted us. "You shouldn't be—"

Astor punched him. The guard caught the blow, his hand moving with blinding speed, and my blood iced over. He must be an Elite.

Will disappeared. *The shadow spell.* Problem: that left Astor and me alone on the balcony with our adversary. The Elite's hand enclosed Astor's fist, his other hand reaching for his gun.

I kicked viciously at his leg, wishing I'd worn heels after all to get the full effect. Even an Elite had a hard time not stumbling after taking a hit to the kneecap, and Astor freed his hand, lifting his own gun.

Don't! I thought, knowing a gunshot would give us away, and kicked out again. The Elite dodged, and this time he managed to pull his gun.

His shot missed, but the sound rang out like a bomb blast. Luckily, in the same moment, a large shadow fell over us, dark enough to block out the sunlight on one side of the house. Even the Elite's attention went towards the fearsome winged beast casting a shadow over the rooftop, visible only as a dark outline in the air.

"Dragon!" yelled the Elite, and all hell broke loose below. The sound of panic echoed up from somewhere downstairs, and I dragged my gaze away from the shadow and punched the hunter full in the face. Bone and cartilage crunched beneath my fist, blood spurting over my knuckles. It was the chance Astor needed to give him a shove over the edge and send him tumbling off the balcony.

"We need to move." Astor climbed onto the drainpipe. Did he seriously expect me to climb while wearing a dress?

Not like I had much choice. Thundering footsteps on the stairs warned me that the other Elites would be heading to the high ground to take aim at their target, which left us in the worst possible place. As more noise erupted from below, I glimpsed people running out onto the lawn in front of the house to stare up at the spectacle. All they'd have to do was lift their heads and they'd see us, too.

Dammit. Hoping Will avoided getting hit, I followed Astor onto the balcony's edge. I didn't possess anything close to his level of balance, and I groaned when he began to climb up the drainpipe instead of down.

"We can't land directly in front of that crowd," he said. "Why did you pick somewhere this exposed to meet with Becks?"

"Why did *you* push a guy to his death from the upper floor?"

"He was a dick when I was a new recruit."

I snorted despite my fear. "Admit it, you're enjoying this."

I, however, was not having a good time. Hunters swarmed the balconies below, and more still had joined the growing crowd in front of the mansion. We'd need to get around the corner to have a hope of descending without being seen, and Astor seemed content to risk the wobbling drainpipe and uneven footing. My flat shoes fell off halfway along, while my dress snagged on obstacles until I lost patience and hauled the skirt up to my waist with one hand to climb more easily. Will continued to fly above, wings spread wide directly underneath the pale sun to make his shadow look larger than it actually was. I had the distinct impression he was enjoying himself as much as Astor was.

What seemed like an eternity later, I pulled myself onto the last balcony with wobbly hands. This one was unoccupied; no hunter would be able to take aim at Will from this angle, so we were safe.

"About time," said Astor, who waited on the balcony, eyeing my ripped dress with raised eyebrows.

"Wait, I need to change. Don't you dare peek."

I opened the glass doors onto a pristine bedroom belonging to someone with more money than aesthetic sense. Everything was a horrible shade of puce. I yanked the ruined dress off and pulled the crumpled uniform from my shoulder bag. Glad I'd also brought spare shoes, I pulled them on and shoved on my mask, tucking my hair into the neck of the black jacket.

When I was done, I caught sight of my reflection in a gilt-framed mirror. Gone was the human woman, a terrifying masked Elite now in her place. All I needed was a gun for a prop. I grimaced, tugged the mask down, and joined Astor again.

Outside, the other Elites were still taking aim at the 'dragon'. Will had wisely dipped out of sight to avoid being hit, which meant we didn't have long to get away from the mansion before we were spotted. At least it would be easier for me to climb while dressed in hunter gear.

"We need to meet the others," I said. "The jail's entrance—do you know where it is?"

"On the east side of the mansion, but there's another problem."

"Which is…?"

"Security."

Howls broke out again, as if to underline his point. The sound slid beneath my skin, threatening to shake off my balance, but I forced myself to focus on our new destination as I climbed back onto the drainpipe and readied myself to descend.

We were halfway down when the screaming started. I swore, picking up speed, my hands blistering as I slid down the pipe and dropped the last few feet into the bushes. My strong shifter bones absorbed the impact, and I straightened upright, not looking back to see if Astor was behind me. The howls were louder than ever, calling to something primal deep within me.

"Wait," he hissed, following me down the incline away from the mansion. "You can't go near the crowd."

"What's making that racket, guard dogs?"

"Of a sort."

I saw them, then. Three large wolf-like shapes were approaching the mansion, slavering and hungry for blood.

17

"Ember," Becks whispered from the shadows. She'd turned back into human form but was hunched as small as possible under a bush.

"Becks, are you hurt?"

She whimpered a little. "No, but—look at them. The wolves."

I peered out of the bush, my heart thumping. At a closer look, the hunters' wolves were far larger than the usual sort, more bear-sized. Had the hunters bred them specifically to use as security? It seemed like the sort of thing they'd do.

The wind turned, carrying a familiar scent, which struck me with the force of a blow.

They weren't wolves, but shifters.

My body froze in an instinctive reaction of horror. There was no way shifters would be serving the hunters of their own free will. What had the League done to them? Common sense warned me to get the hell away, but my body refused to move, my gaze riveted on the wolves. They padded quietly, sniffing the ground for their prey.

Another blow hit my heart. If the shifters were truly working for the hunters, voluntarily or otherwise, their sharp senses would identify me as a dragon shifter. Even shadow-spells wouldn't do anything to hide our scent.

My breath rushed out when Astor hit me in the shoulder from behind. Hard. I bared my teeth, whirling on him. "What?"

"Don't panic," he said in a low voice. "Now is your chance. The guards are looking for the intruders. They aren't focused on the jail."

"Did you know?" I couldn't help asking. "The shifters. What did the League do, put them under a spell?"

"No, and we can't talk about that now. You can't free them either. I'm sorry."

Each word struck with the force of another punch.

"They can smell us, remember?" I said through clenched teeth. "Once they figure out what I am, we're fucked."

Even if I ignored the sheer inhumanity of this situation. I'd never in a million years have thought the guards would be *shifters.* Whether Astor agreed or not, I'd set them free on the way out. I refused to believe they'd chosen to fight for the League of their own free will.

I kept both eyes on the prowling wolves as I backed out of the bushes, walking at a crouch. With my stolen uniform and mask, I looked more like a hunter skulking around than anything else, but that wouldn't fool the wolf shifters' heightened senses. As they continued across the grassy slope, I saw the moment one of them lifted its head and looked directly at us. A rumbling growl travelled through the pack.

They knew we were here.

As they broke into a collective sprint right at our hiding place, a bang like a firework resounded, followed by a shower of sparks rising above the hillside. The wolves didn't slow, but the sparks would surely have caught Malkin's attention at least.

Which left me to deal with the wolf shifters.

The first shifter leapt, ready for the kill, and I pulled out the charcoal-shaped stick and set off the knockout spell. The blast was tame compared to the shower of sparks still erupting in the sky, but the effect caught the advancing shifters head-on. One was sent sprawling several feet away, while two more collided, landing in a heap. Relief that Will's spell had worked warred with horror that I'd had to use it in the first place.

"Ember." Astor came up behind me. "You shouldn't have done that."

"I can't kill them, Astor. Don't ask me to do that."

"I didn't," he said, "but there are more of them outside the jail. You can't get in without bypassing them."

"Fuck." I'd used my only knockout spell. The others had one left each, but Will had said the full effect would only work on one person, and if it hit several at once, they'd only be unconscious for a fraction of the time. "Which way?"

"This way." He trod lightly across the hillside, following the curve around the mansion's side.

I didn't see the others. Becks would have taken cover after setting off the diversion, while I'd lost sight of Will, too. I hoped he'd got his feet on the ground before the Elites shot him out of the air. I couldn't hear any bullets flying, but the continual howls warned me more wolves were on the way. We needed to move.

Astor led us to an area where the ground was slightly raised in order to conceal an opening like an abandoned mine shaft. If he hadn't been leading the way, I'd never have spotted it myself. Beyond the opening was a tunnel of a few metres which evidently been dug straight into the hillside.

Inside, two more wolves waited for us. My steps slowed. I still wore my hunter gear, of course, but again my scent gave me away. Already the wolves stood on high alert, their hackles raised.

Astor held out an arm, preventing me from advancing forward, and overtook me. My heart rose into my throat, but the wolves didn't attack him as I'd expected. Did they think he was a hunter? I supposed that if their human minds had been entirely taken over by the beast within, they wouldn't know otherwise.

As he slipped past them, a harsh voice spoke from behind the wolves. "Identify yourself."

There are human security guards, too. I withdrew out of the tunnel, listening out. Astor's reply was lost under the wolves' growls, but I heard the subsequent thud of a body hitting the ground.

A second chorus of growls, angrier, suggested that the wolves had turned on Astor. *Shit.* As I moved in to help him, Becks ran up behind me in cat form, carrying a stolen keycard between her teeth. The sweep of wings followed, and I glimpsed Will's shadowy gargoyle form coming in to land.

"Is this it?" he asked in an undertone. "Shit, there's a tunnel under here."

The wolves' growls became louder, and a blur of movement showed me Astor moving among them, dodging their teeth. He caught my eye with a clear message telling us to get in while the beasts were distracted. This might be our only chance.

I sprinted flat-out, aiming for the gap at the leftmost side of the tunnel. My claws itched to join the fight, but I held back and focused on speed. As I skimmed past the wolves, teeth snapped on my heels, but the wolf's feet stumbled when

Becks ran underneath them on her way past. Will's semi-visible gargoyle form followed, half-running and half-flying.

On the other side of the wolves, Becks took the lead, her paws making no sound on the earthen floor. Soon the packed soil changed to metal encasing walls and floor. A shiver of fear ran across my skin when we ran past the bodies of two hunters. Astor's work. He'd known he'd put himself at risk of death from those wolves to give us a fighting chance of entering the prison, and I refused to waste that chance.

A pair of steel doors blocked our way, but Becks lifted a paw to a keypad on the right and produced one of the stolen keycards.

The door glided open with barely a sound. Becks went in first, then Will. I hesitated, turning to Astor, and found myself instead faced with a wolf's crazed eyes.

Dammit. I got the message, and I fled through the doors as its teeth closed on my heels.

Leaving Astor on the other side.

"Come on," Will hissed. "Use the shadow-spells, both of you. There'll be guards up ahead."

Becks vanished in shadow, but I hesitated. My disguise was enough for me to be taken for a guard. I'd be better off saving the spell for when I really needed it, as the effect had a time limit, and Will was already flickering noticeably around the edges. It wouldn't be long before he was fully visible again.

The corridor ahead looked like the entrance to a high-tech building, not an underground prison. Modern linoleum floors and tiled ceilings and walls, lit by fluorescent lights, easily wide enough to accommodate a wolf in shifted form. Not a dragon, but my nerves spiked into high gear all the same. I walked forward until we reached another door. When Becks used her keycard to open it, a lift appeared on the other side. The only floors listed were below this one, descending to five storeys below the earth.

Calm down, Ember, I told myself as my rising panic threatened to overcome me. *You're not literally going to the earth's core.*

A change in the wind followed by a faint metallic sound told me that someone else had come in through the front doors. Swift footsteps followed, then a thud, and Will turned visible again, pinning down the person who'd entered.

"Let me up, fool," Astor hissed. "I closed the door on the shifters, but we have to move fast."

"Are they—?" I couldn't say *alive.*

"Yes, but we might all come to regret sparing them." The lift doors had begun to close, so Astor employed his borrowed keycard to open it again. "Use the shadow spells while you have the chance. I doubt you'll have many places to hide down here."

"You don't have a spell." Damn. I'd worried about his chances while fighting those shifters out there, but inside the Stronghold was another matter entirely. As a deserter, he'd have no more hope of escaping than the rest of us did, should we get caught.

Cori is in here. That thought alone spurred me into the lift, and as the others joined me, my pulse began to race.

"Which floor is it?" I whispered, reading the glowing numbers. "We can't search the whole prison. The hunters will get suspicious if the lift keeps moving by itself."

"Then we'll start at the top floor and find some stairs," Will said. "I'd turn on your shadow-spells now, just in case."

Becks disappeared first, leaving a cat-shaped outline in her place. I reached for the band wrapped around my wrist and flicked the switch. A faint shimmering radiated outward, spreading up and down until my body was encased. The world didn't look any different, but being semi-invisible gave me an uncanny feeling. As if I was a ghost.

None of us spoke a word as the elevator descended. The shadows cloaking Will, Becks and me made Astor's lack of any real disguise even more obvious.

"Astor," I whispered. "You really shouldn't walk out in the open. They'll know you're a deserter."

"I'm good at bluffing." He pulled the mask down over his face. "You have more at risk than I do. And remember— whatever else you might find in here, getting to your sister is primary."

"I know." I *did* know, but being in a place designed to torment every shifter who passed through made it difficult to conceive of walking away once I'd saved Cori, leaving the hunters to continue their depravity unopposed.

The lift glided to a halt, and I took a deep, steadying breath as the door slid open. I half-expected a contingent of enemies to wait for us on the other side, but another metal-walled corridor greeted us. Its narrow space carried the same oppressive sense of being caged in. I could only imagine how painful it might be for a faerie, who were highly allergic to iron. No wonder the invasion had never touched this place.

Becks's cat-shaped shadow form scampered into the lead, hurrying to yet another keycard-operated door. The next part of the corridor had walls of glass and not metal, revealing open-plan offices on either side. All seemed to be empty, which struck me as odd.

"The staff must be at the party up at Malkin's house," Astor breathed. "I bet they have a list of prisoners somewhere."

I didn't dare hope for that much, but Becks's keycard got us through a door into the office on the right-hand side. We found ourselves in a wide spare filled with filing cabinets and desks topped with computer monitors and stacks of documents.

I didn't even know where to start, so I picked up the topmost paper on a desk and found inexplicable jargon scrawled in semi-legible handwriting. "Do they have a map?"

"Actually, yes." Astor held up a piece of paper. "The cells are on the fifth level below."

"What's that?" I took the paper from him and snorted. "Fire safety regulations?"

"That's priceless." Will laughed so hard that Astor shushed him. "*Fire safety.* For people who capture dragon shifters."

"Yeah." I sobered up fast. "The fifth basement level… there's no way we won't run into guards down there."

And we still needed to locate which cell they were keeping Cori in. The other levels were mostly labelled as offices and labs.

Is that where they make the bullets? Where they use us as test subjects? I had no doubt something of the sort was responsible for those shifters attacking us aboveground, but I couldn't worry about that now when we were so close to my sister.

Get Cori first. Deal with the rest later. I repeated those words in my mind as I scanned the map and committed the layout to memory the best I could. The fifth floor contained hundreds of cells, with offices filling the space between. The prison was vast, but my senses would tell when I was near Cori. I was sure of it.

Back to the lift. When Becks and Will were both in, I waited for Astor to join us.

"I'll find another route down," he told me. "If one of us figures out where the stairs are, we can use them later."

"All right." I should have expected as much, but my heart sank a little all the same. I hadn't wanted to split up.

"Are you sure he's not going to raise the alarm?" Will whispered in my ear.

"Don't be ridiculous." I wouldn't blame Astor for making a run for it, though. He'd risked too much already. "We need to find whereabouts they're keeping the keys to the cells and then steal the right one."

"I'll do the stealing," Becks said, "but I'm having real trouble reading the signs. And being invisible isn't helping either."

Right. Our current shadowy state didn't help her short-sightedness, but at least she had the advantage of being small and able to slip into tight spaces. "I'll sniff out Cori."

The lift came to a halt, and I held my breath as the doors slid open again.

This corridor was lined with locked metal doors, all of which had barred windows. A pair of uniformed figures patrolled in front. Ah, crap. We might not be fully visible, but the fluorescent lights would without a doubt alert the guards that someone was present. If the lift's arrival hadn't already done so.

Sure enough, one of the two black-clad guards closer to us called out, "Who's there?"

As the guard moved closer to the lift, his partner asked, "What's going on?"

"I thought I saw—" He cut off, and I pressed myself flat to the wall as a shower of sparks flew out inside the lift. White lights bounced off the walls and ceiling, and both guards exclaimed in surprise.

Holding my breath, I ducked around them and glimpsed Becks's cat-shaped shadow doing the same as the sparks continued to fly in all directions inside the open lift. Will had presumably thought they'd assume there was something wrong with the electrical system rather than deliberate sabotage, but in doing so, he'd trapped himself inside the lift behind two curious guards.

One of the guards sneezed. Then the other. The cacophony masked Will's escape, and he slipped past the guards without them being any the wiser. *Nicely done.* The subtlety of the spell might easily be mistaken for dust in the air, but we wouldn't be able to maintain the stealthy approach for much longer.

With the guards now behind us, we had a clear path through the corridor, past the rows of cells on either side. As I neared the first one, a faint sobbing caught my ear.

Shifters.

I inhaled, my heart jackhammering. Cori wasn't here, but there were so *many* cells, more than I'd ever expected of an organisation whose goal I'd always assumed was to simply shoot shifters on sight without taking prisoners.

I'd been wrong. Horribly so. Untold suffering had taken place in here, maybe for decades.

The fluorescent lights made hiding in the shadows difficult, and when we rounded another corner and found another pair of guards, I halted, holding my breath.

Becks ran between the guards' legs, causing them both to stumble. I swiftly moved past and sniffed the air again. Still no Cori. We made it past two more guards before we reached an office, smaller than the one upstairs. A pair of keycard-operated doors barred the way, but the clear window in the side showed me rows of keys hanging on the wall.

We still don't know which one we need. Not to mention it would be all but impossible to steal even a single key when there were at least four staff members inside the office. Making a mental note of the location, I forced myself to keep walking, rounded another corner—and stopped.

One of the cell doors was open. Two hunters stood in the entryway, speaking to the person inside.

"Now, you don't want another night in the dark room, do you?" taunted a female voice. "I'm sure you'd rather cooperate."

I didn't hear the reply, but it ended in a pained grunt when the second guard kicked the person behind the door.

Becks nudged my ankle. I'd begun to growl without realising. I clenched my teeth together and continued past the guards. I glimpsed the prisoner—an emaciated figure whose wrists were encased in heavy-looking metal cuffs—and faltered.

Another nudge to my ankle. *Damn.* I couldn't stop. Not now. Shoulders tensed, I kept walking until I'd left the cell behind.

"You're coming with us." The scrape of metal told me the hunters had dragged the prisoner out of the cell. I kept walking, ears strained to pick up their muttered conversation.

"Waste of time if you ask me," murmured the female guard. "This one's useless. What's Malkin want him for?"

"Beats me. He's too occupied with that pet project of his to care."

My heart stumbled. *Pet project?* Could that be—?

"Have you seen her yet?" whispered the first guard. "Tiny thing. Sure doesn't look threatening."

"They never do, do they?"

Cori. Despite myself, I slowed, biting back the urge to rip out their throats or to pin them down and demand they tell me where my sister was. If she was Malkin's personal project, she'd likely be in isolation, separated from the others... but where?

The scrape of metal told me they were right behind me, so I picked up speed again, coming into view of a door. Beyond lay what appeared to be a lab, from what I could see through the narrow window at the top. I held my breath against the sickly metallic smell emanating from within. My heart contracted, and my skin went clammy.

Behind me, the doors slid open and the guards dragged the prisoner inside. I glimpsed metal chairs equipped with cuffs, long tables covered with equipment—and shifters, in varying states of distress, watched over by lab-coat-wearing guards. My vision flashed white with rage, and I swiftly closed my eyes in case they saw the glow. A faint meow came from near my feet, a tortured sound that told me Becks was as horrified by the sight as I was. My rational mind warned that we had less than an hour's use out of the shadow spells, and we still didn't know where Cori was, but the extent of the operation in here took my breath away. I hadn't known they'd taken in so many shifters alive.

I forced my eyes open, shoved my shifter side to the background. As the door began to slide closed, I slipped over the threshold. Regret hit me a second later. With a full view of the lab, I could see that most of the shifters present were either children or teenagers. Two young boys crouched inside a glass-walled cage while an onlooking hunter operated some kind of mechanism from the outside. A heartbeat later, one of them fell to his knees, his body contorting, hair sprouting from his shoulders as the first signs of a shift began to appear.

They're forcing kids to shift?

Were they doing the same to Cori? I wrenched my gaze away, scanned the wide space of the lab, but no sign of her bright hair leapt out at me. Even with the metallic stench in the air, I'd know if she was in here.

I'd seen enough. I backed out before the door had fully closed and collided with an unseen figure on the other side.

"Ember," Will breathed in my ear. "There's a problem."

"Aside from that?" I nodded in the general direction of the lab.

"He's here. Malkin."

My mouth went dry. "Where?"

"Stairs. Not two corridors from here."

I swore, cut off when Becks's claw jabbed me in the ankle, warning me of two more guards coming around the corner. If Malkin was ahead of us, my sister must be, too, and if he had her in isolation, I'd bet he had the only key. That left me with little choice but to keep going. The murmur of voices told me I was on the right track, and all too soon, I rounded a corner to see the man himself, walking down the corridor with his back to me. He was still dressed in his army-style uniform, with two guards behind him.

And at his side was Astor.

18

My body locked to the spot, my eyes fixed on Astor. He wasn't wearing his mask, and with his real face on full display, there would be no mistaking him for anything but a deserter.

And yet Malkin hadn't shot him or put him in cuffs. Instead, from what I could see from the back, his body language was that of someone talking to a confidant, an equal.

"… you've always been too wilful for your own good," Malkin was saying as they walked. "Am I to understand the unnaturals told you nothing of their strategy for entry?"

"I wouldn't know," Astor said. "I parted ways with them as soon as we left London and came here immediately to head them off. I was unaware that you were hosting an event aboveground, given the circumstances."

It can't be. Lightheadedness washed over me. He'd told Malkin he'd brought us here? If this was some kind of ruse, how could Malkin of all people have fallen for it?

"Someone mentioned seeing you at the mansion," he said to Astor. "More than one person, in fact."

"They were right, but I didn't stay long. I'm not generally welcome among my fellow Elites, as you might imagine."

"No, I expect not. As for the unnaturals… you're quite sure you don't know how they're hiding themselves?"

"Wards, I expect. They didn't trust me with the details."

"And yet they trusted you."

"They did." He sounded almost… amused. I caught myself starting to growl again and bit the inside of my cheek to silence myself. Of course Astor would have had to pull together a cover story in case he ran into the hunters' leader, but it seemed impossible that Malkin believed him when Astor had shot hunters dead right outside this very prison. Not to mention the ones he'd killed in London. There hadn't been many surviving witnesses, true, but if he'd truly left the hunters two years ago, why would Malkin have welcomed him with open arms?

No. The only way that Malkin would have accepted him back that easily was because they'd been in contact from the start. In other words, Astor had been playing for both sides.

The question was, how much of what he'd told me was the truth? *I'm good at bluffing,* he'd said, but how was I to tell truth from lie when he'd duped me so thoroughly in the past? Yes, there was Giselle to consider, too—she *was* marked as a deserter, and Astor hadn't mentioned her to Malkin so far— but he'd also revealed far more than someone who should have been trying to help us stay hidden until we achieved our goal.

Malkin reached a door, pulled out a key, and unlocked it. He entered first, then Astor, then the two guards. One of the pair stumbled as Becks's cat-form streaked between his legs, and his companion looked at him. "What is it?"

"Something went under my—"

A flash-bang went off, sparks skittering off the walls. I seized my chance and ran through the open door.

The smell hit me first, bringing me to a halt. Blood. Iron. And… *Cori.* My sister, and other shifters, too, their scents overlapping. The space was arranged like a lab, but neater, less chaotic than the previous one. Most of the equipment was pushed against the walls to make room for several large glass cages. My heart stopped when I caught a bright flash of red hair at the end.

There came a dull thud from behind, and Becks appeared in a blur of tabby fur, collapsing onto her front as she turned human again. For a moment I thought she'd been shot, but I hadn't heard a gunshot. Rather, a sharp object resembling a dart protruded from her shoulder. A tranquiliser? How could it have turned her human?

"Got one of them!" said the guard. "There's another somewhere—I heard them."

"Three of them came here?" Malkin addressed Astor, his sharp eyes scanning the room. "Yes… I can see one. There."

He pointed at Will. Astor hadn't been kidding about the hunters' sharp senses, but this went far beyond what should have been possible for a human. I'd seen enough in the lab to know the League's hunters were open to experimenting with magic when it suited them, but I had seconds at most before they found me, too.

My claws slid out, and I leapt at Malkin's throat.

An invisible force slammed into me, sending me flying. I hit the floor, sprawled on my back, head ringing from the collision. A click sounded, and Will collapsed onto his front, his half-shifted form returning to full human, another dart sticking out of his arm.

"Don't shoot her." Malkin pointed to the spot where I'd hit the ground. "This is the one I've been looking for… Ember, is it? You might as well turn off whatever spell you're using to hide yourself now."

"Eat shit," I said, and tried to jump at him again.

I say *tried*, because that was the moment when a dart slammed into my leg, and everything went black.

———

I CAME TO AN INSTANT LATER, or so it seemed, opening my eyes to see Malkin peering down at me. "I tried to tell them not to shoot you."

"And I told you to eat shit." Not my best comeback, but the world was spinning in dizzying circles, and my head felt as if it was filled with cotton wool. What kind of drug had the hunters hit me with? From the angle, I lay on my back, within a glass-walled cage. Cold metal pressed against my spine, and my hunter's mask had been removed, and so had my pilfered uniform. Instead, I'd been dressed in plain prison-style grey clothes.

"You're so much like your sister."

Alertness flooded me. I lurched upright, willing my claws to slide out, but nothing happened. Malkin watched me with an almost pitying expression, safe on the other side of the glass. His sleek uniform gleamed in the fluorescent light.

There was no sign of Astor. Nor my other friends, and I hadn't seen Cori at all.

"Your name *is* Ember, isn't it?" said Malkin. "Your sister said that name a few times."

While you were torturing her? Rage flickered through me, but my claws remained dormant. I glared at him instead of speaking, refused to let him see even a trace of my pain.

"Nothing to say?"

"Not to you. Where are my friends?" Doubtless Becks and Will would be locked in regular cells alongside the other shifters, but I was a prize. Like Cori.

"Alive, for the time being," he said. "We don't normally

take in subjects voluntarily, but they did seem so willing. Unlike your sister."

Furious tremors travelled through my body. This man was the enemy I'd trained to fight for my entire life. The reason I had no past, the reason Cori and I were hunted. Yet he was so utterly, insultingly *human.*

"She's a kid," I growled. "What you do here is despicable. And you call us *unnaturals.*"

"Perhaps you would define the term differently," he said. "I've seen evidence of your handiwork in the bodies you left in your path, and let's not forget that you and your friends also attacked my guests at my own home."

"I didn't leave a mark on a single human." As well he knew—but there was no point in arguing. He was set in his beliefs, and for whatever reason, he'd decided dragon shifters were the reason for all of the world's problems. "They don't deserve to die for believing a bunch of bullshit spewed by someone out for themselves alone. Why didn't you use the crap you're making in here during the faerie invasion?"

"The invasion was a terrible crime, yes," he said. "Unfortunately, we were no more prepared than anyone else was. What you see here is a result of two years of painstaking research intended to ensure that should the Sidhe attack humanity again, we shall strike back."

"If that's supposed to excuse you turning shifters in lab rats, you're barking up the wrong tree." The level of sadism I'd seen was proof that their motives were anything but altruistic. "The mages are preparing, too, and I doubt they're torturing anyone in their basement."

"The laws set out by the Mage Lords also forbid murder, which you have committed yourself, several times. If you'd prefer to rot in one of *their* cells..." He trailed off suggestively.

"You'd let me go that easily?"

Also, did that mean *he* was in touch with the Mage Lords? It was clear the League had friends in high places, but there was absolutely no chance the mages would condone anything that was happening here. They shouldn't even have tolerated the League's existence. But then again, they weren't the victims, and their own biases against shifters would prevail over the need to investigate any further.

"Oh, I'm not letting you go, Ember," he said. "I think we both know that you're a vital part of my research, as is your sister."

Searing anger rose inside me. There was nothing I could say to save my own skin, but I'd gladly give myself up for my sister's sake.

"Let her go." I wished I had the claws to back up my words. "Cori's a kid, and I'm the one who killed your people. Not her."

"Lying does you no favours," he said. "I received the report directly from the hunters who captured her, who confirmed she's as much a killer as you are. She won't be going anywhere, but rest assured that she'll have a much easier time now you're here. Some of our tests will be more effective on someone who's already achieved a full shift."

The sick bastard. Had he tried to force her to shift, like the others? As a growl built inside me, Malkin's eyes flickered with amusement. "I'd like to see your claws, little shifter, but the serum won't wear off for a while yet."

"When it does, I'll rip out your throat." Last time he'd thrown me into the air without touching me. How? Was he wearing a shielding spell? "Do you have a bunch of witches locked up in here, forced to make spells for you?"

"Actually, most of them serve us quite willingly," he said. "They're paid well and offered all the benefits of regular employment. We also have a number of contacts on the outside, as I believe you've seen for yourself."

Like Twill. Bastard. "So you're good at bribery. Big deal."

"Oh, your friend required no persuasion. I have to admit I'm surprised at how readily you came to trust in your natural enemy."

Astor? I hadn't figured out a cover story, but Astor himself clearly had, and he hadn't told any of us. If he intended to break us out later, I'd have to go along with the ruse. "He told us he deserted."

"Of course he did." A smile tilted his mouth. "He's a good liar, but he was trained by the best."

So well-trained that he'd fooled Malkin himself? I wanted to believe that, but wanting didn't make it real. "I should have known it was too good to be true."

"Yes, you should." His smile widened. "Did he ever tell you what happened to his family?"

My heartbeat kicked into gear. "Yeah, he said they were killed by a shifter."

"A dragon shifter," he corrected. "Some fifteen years ago. I assume you and your sister were in London at the time, but do correct me if I'm mistaken."

No way. It can't be true. I stared at him, all words fleeing my mind. Fifteen years ago… I didn't know *where* I'd been, nor the other dragon shifters either. My memories only started a dozen years back, and if Malkin told the truth, there was no possible way to be certain I hadn't known the dragon shifter who'd been responsible.

I might never know. Not if I can't leave this place. Malkin sure as hell wouldn't tell me, and I wouldn't fall to my knees and beg for the information. I'd always been secure in the knowledge that he wouldn't be able to torture any information out of me about the other dragon shifters, but I had the sickening feeling that he already knew. He'd had his eye on us for years. Maybe since before I was born.

"Now you see where you stand," he said softly. "I'm

offering you a choice. If you choose to serve me, your sister will be spared. If you fight, she will be the one who suffers in your place."

Fury tasted metallic on my tongue. "As if you *ever* planned to spare her. I won't be your lab rat."

My skin prickled along my hands, and I willed my scales to break through the fog and appear. I wanted to swipe his head off and torch the remains. I'd seen all manner of fae monsters inflict terror and pain on humans, and yet they didn't repel me as much as this man. Wild fae had no concept of morality. Malkin, on the other hand, had made the active choice to torment supernaturals because he *enjoyed* it.

"You might change your mind when you see her." He reached for the cage door, and my body thrummed with anticipation. *Cori.*

Malkin reached into the cage and grabbed my arm. He was stronger than he should have been, and I bit down on my tongue to avoid screaming as my shoulder wrenched to the side. He pinned my arms behind my back. A pair of cuffs snapped into place.

Malkin dragged me out of the cage and threw me to the floor, bruising my arm. I spat at his feet.

"Animal," he said softly.

"Speak for yourself." I bit back a wince when he dragged me upright by my cuffed hands and roughly shoved me forward. "I wondered why you took us in alive, but I guess it's because you can't be satisfied unless you have someone underfoot, at your mercy. You're so fucking fragile that you'd rather torture a teenager than accept that you lost. That the supernaturals you hate so much are the ones that came out on top. That'll be true whether I see the light of day again or not."

"You're wrong," he said. "Even the Mage Lords think shifters are a blight on the world, and they have no idea how tenuous their grasp on power truly is. Now, I think you should meet one of my other guests."

He gave me another shove, and when I saw the next cell along, I couldn't restrain my gasp. A large dragon was harnessed to a table, hunched up, obsidian scales dull underneath the harsh lighting.

Cori and I weren't the only dragons he'd captured.

19

The dragon was much larger than my shifted form. Maybe eight feet long, and twice as wide despite the narrow table he was tied to. I knew he was also much older, and male. How, I didn't know, maybe his scent. I also knew he was unconscious, his head on his front claws, faint puffs of smoke emitting from his nostrils as he exhaled. He was hurt, too. Even through the dark scales, crimson blood stained both legs and his back. His wings were torn in places and hunched up as though to take up as little space as possible. The sight punched me in the chest, and my vision wavered as every inch of me reacted on a visceral level. This dragon… how long had he been here?

"You sick *bastard*." I curled my fist, turned on Malkin and aimed a punch.

He moved, shifter-fast, and caught my fist in his hand. Then he twisted my arm until I gasped. "He's taught us a lot, but he's outlived his usefulness. You'll be his replacement."

"I'd rather die." How many other shifters had perished here, trapped behind iron and glass until they'd breathed their last? Blood thundered in my ears as my dragon nature demanded to break free, fighting against whatever drug he'd used on me.

A blaring alarm rang through the lab, echoing from the walls and ceiling. Red lights flashed. Malkin didn't let go of me, merely raising a brow. "Fire alarm? Is that your friends?"

Will and Becks. One or both of them must have escaped.

As I fought against Malkin's hold, a strangled yell came from behind us. Teeth bared in a snarl, Malkin dragged me back past the dragon shifter, past my own cage, to the lab's entrance. There, a body lay sprawled on the floor in a pool of blood. A knife had been embedded in his spine.

Astor came running in an instant later, mask off, eyes wide. "They escaped. They must have smuggled something inside. An explosive—"

As if on cue, a loud blast went off. The walls trembled and the floor shifted underfoot as if a quake had shaken the earth. My ears burned, and my arm wrenched out of Malkin's as the unsteady flooring broke his grip. Seizing my chance, I ran. My feet slammed against metal as I raced for the door Astor had left open behind him.

He did it on purpose. At a guess, Astor had put himself in charge of escorting my friends to the cells and had either let them keep their hidden spells or otherwise helped them out. As far as I knew, none of Will's spells was strong enough to create a blast that strong.

I skidded around a corner and ran smack into Will. "Whoa. What did you do?"

"I may have destroyed one of their labs," he said. "Problem is, they still have Becks. I know which cell she's in, but—"

A second blast rocked the walls. Will grabbed my arm and pulled me after him as the impact reverberated in the air, making my ears throb.

"Oops," he said. "I found out the raw spell ingredients I

was carrying don't mix well with some of the shit they're keeping in the lab."

"Damn. Good one, Will." My teeth rattled as the impact continued to rumble through the floor and walls. "They're using witch ingredients. Malkin said so openly. He has no problem working with supernaturals if it means figuring out new ways to torture us."

His expression darkened. "Yes. I have a score to settle with a certain someone, if we get out of this godforsaken place."

"Find Becks first," I said. "Wait—there wasn't anyone else in the lab, was there? You know—the shifters we saw earlier?"

"Oh, the lab was already empty. That assassin of yours is nothing but not resourceful."

He set the shifters free. My mind reeled, struggling to process the turn of events. Then I remembered what I'd left behind. "He's with Malkin. And another dragon shifter is there, too."

Will swore. "Another one?"

"Yeah, I'm supposed to be his replacement." Guilt knifed through me. I couldn't leave him to die either. "As a lab rat."

"Fuck that shit." Will ran around the corner and skidded to a halt in front of a group of masked hunters.

Both of us reacted on instinct. Will reached up his sleeve and whispered, "Close your eyes and run."

I squeezed my eyes shut at the same time as a dazzling flash lit up the inside of my eyelids. I ran, elbows out to knock the guards aside, and kept going in a straight line until Will flung out an arm. "It's safe to open your eyes now."

I did so and found myself nose to nose with a solid wall. "That was a close one. Flash spell?"

"My last one," he said. "I'm almost out. And we'll need a way to get into the room with the key to Becks's cell."

"Alternatively, you could just let me handle it." Astor stepped into view, the body of a dead guard falling to the floor behind him. A thin knife gleamed in his hand.

"You…" I didn't even know what to say. "Malkin. Is he still in the lab?"

"No, but you have five minutes to go back there and get Cori out. Maybe less. I did what I could."

"Thanks." An inadequate word for what I owed him if this worked. "Wait. Malkin's got the key for her cell."

"Here." He extended a hand, revealing gleaming metal. "This is a spare I got from one of Malkin's personal guards after I stabbed him in the spine."

"Ember's right, you're fucked in the head," said Will. "But thank god you're on our side."

Astor ignored him. "Go on."

I didn't need any encouragement. My hand closed around the key, and I ran back the way I'd come, past the bodies of the hunters Will had dazzled with his spell. Their bodies lay spreadeagled on the ground, each with stab wounds delivered with precision to the back or neck. *Damn, Astor.*

Reaching the lab, I ran through the open door. Astor hadn't been kidding. Nobody was in here except the man who'd bled out in the entryway. *Cori.* My sister's name thrummed through my head in time with my footsteps. First, I passed my own vacant cell, and a keening noise reached my ears. It didn't come from the dragon shifter—he still looked to be unconscious—but from the cell next to his.

Will swore under his breath when he saw the dragon. "Fucking Malkin."

"I know." I reached the next cell and halted, sickened. The keening noise came from a black-haired boy, who lay sprawled inside a cage in a prone position. His pointed ears told me he was half-fae, and the metal floor must be causing him unspeakable pain.

"Ember!" Will called from the cage on the other side of the half-faerie. "It's her."

My sister was tied to a metal bed, which looked cold and uncomfortable enough without the cuffs on her wrists and ankles. Her eyes were closed, her hair loose and sweeping across her face. Had they shot her with a tranquiliser, too? There was nothing in the cage, save for the table she was chained to. No torture instruments. But she didn't stir as I stepped close enough for my breath to fog the glass. The faerie boy moaned, in pain or distress, and the hairs on my arms stood on end. A scent reached my nostrils, like the smoke from a far-off fire. Moonbeam leaves.

"Ember." Will tapped on the glass. "I bet your claws can break this."

"Yeah." I reached inward for my shifter self, for the part of me that the tranquiliser had suppressed, and willed the dragon in me to awaken.

Heat flickered below the surface, and scales rose to cover my palms. As my claws slid out, someone came running into view. A female hunter dressed in the shiny gear of one of Malkin's bodyguards. Shit.

Will lifted a hand and flung something at the hunter. I ducked, expecting another explosion, but instead the guard stopped in her tracks, her legs locking together and her arm struggling to lift her gun. I leapt in, my claws finding gaps in her armoured clothing and tearing into her throat. She let out a gurgling cry, abruptly cut off in a spray of blood.

I returned my attention to Cori's cage. "What spell was that? I've never seen it before."

"Another new one I got from their lab," Will replied. "They had a jar of adhesive lying around, so I combined it with one of my point-and-shoot spells. I sealed a few doors on the way out, too."

"Is that why it's so quiet?" Astor had left a pile of bodies behind, true, but there should be more present than this.

"Yeah, the guards back in the labs aren't having a fun time," he said. "I might have doctored the floors as well."

I snorted. "Trust you."

"Always."

I curled my claw into a fist and drove it into the sheer glass wall of Cori's cell. Again. Again. The impact would have hurt, had I been in human form, but I kept going until splintering cracks spread out across the glass.

An alarm began to blare, not the fire alarm this time, but a siren-like wail that came from the cage itself. Red lights flickered above Cori's unconscious body, yet she still didn't wake.

"Cori!" I launched myself forward, thrust both fists against the pane, and the remnants of the glass cracked outward and made a gap big enough for me to climb through. I leapt, slivers from the broken edges cutting my skin, but I didn't care. I had eyes only for Cori.

Lifting her one-handed, I took the manacles between my claws and squeezed. The metal snapped in my hands, the chains fell away, and Cori collapsed against me. I felt for a pulse, relieved to feel the frantic beat against my hand.

Then my baby sister was in my arms, and nothing else mattered. I held onto her like I did when she woke screaming in the night, like she was five and I was twelve again, the only person she had left in the world. *It's okay, little sister. I'll get us out of here.*

"Ember!" Will's frantic voice snapped me back to the present. "We have to move."

A gunshot. I whirled around, Cori still in my arms, in time to see Will dive for cover as a bullet embedded itself in the wall between cages.

Malkin approached, his footsteps lost beneath the

continual blare of the cage's alarm. He'd lost some of his earlier composure, and his mouth was an angry slant as he surveyed Will and me.

"This really wasn't necessary, Ember," he said. "I would have shown you mercy."

"No, you wouldn't." My heart drummed against my ribs. *Cori.* He didn't need her alive, now that he had me, and it would be infinitely harder to fight him while simultaneously trying to prevent her from being hit by a stray bullet or knife. "You'd have kept me imprisoned until you found my replacement, like you did to the other dragon. One way or another, I'd have died here without ever seeing daylight again."

"You're quite wrong," he said. "You never gave me the chance to explain my aims for you, but I can assure you that your sister would have been treated quite kindly, had you cooperated. As it is, you will stay here alone. I have no need for the rest of your friends."

"Good, because we've no need for you, either," said Will, mottled grey rising to cover his skin. He leapt at Malkin with a shriek that turned into a yelp as he hit the same invisible barrier I'd collided with myself. I winced as Will was sent flying back into the wall, shifting back to human form again as he slid down to the floor.

Malkin calmly pointed a gun at him. "As I said, you are replaceable."

"Not me," said Will. "I'm unique."

"Will," I hissed. *Don't piss off the man with the gun.* We were both unarmed, aside from whatever spells Will had left, and it sounded like he'd used a fair few of them just to get here.

Malkin turned on me with an almost bored expression. "Your friend is tedious. I think it's time we got him a cage of his own. A quick and painless death is more than he deserves."

"He has a name, you know," Will said, with a groan.

Malkin reached for a mechanism on the wall next to the cage containing the captive faerie. The glass door slid open, and Malkin seized Will by the arm, shoving him over the threshold.

The faerie lifted his head as Malkin threw Will into the cage, his eyes dull with pain and confusion. His hair was tangled and unkempt, and he was as thin as a rail. They'd been keeping him in here far longer than Cori, and his feet were bound together by manacles like the ones that had held Cori. Iron was poison to fae. It was a miracle he was still alive.

Cori hadn't stirred in my arms. If I put her down, I'd risk her life, but Will… dammit. I couldn't let him die in here either.

Movement stirred in the corner of my eye. I lifted my head and spied a masked figure treading into view. As my gaze passed over him, the hunter lifted the mask a fraction. *Astor.* Was Becks with him, too? I couldn't see her, but my gaze connected with Will's, and he nodded almost imperceptibly before rising to his feet.

"I find this accommodation unacceptable," he said to Malkin. "I demand to be moved to a nicer one. With a shower. And no roommate."

The faerie skittered away from him, the iron manacles clanking against the metal floor.

"You are in no position to bargain." Malkin kept one eye on Cori and me, but he hadn't noticed Astor's stealthy approach. And while whatever shielding spell Malkin wore made me reluctant to try striking him, if anyone had worked out a way around that, it was Astor.

"And what? I'm supposed to sit down and accept that I'm being imprisoned without a trial when I've never committed a crime?" Will said loudly. "Except against fashion, maybe. It depends who you ask."

A faint popping sounded—not a gunshot, but quieter—and something whistled past my face. Malkin stepped back, one hand lifted to his neck. A dart protruded from beneath his chin. *It suppresses magic.*

For a heartbeat, Malkin stared at the dart. Then he shoved me in front of him as a gun went off. I caught Astor's eye—wide with horror, unable to stop the shot he'd already fired—but Will lunged out of the cage, lifting a hand. A flash went off and the bullet veered sideways, harmlessly bouncing off the metal floor.

"You." Malkin plucked the dart out of his neck and threw it to the floor. If it had any dizzying effect on him like it had on me, it didn't show. "Number three oh eight. I'm disappointed."

Three oh eight? I'd known the League didn't put much value on individual hunters, but not that it manifested in such a literal sense.

"So am I." Astor stalked towards him, lifting his gun again.

"I wouldn't." Malkin pointed his own gun at Cori. I stopped breathing. "Stay where you are—and you, too, Ember."

I didn't dare move. Dread held me in its grip as he approached me, his gun still trained on Cori.

"Please," I whispered. "Not her."

My dragon fought to escape, and the only thing that kept me from fully shifting was the fragile body of my sister in my arms. Wings pressed between my shoulder blades, threatening to break the skin—but if I shifted, I'd lose Cori.

Footsteps echoed. Without taking his eyes off Cori, Malkin said, "Take him to the cells. I want to deal with him myself."

No. God, no. Out of the corner of my eye, I saw two

hunters close in on Astor. Then a shot rang out, followed by a choked sound that drove a steel knife into my chest. *Astor.*

I could do nothing as they dragged him away, nor as Malkin reached out and plucked Cori from my arms with the gun pointed directly at her forehead.

"Walk," he commanded.

I walked. Broken glass crunched underfoot. When we neared the other dragon's cage, Malkin stopped, operating a mechanism on the door. The dragon's cage slid open.

"Now," said Malkin, "you're going to kill him, Ember, or your sister will die."

20

I didn't move. The other dragon remained unconscious, or semi-conscious, his eyes closed, his body hunched up in his chains.

"Your sister, Ember," Malkin said softly.

"Fuck you," I said. "Astor is worth ten of you."

"I have to admit, I'm intrigued as to how you convinced him to switch sides. He was always one of the most ardent of Elites. At one time, he might have been in the running as my successor, in fact."

My stomach sank, but I held his stare, knowing he was trying to rattle me. "Except he realised you're a brainwashing bunch of crooks with no redeeming qualities."

"You have no weapons left but words, which mean nothing to me." Malkin gestured to the other dragon's cage with one hand, still holding Cori in his arms. "She is even less of a danger. I might have offered her a painless end, but you've forfeited that right."

Rage surged to the surface, and only Malkin's grip on my sister stayed my hand, forced me to walk into the cage myself. As I did so, Malkin took my place on the outside and hit the mechanism that closed the door on me.

"Now," he said, "I want you to shift into a dragon."

"What?" I frowned at him through the glass. "You do realise my claws can easily break through the glass?"

"Yes." His gun was still pointed at Cori. A clear message. If I made a wrong move, my sister would die. "Go on. Shift, Ember. You want to. It's your nature."

I did want to. Seeing him holding my sister, and the dried blood on her arm, sent my dragon side into a frenzy that threatened to spill over despite my best efforts to stay human, to stay in control of my conscious mind. Because if I shifted, I couldn't guarantee that I'd remember the other side of me at all. For all I knew, I might end up stuck, like the other dragon shifter, chained to a table and unable to break free.

"No," I said. "Not if it's what *you* want from me."

"You're afraid, aren't you?" he said. "I know enough of your kind to be aware that you have no more control over your dragon side than a wild animal has over their own nature."

How could he know so much? Cori wouldn't have told him a thing, so he must have dragged the information from the other dragon, who couldn't help me even if he'd been capable of it.

"You don't know anything at all." My hands fisted. "Your people slaughtered us, hunted and hounded us to the brink of extinction, but you'll never understand who we are."

"On the contrary," he said, "your fellow dragons alone are responsible for their extermination, without the need for outside intervention. I was merely the spectator, not the instigator."

"Bollocks. You *locked us in cages.*"

"Also incorrect," he said. "Your friend over there volunteered to help the League as part of a vital research programme. He came here willingly."

I choked out a laugh. "You really think I believe that?"

"You can believe as you like." His grip on Cori didn't waver as he lifted his gun to point at the dragon chained to the table. "Following the faeries' attack on this realm, the need for such research has become even more essential than ever. After all, dragonfire is one of few weapons capable of causing damage to other unnaturals, even the Sidhe."

"What's your point?" The Sidhe weren't the danger here. *He* was, and nothing in his treatment of his captive indicated that he was in any way acting for the good of humanity. He wasn't training the dragon shifter to fight the fae, but simply torturing him for his own gain.

"My point is that the Sidhe remain a threat to humanity, and the damage they wrought on our world deserves to be met with retribution," he said. "The Mage Lords have no intention of taking action. They believe we should peacefully coexist alongside the very invaders who destroyed our world. In doing so they betray the humans they claim to serve, and as you saw for yourself, many people are dissatisfied with that. They want better, and they deserve it."

"Funny," I said. "All I saw was a group of rich fucks trying to convince desperate humans to blame the wrong person. Oh, and you've spent more time torturing innocent shifters than punishing the fae, so don't pretend that you're acting in the interests of anyone except yourselves."

He knows that. He couldn't possibly believe his own bullshit enough not to be aware of precisely what he was doing when he'd invited those people to the mansion. He'd pretended to have the answers, but he'd lied. He hadn't known the Sidhe were coming, and I suspected that if they were to attack again, he'd hide here in his underground Stronghold just like the first time.

"You continue to misunderstand me, Ember," he said. "Really, I'm offering you a boon. The humans you share this world with will never tolerate your existence. They would hunt you down themselves if they knew a dragon walked among them. As it is, you have the chance to be useful. You will win me this world, starting with the city you call home."

"Like hell." I'd had enough. My claws slid out, scales creeping up my arms.

Malkin's eyes gleamed eagerly. "Yes… shift, Ember. Go on. Strike him dead."

My gaze went back towards the dragon shifter. This time, his eye slid open but didn't focus on me. He was drugged, like I'd been, but rather than being stuck as a human, he was trapped in dragon form.

"Kill him, Ember," Malkin said. "And I'll spare your sister's life."

Bile burned the back of my throat. If I shifted, I might well lose enough awareness of myself to kill the other dragon without suffering as much guilt. At least until I turned back into a human. Obeying Malkin's command should have been out of the question, but when he held Cori up against the glass, her head lolling, red flashed before my eyes, then white. My claws lifted, and I swiped at the dragon's chains, slicing straight through the metal. The chains fell away, and the dragon growled with a rumble worthy of the spell that had made the floor tremble underneath our feet. His eyes slid properly open, and while his body remained hunched on the table, there was an intelligence in his gaze that took my breath away.

Intelligence… and anger.

"Hey," I whispered. "I'm Ember. I'm here to get you out."

The dragon's clawed feet shook as he adjusted his position, moving slowly. He must be in pain from being chained up for a long time, but his eyes radiated hate enough that my own eyes began to glow.

Then he lifted a claw and swiped out, the edge catching me full in the face. I flew across the cage, and my back slammed into the glass wall.

"He's too far gone, Ember," Malkin called to me. "You'll only be showing him mercy by ending his life."

The dragon half-slid off the table, clawed feet hitting the ground with another bone-shaking thud. I rubbed the back of my head, wincing, and saw the cage door slide open and Malkin throw my sister into the room. Her limp body hit the ground, and white light flashed across my vision again. I sprang at him, colliding with the glass door, a snarl on my lips. He'd let go of Cori, so I could rip out his throat without risking her life. Only a flimsy sheet of glass was in my way.

A claw swiped at me again, snagging my ankle, and bodily hurled me across the room. I landed on my shoulder hard, pain ripping up my arm. The dragon growled, lifted his claw again, and this time aimed at Cori.

"No!" I lurched upright despite the pain as his claw snagged Cori around the waist and flung her across the cage.

I lunged, catching her in my arms. The impact sent us both crashing to the floor, further jarring my aching shoulder and back, but I'd spared Cori further damage. I couldn't keep taking hits while in human form indefinitely, but shifting would come at the price of my reason.

Or would it? Maybe Malkin was right, and I had good reason to be afraid of losing myself, but I didn't need to be afraid of my own nature. When it came to two matters, my dragon side and I shared the same goals.

Protect Cori. Destroy the hunters.

The shift came on me, claws sliding out first. Scales spread up my arms, my shoulders, and as my body trembled with the oncoming shift, Malkin slipped away.

He'd gone, left me here to kill the other dragon or risk my sister's life.

"Fuck that!" I shouted, the sound turning into a growl as wings sprouted behind my shoulder blades.

I crashed into the other dragon head on. This time the impact didn't leave so much as a scratch; we skidded across the floor, feet scratching the metal, claws locked in a bitter struggle. His sharp teeth grazed my neck, trying to gain purchase, his eyes wild and unseeing. Maybe he'd forgotten how to turn back into a human. He didn't even seem to recognise me as one of his fellow dragon shifters.

"I'm on your side!" The words came out in a growl that nevertheless should have been understandable to him.

His answering growl was one of wordless anger, and he opened his maw in a flash of white fire.

I flung myself flat, and a jet of fire shot overhead, burning a trail through the glass wall. I called upon my own fire as the dragon swiped at me again, his claw skimming over my head.

Fire obliterated any lingering traces of human instinct left in me. I planted my feet next to Cori and roared. The resultant blast of flames caught the other dragon full in the face, sending him reeling back despite his fireproof scales. The next second I was on him, my claws sliding between the scales of his neck. Blood gushed out, its metallic scent filling the air, as the dragon shifter crumpled to the floor.

"Ember!" The hoarse shout drew my attention to the gaping hole that had once been sheer glass. Will stood outside the cage, a cat sitting at his feet.

Becks. She'd been the only one of us who still walked free, and she must have opened Will's cage as soon as Malkin had left us alone. As I watched, he trod forward, one hand reaching uncertainly towards my sister's unconscious body.

Cori. I turned back into a human, reeling, a sob catching

in my throat as I looked down at the bloodied body sprawled across the cage floor. I'd killed my fellow dragon shifter and played into Malkin's hands. I'd done exactly what he'd expected, what he'd wanted.

"Malkin," I said, my voice shaking with anger. "He—"

"Has Astor, I know."

My head snapped up. "What?"

"I heard him talking to two of those guards. He mentioned—an execution."

"No." Horror shocked me to the core, blanketing the guilt and regret roiling inside me.

There'd be time to grieve later. Time to process what I'd done when we were free from this horror. For now, I owed Astor my life, and that meant I had to help him.

"You can't help him," Will said. "The hunters will have him surrounded, and I don't have any spells left."

"Malkin's been hit by one of those darts. His magical protections are nullified."

At least, they had been. I didn't know how long those darts usually lasted, and he might have some contingency plan in place in case he ended up getting shot with one himself.

Will swore. "Look, I owe him my life, too, but Cori can't get out in the state she's in now, and neither can Kit."

"Who's Kit?"

Will gestured to the cage he'd stepped out of. The faerie crouched on the metal floor, hands over his head, rocking back and forth. "He won't come out. I don't know why."

"Shit."

I trod into the cage myself, having no idea what I could possibly say to make the prolonged torture the half-faerie had suffered any more bearable. Faeries had powerful magic, but it was anyone's guess as to whether he'd be able to access it after so long in captivity.

When I entered the cage, my foot caught on a piece of paper that had blown across the floor. Words snagged my vision, and I stared for a heartbeat.

The text was written in the same language I'd found inside the notebook Cori and I had travelled to London with. The part I'd never been able to read. Why would the hunters have something written in the same language as the notebook I'd been given by my fellow dragon shifters?

"Ember," Will hissed. "What are you doing?"

"Nothing." I gave myself a mental shake and crouched beside the faerie. "We're going to help you get out of here. I promise. But you'll need to walk, if you can."

He rocked back and forth, moaning to himself. "Hurts. Iron."

Oh. Shit. He was barefoot, so every step he took on the metal floor would be agony. I turned to Will. "He needs shoes."

"For god's sake." Will hopped on one foot, pulling off his boots. "He can wear these, if they'll fit, but seriously—the only reason we haven't been overrun is because Astor killed half the patrolling guards before he got himself hauled off."

"Then we'd better finish off the other half," I responded, helping the faerie put on Will's shoes. He wouldn't be able to move fast, but at least he could walk without pain.

Carefully, I lifted Cori off the ground and carried her out of the cage. I couldn't rescue Astor while holding her, but there was no way in hell I'd leave her behind again.

"I'll take her." Will extended his arms. "I know you want to get Astor out yourself, and you have more fighting power than I do."

Like my claws, which had pierced the other dragon shifter's throat. Tears burned my eyes as I stepped past his crumpled body. *I'm sorry. I'm so sorry.*

Becks meowed, perhaps in sympathy, but I couldn't look at her either.

"Come on." Will took Cori gently in his arms and addressed the faerie.

After a short pause, he staggered after Will, while Becks padded ahead of us out of the room and into the corridor once again.

The first hunter who stepped into our path died on the spot, my claws moving on autopilot to rip out his throat. I stepped around the body, ears strained to hear the murmur of voices from somewhere ahead.

We came to a locked door as sheer as the glass cages, through which I could see Astor lying on the metal floor. He'd been shot. Several times. Blood soaked his ankles and wrists, and his jacket had been ripped off, exposing blood-streaked tattoos. As I watched, horrified, a hunter took aim and shot him through the upper arm. Three more hunters circled him, overlooked by Malkin.

None of them had shot Astor anywhere fatal, but I'd bet that was deliberate. Malkin had ordered a slow, painful death, and though the bullets would do their work eventually, he was in for hours of suffering first.

Rage lanced through me. I was barely conscious of stepping up to the door until my nose pressed to the glass, a growl slipping through my teeth.

Malkin's head lifted. His expression displayed no surprise at seeing me and the others outside. His mouth moved, speaking, but a loud report like static cut through the air, followed by a muffled voice spoken through a loudspeaker. *"All... to the exits... immediately."*

"What are they doing?" Will took an alarmed step back. "Ember—they called an evacuation. Wait."

Too late. I dug my claws into the door and ripped it away

from its frame before I launched myself into the room. Immediately, three guns pointed at me.

"Stop," Malkin called to the hunters. "Don't shoot her. She's too valuable."

"So valuable that you took your eyes off me to torture Astor instead." My chest tightened at the sight of him sprawled on the floor, drenched in blood.

"Since you're still alive, I assume you did as I asked."

I killed him. My stomach turned, but I refused to let Malkin divert my attention from Astor. "Let me guess, you're going to use his life as a bargaining chip this time. Do you have no other tactics left but cheap threats?"

The hum of static from outside told me the loudspeaker had made another announcement. The three hunters didn't lower their guns, but they all turned that way, evidently trying to hear, too.

"As a deserter, number three oh eight is of little use even as bait." Malkin aimed the gun at the back of Astor's head.

Becks got there first. She leapt at Malkin, claws outstretched, and collided with an unseen shield. With a yowl, she flew back, barely landing on her feet.

"So you're the one who's been running around causing trouble," Malkin said to her. "I suppose it was you who set her free." He pressed his foot to Astor's back, against one of the bullet holes.

A gasp caught in my throat when he stirred. He was awake, and probably in terrible pain. My friends had yet to use the healing spells we'd brought, but I didn't think any spell could heal that many bullet wounds at once.

"It doesn't matter how many of you there are, not when your fates will all be the same." Malkin dug his boot in harder. Astor made an indistinct noise, tried to push to his knees, and then collapsed again. "So will his. It's time. Leave us. I shall join you on the surface."

To my bemusement, the three hunters obeyed him, trailing out of the room without so much as a glance at their former comrade. I didn't hear any confrontation outside—Will and the faerie must have hidden out of sight, together with Cori—but it made zero sense for Malkin to tell the hunters to leave when he already had the upper hand.

"What are you playing at?" I asked. "You're running away?"

"I confess, your friends caused a little too much damage to the structural integrity of the Stronghold," he said. "Luckily, we were prepared for an evacuation, and it will be no trouble for us to relocate elsewhere."

"Excuse me?" He couldn't be serious. Yes, Will had caused one hell of an explosion back in the labs, but I hadn't expected the hunters to leave outright, taking my shot at revenge with them.

Cori is all that matters, I reminded myself. Revenge could wait.

Malkin reached into a pocket and produced a mask. Unlike the ones carried by Elites, his looked metallic and glimmered in a similar way to the shielding spell he wore. Placing it on his face, he said, "You will come with me personally, Ember. If not, I will kill your friends one by one."

"Over my dead body."

"Or your sister's?"

"What's the plan, leave everyone left in here to starve to death?" Becks was back on four paws, but she looked shaken, and the two guns gleaming at Malkin's belt left little doubt as to how he planned to execute anyone who stood in his way. Except, apparently, me.

"Not you, Ember," said Malkin. "I'm offering to spare your life. Walk with me, or I will be less patient with you."

When I didn't budge, he seized my arm in a grip that was even stronger than it had been earlier, and more than any human's had the right to be. *Another spell?* I dug my heels in, but he pulled, hard enough that my shoulder threatened to dislocate.

"What the hell are you?" I snarled through gritted teeth. "You're no simple human."

"I'm quite human, as is he." Still holding me, he surveyed Astor's broken body with a half-smile. "I suppose it's worth explaining, Ember, though I have to admit that part of me thought you would have already guessed."

"What?" I tried to free myself again, earning another spasm of pain up to my shoulder. "What have you done?"

"Those of our number who prove themselves worthy of promotion to the Elite rank are rewarded with certain advantages," he said. "An enhancement, I suppose one might say, to aid them in their goal of subduing shifters and other unnaturals."

He extended his foot towards Astor's limp arm, nudging at the tattoos running from shoulder to wrist. Astor's head turned, and as though pulled by a magnet, my gaze connected with his. Shock and disbelief shone clearly in his half-open eyes. He hadn't known.

"I saved the best for myself, of course," Malkin added. "So that no shifter will ever get the better of me."

"You're deluded."

I ripped my arm free, and there came a crash and shout from outside. The smell of burning filled the air a moment before glass shattered and a plume of fire filled the room. Malkin grabbed my arm again, dragged me to the floor as the flames raced overhead, singeing my hair.

Holy shit. The dragon.

He was alive, and ablaze in dragonfire. Malkin shouted something that was lost in the roar of oncoming flame, but despite the heat, my skin didn't burn. I lifted my head, seeing the dragon's huge scaly form shoving its way through the shattered glass. His jaw opened, readied to breathe fire again.

I twisted my arm free of Malkin's and heard the sickening crack of a bullet. Malkin had raised a gun with his free hand, and the dragon vanished at once. An emaciated old man with white hair crouched in his place, blood blossoming on his chest. The old man's head lifted feebly, and his gaze locked with mine.

"Find the… moonbeam…" His words trailed off as his head lolled back and he crumpled into a heap on the metal floor.

"There," said Malkin, his voice slightly muffled behind his mask. "Now, you'll come with me."

Dizzy with shock, I tried to move, but Malkin's hand shot out and hauled me out of the room. A faint haze overlaid my vision. At first, I took it for smoke from the fire, but when I started coughing, I couldn't stop.

"Come on." He pulled harder. "The air on this floor has been flooded with poison. If you stay here, you won't last twenty minutes."

Poison. That was why he'd ordered the hunters to leave without taking the shifters with him. He knew there was no danger of them escaping their cells.

He dragged me around a corner, and we came within sight of the lift. "All other ways off this floor are sealed. The upper floors will be mostly empty by now, too. All that remains is to reach the surface."

"You—" I fought hard, to no avail, as he dragged me into the lift and pressed the button to seal the doors. As the lift began to climb, the tickle in my throat faded a little. I swallowed, wheezing, "Bastard."

"Now, you're very fortunate. It looks as if you'll get another chance to see daylight after all."

But my friends wouldn't. And my sister. Panic sliced

through my mind, and my claws emerged, reaching for his mask, for the smallest gap between the chin and the neck. His hand latched around my claw, pinning my arm to my side with a strength that shouldn't be possible without magical assistance.

"What the hell did you do to yourself? You have some nerve calling us *unnaturals.*" I twisted, fighting against his grip. Beneath his sleeve, I glimpsed the band of a tattoo, like Astor's. "Don't bullshit me by claiming it's some kind of upgrade. You're as unnatural as I am."

"I am willing to make any sacrifice to rid the world of the stain that is your kind, Ember." His fist came at my throat, fast as a whip, and my breath escaped in a pained rush.

My claws appeared and vanished in the same instant as he shoved me to the floor. My head cracked against solid metal, and sparks danced before my eyes. I dug my hands into the floor, willing myself not to pass out.

Not human. A gasp tore from my lips as he seized me by the shoulder again and twisted my arm behind my back. My eyes watered, and I fought to cling onto consciousness as the lift climbed higher and higher.

Then we came to a stop, and the doors slid open. Impulsively I gave a lunge for the control panel, slammed my fist into the button for the fifth floor as Malkin seized me bodily around the waist and hauled me out into the open.

Not for long. With my last ounce of strength, I twisted free and reached for the metal doors where the lift had been. My claws dug in and ripped the doors open, revealing the empty elevator shaft.

Malkin shouted, tried to grab me again, but I'd already flung myself over the edge and into the darkness.

21

I fell. Far too fast, the lift came up to meet me. I landed in a roll, cold metal digging into my back and shoulder, and rode the lift the rest of the way down. When I emerged, I crawled out into the corridor and immediately broke into an uncontrolled coughing fit. *The poison.* How long had Malkin said I'd have before the poison finished me off? Twenty minutes?

"What the fuck, Ember?" Will said. "Did you forget you can turn into a dragon?"

"No time." I coughed, pushed to my feet. "Shit. The poison… the prisoners…"

"Becks is busy setting everyone free." He gestured to Cori, who lay beside the frightened half-faerie. "I was trying to open the door to the stairs."

"Astor." I coughed again. "Where is he?"

"He refused to come with me."

"He didn't." Shit. He'd been shot in both ankles. Walking away was an impossibility, and Will could only carry one person at a time. His half-faerie companion could barely walk himself. "I'm going back for him."

Will didn't look surprised in the least. "Try not to breathe too much."

I rolled my eyes. "Sure, I'll go ahead and do that."

Already my breath came short and my chest felt tight, and there was no telling how many other shifters were imprisoned in here. The doors were all sealed past this point, including the one Will had come through, but I pried it open with my claws and kept going, coughing harder with each step.

A body blocked my path. Astor. He'd pulled himself out of the room in which he'd been tortured, leaving smears of blood all over the metal floor. Upon seeing me, he lifted his head and tried to prop himself up on one elbow.

"Stop. Don't hurt yourself even more." I might be able to carry him for a bit, but I didn't want to cause him any more pain than he was already suffering. "I'll get you out of here. Becks is freeing the other shifters. The other floors already evacuated ages ago."

"I know." His head drooped. "You can't save everyone, you know."

"I have to try." I hadn't been able to save the other dragon shifter, but I was damned if I let the other prisoners suffocate in darkness. "The stairs…"

"Malkin has the only switch."

I swore. "Fine. We'll have to go out via the lift." At least it was still in working order despite the damage my claws had done, but the more trips we took, the greater the odds of the poison seeping out onto the other floors. Or Malkin coming back. He was the only person in here with a protective mask, and I'd bet he was loathe to let his prize prisoner go so easily.

I lifted Astor around the waist, or tried to. He protested, trying to push me away. "Get your friends out first."

"There's room in the lift for all of you, you know." I half-dragged him upright, trying not to jostle the bullet wounds.

Dragging him down the corridor was painfully slow, and the amount of blood we left behind us made me conscious of how close to death he must be.

The loud thump of footsteps prompted me to slow down. Becks's cat form came running around a corner, pursued by a number of other shifters. Some were in human form, others animals. Wolves, mostly, but a couple of gargoyles too, all painfully thin and many of them bleeding from fresh wounds. Anger lanced through me, but Astor's increasingly limp body brought me back to the present moment.

"Get in the lift." I nodded down the corridor. "Will and Kit—the faerie—are there, too. You need to get out. All of you."

Becks meowed an objection, but I lifted Astor's arm around me again. "We'll catch up to you."

Astor muttered something that sounded like 'too stubborn for your own good'.

"Yeah, that's the thing about shifters." I continued to drag him along, coughing with each step. "We have this tendency to latch onto things we want and refuse to let go."

I *think* he said, "And you want me?", but his words were muffled when he too began coughing, his body shaking in my arms.

"Guess you got under my skin," I added, more to drown out my own panic than anything else. "Or scales, as it were."

The shifters overtook us, some running, others only able to limp. When Astor and I rounded the corner, a commotion came from among the shifters, and I heard Will shout, "The lift has gone!"

"Shit." Had Malkin or someone else called it back to the upper floor? There was no other lift, and while I could climb out through the elevator shaft, doing so with a passenger was another matter. Let alone a bunch of weakened, tortured shifters, most of whom weren't able to fly. "I'll have to tear open the way to the stairs."

Nothing for it. We'd have to go up the slow way, racing against the clock to escape before the poison reached the upper floors. Becks led the shifters back the way they'd come. Some were outright panicking, but far more of them moved with the sort of numb expressions I associated with people who'd given up hope.

I began to drag Astor, too, but he shook his head. "I told you to leave me here. You need to open the stairs."

"I'll come back for you." I'd carry him up the elevator shaft myself if I had to. "Just give me a minute."

I ran, each step pounding through my lungs and drawing out a rattling cough, until I reached the stairs. The sealed doors refused to budge when I tugged on them, but my claws easily dug into the edges of the frame. My shoulder wrenched with fresh pain as I pried them open, inch by inch, until there was a gap large enough to climb through.

The shifters didn't need any encouragement. They approached in a surge, supervised by Becks, who helped some of the more injured or older shifters climb through first. When the last had vanished through the gap, Will helped the half-faerie climb out, too.

"Take Cori," I told him. "I'll grab Astor and I'll meet you at the top."

"You'd better." Will put one leg through the gap in the doors. "Or else I'll hire a necromancer to bring you back as a ghost so Becks and I can berate you for the rest of our lives."

"Love you too." I looked at Cori, draped in his arms, and my heart squeezed. "Please take care of her. I'll come back."

I promise.

I ran back the way I came, my coughs echoing off the walls, and rounded the corner to find Astor where I'd left him. He hadn't even tried to pull himself after me, and the blood soaking into the floor wrenched my heart as much as seeing my baby sister carried out of sight.

"There's no time," he whispered, his voice raspy. "He's coming."

"What?" I reached for the lift doors to wrench them open and recoiled when a metallic scraping sounded from beyond.

Then the doors slid open, revealing Malkin, still masked, still holding a gleaming gun in one hand. *I should have known.*

"Ember." Surprise flitted across his face when he saw Astor lying at my feet. "You'd truly risk so much for him?"

"I guess loyalty isn't a concept that you're capable of understanding," I shot at him. "Get out of my way."

"I don't think so." He pointed the gun, not at me, but at Astor. "You both have minutes at most before you suffocate to death. He'll die before you do, whether I act or not, but I'd hate to lose my new test subject so soon."

"Give up." Dammit. Malkin was right—Astor would die before I did, no matter the outcome of our struggle. "I told you I'd rather die trying to escape than live trapped in a cage."

My claws slid out, and once again I collided with Malkin's invisible shield as I lunged at the lift. My fist slammed down on the button to close the doors. Malkin grabbed for me and missed as something moved in the corner of my eye—a cat, sprinting across the corridor. *Dammit, Becks. You were supposed to go with the others.*

Malkin lifted the gun and fired at her, missing. She leapt, high, bouncing off his shield, and the distraction was all I needed to dig my claws into the metal doors and wrench open the empty elevator shaft.

"Stop!" Malkin pointed the gun at Astor next. I spun on him, a snarl on my lips, and he offered a smile entirely without warmth. "I'd suggest you make up your mind,

Ember. Will you come with me, or will you die here in the darkness with him?"

"I'll take my chances." I saw Becks move, leaping at him again and throwing off his aim. Claws digging in, I ripped a chunk out of the lift door and flung it at Malkin. The metal also bounced off his shield but gave me an opening to grab Astor's arm and pull him out of range.

Becks yowled in warning as Malkin fired off another shot. Astor's body gave a faint jolt, telling me that he'd been hit, but it didn't look to have been anywhere fatal. I pushed him ahead of me towards the gaping hole in the lift doors and shouted to Becks. "Get on my back!"

I shoved Astor through the open shaft and leapt after him, shifting as I did so. Wings shot out between my shoulder blades, and my body lengthened as the scales spread from my arms to my shoulders, and my clawed hand caught Astor before he fell. Immediately my head felt clearer than it had when I'd been in human form, and beneath the dizzying scent of the poison came the familiar smell of fresh air. The scent of freedom.

Once I was sure Becks was safely on my back, my wings beat in the dark shaft, carrying me higher. I'd never flown like this, let alone while carrying anyone, but my muscles knew what to do without prompting. The space was cramped, but the tantalising scent of fresh air spurred me on.

As the hulking outline of the lift appeared, blocking my way, a plume of orange-red escaped my mouth, turning to white dragonfire. Metal melted, walls buckled, and the earth itself trembled as the fire ripped through any obstacle in my path. The charred remains of the lift fell away around me as I beat my wings again, again.

Solid earth formed a ceiling above me. I kept flying, claws outstretched, hoping that anyone on the surface would have had the sense to get out of the way.

My claws ripped through soil, through stone, through metal. The smell of clean air mingled with dirt as I tore my way to freedom. Layers of grass and earth collapsed under my claws and clean air filled my lungs, washing away the poison.

In one glorious beat of my wings, I flew out into the sky. I soared high, caught in the dizzying joy of unexpected flight and the knowledge that this was as natural to me as breathing, that I didn't want to come down.

"Ember!" someone shouted. "They're going to fall off!"

Below, Will stood on the hillside, my baby sister draped in his arms and injured shifters gathered all around him. The sight of Cori rang through my core, reminded me of who I was. Human and dragon both, melded into one.

Cold wind whipped past as I plunged towards the ground. I landed, claws splayed, heard Becks's panicked yowl as she slid from my back. The thud of a body hitting the grass followed a moment later. Astor had also fallen into a limp heap, blood soaking through his clothes.

As I shifted back into my human form, I fell to my knees and broke into a coughing fit that shook my entire body. The world swam as my vision fractured into pieces.

"Ember." Through the haze, I saw Will crouched beside me, still holding Cori in his arms. I reached for her, my breath heaving, and my hand found Cori's and held on as consciousness fled.

22

Bright sunlight poked me in the eyes. I opened them slowly, soft pillows cushioning my back. I lay on a bed, more comfortable than I'd been in a long while. I didn't recognise the room, but it looked like the inside of a hotel room. A second bed lay adjacent to mine. Cori's red hair stood out against the white pillows.

"Cori." My voice came out in a croak. I tried to sit up and broke into another coughing fit so intense that I nearly passed out again.

"Whoa." Becks came hurrying in through the open door. "Don't move too fast. You inhaled a ton of poison."

"So did you." Will followed her, fixing me with an accusing stare. "You both scared the shit out of me."

My coughs faded to a feeble wheeze. "How'd you save us?"

"Healing spell, but I've never had to brew something for inhaling poison gas before, and there were an awful lot of shifters who needed help."

"Are they... all right?" A flurry of questions hit me like a jackhammer. "Is Cori?"

Ignoring the others' protests, I pushed upright and managed to climb out of bed. On shaky legs, I crossed the room to Cori's side and sank to the carpet next to her bed.

"She's fine," Will said, exasperated. "*You* won't be, if you keep walking around like that. Between you and the other shifters, it's a miracle I've been able to keep any of you alive."

I sagged against her bed, gripping the bedsheets in my hand. "Does that mean… Astor?"

"He's alive," said Will. "Those assassins are made of freak-ishly strong stuff."

He's alive. "Where is he?"

"Back with Giselle," he said. "He refused to come back into the city with us."

Right. Of course he'd wanted to stay with her. "Uh. *Where* are we?"

"A hotel," Becks replied. "Now will you get back into bed?"

"Since when could we afford hotels?" I rose shakily to my feet again. "We lost two hideouts and never did get paid for that mystery monster job."

"Yeah." Will glanced at Becks. "So, I got a call from the Mage Lords yesterday."

"Huh?" I sank back onto my bed and broke into another coughing fit, my body doubled over. "The *Mage Lords?* What did they want, to charge us for damages?"

"Not quite." Will grinned. "The mages—well, their assistant—called me asking if I knew about an incident involving a bunch of trigger-happy vigilantes deciding to have a shootout on the street. Seems they were calling up people on Magic Avenue, and I was the first to answer the phone. I was more than happy to point them towards the culprit."

"Twill?" I spoke between coughs. "The mages actually did something?"

"I'm as shocked as you are," he said. "Even the mages couldn't ignore that automaton the hunters set loose, even if you did burn it to cinders."

"They know?"

"Sure, they know someone shifted into a dragon and breathed fire, but not that it was you. What you did yesterday was considerably more conspicuous."

"What I did?" Oh. I'd dug my way out of the ground and taken flight over the countryside in full view of whoever had been left at Malkin's party. That was bound to have drawn a fair bit of attention. "Did the mages catch Twill?"

"Yes." A dreamy expression passed over Will's face. "Supposedly they found him hiding in another witch's basement in central London. I wish I'd seen his face when they hauled him in."

"So we're back in London." I gave another wheezing cough. "How on earth did you bring all those shifters back here, given the state some of them were in?"

"I didn't," he said. "I took them to Giselle a few at a time, using Astor's car—she *loved* that, by the way—while I treated them for the poison. Half of them had left her house by morning."

"And I've been out cold the whole time?"

"I had to use a super-strength healing spell on you, so yes." He cut me an accusing look. "Since you inhaled half a gallon of poison and dislocated your shoulder to boot. Only Astor was worse off than you."

"But he survived." If I knew anything about Astor, he was probably in an even worse state than he'd wanted anyone to know. In addition to all the bullet wounds, he'd also have to contend with everything that Malkin revealed about the nature of his tattoos. That they were no ordinary markings, but magical.

"Because of you," Becks said. "I can't pretend to understand why, but he did save all our lives back there."

"Some of us more than once." Will rubbed the back of his neck. "I can't pretend it doesn't feel weird, owing a life debt to someone who once hunted shifters for a living."

"It's fifteen levels of fucked up," I agreed. "As well as the personal shit that happened between the two of us, Malkin told me… he told me that a dragon shifter killed his family."

My throat tightened. I hadn't been in any state to take in the implications back in the Stronghold, and frankly I wasn't much better off now. Hell, it might not even be true. I'd know if my people were ruthless killers of innocent humans. Surely.

"Ember…" Becks hesitated.

"Don't," I said. "I—I'll come back to it another day. When Cori's awake."

"Of course," said Becks. "Instead, let's talk about your ridiculous plan to climb out of an elevator shaft while carrying a cat shifter and a half-conscious assassin. Because Will and I both have words to say about that."

"You came back to attack Malkin," I protested. "There was no other way out. And, you know, I'm a dragon."

"You don't say?" Will shook his head, looking mildly awed. "I still can't believe it, personally."

"You've known me for two years."

"Yeah, but I've never seen you shift until a few days ago, remember?"

"Guess it's no wonder Malkin wanted to keep me as a pet." A growl rumbled in my throat, turning into another cough. "I left him behind. I suppose it's too much to ask that he suffocated to death."

"He was wearing a mask, so I bet not," said Becks darkly. "I hope he's a long way from here."

So did I, but I knew we hadn't seen the last of him. He and I still had a score to settle, after all.

A faint wailing echoed through the wall. My head lifted, alarm filtering through my relief. "What was that?"

"Our faerie friend is having a rough time." Will's mouth turned down at the corners. "As soon as he reached the surface, he started freaking out. I think he's been trapped in the dark for so long he can't deal with being exposed. That, or the iron poisoning affected him worse than it looked."

"He can stick with us for the time being." The poor guy had been trapped in jail for what might have been years. Like the other dragon.

Grief welled inside me all over again. I hadn't known him, but I'd spent so long thinking Cori and I were the only dragon shifters left. To see another... and then to watch him die...

I crawled back to Cori's bed and stroked her hair, murmuring to her.

It's okay. We aren't alone. I'm sure of it. When you're awake, Cori, we'll figure this out.

———

CORI DIDN'T WAKE up that day, but I gradually gained the stamina to get out of bed. Will, Becks and I ordered room service and played a half-hearted game of Monopoly before we all turned in for the night.

I woke to the sound of a window being opened. My eyes slid open when someone climbed into the room with the quiet sureness of an assassin who regularly spent his time running over rooftops.

"Astor." I half sat up in bed. "Good to see you."

"You should be warier when an assassin creeps into your room in the dead of night."

"You're not that scary." Abruptly I became aware of my exposed skin—I'd slept in my underwear—and my dragon side registered his approach with interest. He was dressed in plain black, and if his face was a little paler than usual, not a visible trace remained of his wounds. "Also, didn't you get shot seven times?"

"Nine." He ran a hand over his shoulder, the movement a little stiff. "Giselle says I'm more scar tissue than skin."

My own skin burned at the thought of him being unclothed, exposed, and desire stirred in my core. When I properly sat upright, I immediately broke into a fit of coughing. *Typical.* Astor trod softly to my bedside as I struggled to get my body back under control.

"How are you—not like this?" I wheezed.

"Got lucky."

Or those tattoos protected him. Given his reaction to learning he wasn't entirely human, I suspected he'd prefer it if I didn't bring that up.

"What?" he said, apparently reading more into my expression than I'd meant to convey.

"Nothing." Still coughing, I tried a smile, but it felt strained. "I'm just… glad you're alive."

Incredulity crept over his face. "I know you've been unconscious for more than a day, but you saw me with Malkin, didn't you? You saw him let me back into his confidence."

"You were pretending to spy for him for the past two years, I know." I swallowed against my dry throat. "Do you think he's alive?"

His expression darkened. "I drove back to the estate on my way here, and it's completely empty, at least from the outside. It's like someone cleared out the whole place overnight."

"Weird." I hadn't seen the last of him, I was sure. "Well, I guess the hunters won't be hosting any more high-class parties for a while."

Maybe the Mage Lords would invite us to one, if they really had taken notice of us, but I had my doubts.

"No." He took a step back from my bed. "I should go, anyway. I just wanted to check on you."

"Wait." I struggled upright, eyeing the half-open window. "Aren't we on the tenth floor? Are you sure you didn't fly up here?"

Shouldn't have said that. Astor stiffened at once, picking up on the underlying implication. "No, I climbed."

"It was a joke." He knew that, too, but I couldn't help myself from digging deeper. "I've spent my life surrounded by supernaturals, remember? I don't give a shit what super-powers Malkin gave you."

He looked straight past me. "You don't understand. I was a lab rat as much as…"

"As the other dragon shifter? And me?" Bitterness choked my throat. "I know all the rumours about Elites, and at least half of them aren't true. Just like it isn't true that all shifters are murdering—"

"Some are." His hands clenched at his sides. "I know Malkin talked to you. That he told you—about my family."

"A dragon shifter killed them." Glass shards dug into my throat. It was true? What did that mean for us? My own absent memories made it impossible to know for certain of my own role in my fellow dragon shifters' actions. "Why didn't you tell me?"

"You know why." His mouth twisted. "You don't—"

"Understand?" I finished. "Understand what, exactly? It's in the past. We can't change it."

"Exactly," he said. "Shifters killed my family. I thought they were evil incarnate. The day I saw you was the first time

I considered I might be wrong. I can't erase anything I did before then."

"Because dragons can't change their scales, right?" I didn't believe that. What he'd done for me in the Stronghold was proof of that.

Disbelief crept over his face as I rose from the bed, crossed the short distance to the window, and pulled his mouth down to mine. Heat flared between us, all too brief. He broke off the kiss first, took a decisive step back.

Then he pulled himself out the window and disappeared into the night.

———

WE PACKED up ready to leave the hotel the following morning. My cough had mostly faded, but my memories of the previous night felt more like a half-remembered dream than reality.

Besides, we had bigger problems. Cori still hadn't awoken, while the faerie was so hysterical at the idea of going outside that Will had had to leave him confined to his room while he went to fetch breakfast for us. When he came back, he also held a copy of a local newspaper.

"Hey, you're famous, Ember." He showed me the first page, which was half occupied by a giant photograph of a bright-red dragon.

I stared. I'd never actually seen my full shifted form in the mirror, but the red-scaled beast soaring over the rooftops looked like something out of a storybook. The memory of flight trickled back in—feeling the rush of the wind against my scales, spreading my wings wide and unleashing the fire from deep inside me—and then reality slammed back into me. If the newspapers had picked up on the story, any remaining hopes we might have had of staying under the radar had vanished along with the Stronghold.

"We made headline news?" said Becks. "Wish someone had offered us payment for it."

"Does it mention the League?" I asked as Will flipped the paper back over. "And that they've been experimenting on shifters for decades?"

"I wish," said Will. "There's no mention of the League, and barely a footnote about the automaton incident. I think the mages want to avoid sparking a panic."

"Gimme that." Becks snatched the paper from his hands and swore. "Is it just me, or is this article implying *we* were responsible for the criminal damage? *Destructive dragon wreaks terror on London?*"

"Great." I snorted at the headline. "The mages know that isn't true. They wouldn't have ordered Twill's arrest if they didn't."

"God forbid the press actually report accurately," Will said with an eye-roll. "The good news is that nobody got any photos of us in human form, that I could find."

"No." Becks flipped the page open and squinted at the text. "I can't read this, but isn't that a picture of Malkin's house?"

"What?" I leaned over her shoulder, my heart racing in my chest. There was indeed a photo of the ruined countryside around Malkin's house, together with an eyewitness account from an 'esteemed local gentleman' describing the vandals who'd attacked his property. Several other reports from attendees at the party also confirmed the incident.

"Arseholes," I said. "We saved their lives, even if they don't know it."

Except for Malkin, and if he wanted war, I'd give it to him. I'd already destroyed the Orion Stronghold.

Next time? I'd bring down the whole Orion League.

PREVIEW OF ARISE

"If you can't take the heat, stay away from the enraged dragon."

It was with those words that I addressed the giant tentacled monster that had wrapped itself around a middle-aged woman carrying a shopping bag and was slowly squeezing the life out of her.

"Help!" screamed the woman, clinging onto a lamp post with both hands as she attempted to climb to safety. "The shadows are eating me!"

A few years ago, hearing that phrase in the middle of London would have resulted in raised eyebrows, even from supernaturals. But times had changed. On the plus side, shifters, witches and mages were able to live out in the open without hiding what they were. On the minus side, monsters from Faerie were as common a sight as pigeons in Trafalgar Square. This one did look a bit like a shadow, albeit one made entirely of tentacles and capable of spitting ambulant slime. Lovely stuff.

I reached for my knife. Iron or steel was always a sure bet to kill a fae, but I'd have to be careful to avoid hurting the victim in the process. On the woman's other side, Becks stood in wait, ready to shift into cat form if need be. The three of us had to trade shifts watching over Cori, my sister, who'd been unconscious since we'd rescued her from the Orion League's prison two weeks ago, and we had to fight monsters as a two-person team rather than three.

Knife in hand, I lunged, swiping at a tentacle. Despite its semi-transparency, the iron sliced straight through, and the wriggling tentacle dropped into the road. Urgh.

Becks cut in with her own knife, severing another tentacle, but the thing had at least twenty and the woman was running out of oxygen fast.

Taking careful aim, I stabbed at the tentacle holding her. Shadow shrivelled to grey ash as the iron took effect, and Becks joined me, one sharp knife in each hand. Kitchen knives, but they'd do the job. The woman wriggled free, and I seized the chance to leap at the pulsing mass I could see beneath the tentacles.

The creature spat at me, a wad of viscous black slime that hit the pavement and immediately reared up like a fast-growing plant and grasped at my ankles. I swore and hacked at it, glad I had at least one solid iron weapon to hand.

Nearby, Becks reached the monster's heart. Her twin knives struck home, and the creature collapsed into a mass of tentacles that shrank in on themselves until nothing was left but a greyish mess.

The woman screamed again. Her arms were lifted above her head, and from the angle of her body, something invisible had grabbed her.

Ah, shit. Even shifters didn't have the Sight—the ability to see through faerie glamour—and I'd had no idea the monster had brought backup.

I left the tentacled creature lying in a heap and took aim at where I thought the new enemy was.

My knife passed through empty air. Becks shouted a warning as the target appeared in a burst of light—a fey creature with hook-like hands reaching for my throat.

I raised my own hands in defence—hands now turned into red-scaled claws—and caught the creature's hand before it reached my neck. My claws found its throat, and it went limp.

The woman pointed at me, gaping. Oh, crap. I'd been trying not to use my claws. As a dragon shifter—the only one in London, aside from my sister—keeping a low profile was kind of essential. Especially as I'd been all over the local news a few weeks ago. I'd hoped the papers would move on, as there was no shortage of news to report in the post-faerie invasion world, but I guessed a dragon was a once-in-a-lifetime story.

In fairness, we hadn't made the front page since that first day and had been replaced with the usual stories. Gargoyle gangs brawling in Soho. Kraken in the Thames. A chimera in Green Park. But not a peep about the Orion League. I knew better than to think they'd disbanded. No, they'd taken their depravity elsewhere. They, and their leader, Malkin, wanted my blood. Not just because I was a dragon shifter, but because I'd escaped the Orion Stronghold, their most notorious prison. I'd also destroyed the place in the process. Oh, and I'd kind of trashed his fancy house. The last part might have been the most offensive but equally deserved, given that he was the kind of entitled arsehole who hoarded wealth while everyone else struggled to stay alive in the post-invasion world. That on top of being a murderous would-be despot.

Hence—low profile. I sheepishly hid my hands behind my back and put on an unconvincing smile. "New witch spell my friend is working on."

In fairness, Will probably could manufacture a spell that

conjured up scaled gloves if the mood took him, but he'd spent the best part of the past fortnight rebuilding his supplies after a combination of an attack on our shop and a rescue mission that had forced us to use every asset we had available to snatch Cori from the Orion League's hands.

The fact that Cori had been in a coma ever since had thrown a bucket of icy water over our victory, and my constant state of nervousness about her plight led to things like this happening. I concentrated for several seconds before my claws turned back into regular human hands and I was able to help Becks pull out the bin bags she'd brought to transport the dead monster back to the local clean-up unit.

Yeah. That's what we did for a living now: killed monsters and then cleaned up the mess for a pittance. And for the security of knowing one fewer human-eating menace was loose on the street, of course. Becks stashed her knives away and lifted a bin bag to dispose of the hook-handed fae first.

"Delightful creatures," she muttered, wiping blood on her jeans. She was an unassuming sight in her human form, maybe five feet tall with deep tanned skin and hair that looked like she'd dyed it in an ombre black-brown effect but was actually her natural colour. "Now let's get that tentacled thing in the bag."

Easier said than done. Shoving a mass of tentacles and dead skin into a bin bag was trickier than it looked, and the slime it had left behind didn't help much either. When we'd finally wrestled the monster into the bag and sealed it, the woman thanked us, handing a ten-pound note to Becks. "For your trouble."

She didn't look at me. Freaked out by the claws, I guessed. Not unusual for a non-supernatural human—that is, someone who until two years ago, didn't know any of us existed. I tried not to feel too insulted. At least she hadn't tried to hit me over the head with a fire extinguisher like one of our last clients had. And she'd given us a tip, too.

Becks and I split the bags between us and began the long and torturous task of hauling our cargo down the street. Being Londoners who'd spent most of our lives in hiding, none of my friends could drive, and taking dead faeries on public transport or in taxis wasn't allowed, for obvious reasons. The local pickup was a half-hour walk from here. What the mercenaries' clean-up crew did with the bodies, I absolutely did not want to know.

"What do you want to spend the extra tenner on?" asked Becks. "We can split it four ways or buy something all of us will use."

"What, like weapons? Or decent food for once?" *It's not like Cori's awake to enjoy it,* said a cynical voice in my head which had been getting louder lately. "If you ask me, the guild ought to pay us twice over for bagging two monsters and not one."

"Buy one monsters, get one free," Becks quipped. "I bet they'll pull out some bullshit rule on us again."

"That's what we get for going official." We'd scraped together a living for the last two years through taking on odd jobs, since our former lives had gone up in smoke along with half the city. After our last independent mission had led the hunters right to our doorstep, we'd signed up to the local mercenary unit to lessen the odds of someone trying to knife us in the back. Except the monsters we hunted, that is.

Most people would pick a less hazardous way to make a living, but shifters had possibly even less chance of being hired than other supernaturals did, because in our trans-formed state, some of us looked too similar to the shape-changing faeries who'd invaded the Earth. The only way to prove ourselves trustworthy was to fight *against* the faeries who'd caused so much damage. And try not to get eaten in the process.

My arms were numb by the time we reached the pickup spot, an old warehouse covered in laminated posters advertising employment at the local guild of mercenaries. They called themselves a guild in an attempt to imitate the mages and their posters proclaimed as much, declaring the guild's purpose to be in line with the Mage Lords' long term plan to clean up London's streets so people could leave their houses without being attacked by monsters.

Becks rolled her eyes at them. "I notice nobody's put a bounty on the League members yet, even though they're the ones who caused criminal damage in the middle of London."

"Malkin never set foot there himself, though," I reminded her. "The others all wore masks. Kinda hard to put out arrest warrants on people who all look identical."

That, and I'd roasted half of them alive when they'd cornered me in Magic Avenue. There was a good reason I'd rarely set foot back there since our narrow escape. Turning into a dragon in front of one's neighbours makes for awkward conversations.

"Where in the world is the pickup crew?" Becks said, depositing the bin bag in the designated area by the warehouse with a revolted look on her face. There were already a sizeable number of equally disgusting bags and sacks in the same area. "It looks like nobody's been here in a week."

"No clue." I didn't particularly want to go *into* the warehouse, because it smelled like a troll had curled up and died in it and then been left to rot for a week. Eyes watering with the stench, I backed away from the revolting pile of monster parts and turned to Becks. "I'm going to report this to old Harwood. He'll bitch at me, but honestly. I know watching a bunch of decomposing faeries isn't a nice job, but if they stay there much longer, they'll attract even more Unseelie."

"True." Becks joined me as we turned our backs on the warehouse and gladly left it behind. The buses were running infrequently now but nobody had cleaned the ghosts out of the Underground yet, so the tubes were on pause while necromancers took care of the rampant undead problem. London had a lot of rebuilding to do. So did the world, come to that.

It took a further fifteen minutes to reach the office of the local mercenary unit, but at least we weren't carrying a sack of tentacles this time around. Such places had sprung up all over the city, as you might imagine, when it had become clear that the monsters who'd accompanied the invading Sidhe were here to stay and not at all picky about their taste in cuisine.

The office had once been a bank, but someone had stripped down the signs and replaced them with a crooked handmade plaque declaring this to be the "Mersenerry Gild." I hadn't wanted to get on the wrong foot with our new employer by pointing out the errors, but old Harwood wasn't exactly known for attention to detail.

We found the boss at his usual place behind a desk. He was a middle-aged guy with pasty skin that looked like he'd never seen the sun and thinning brown hair laced with grey. For some reason, the mercenary units attracted people who'd survived the invasion by sheer luck and didn't want to risk their necks, so they'd taken on admin positions to make other people risk their necks instead. They were almost always unpleasant. Old Harwood wasn't the worst boss I'd had, but his current expression was more akin to a manager about to fire us than someone greeting two employees who'd completed a successful project.

"Hey." I gave him a smile, which he didn't return. "We just dropped off the dead faeries at the warehouse. There were two of them, did you know?"

"No," he said. *Yeah, right.* "What was your name again?"

"Caroline," I said, using my current alias. My auburn hair was now jet black, thanks to hair dye, which made me a little less recognisable than before, and it was lucky the cameras which had snapped me in dragon form hadn't recorded what my human form looked like.

"Surname?"

"Hicks. Why?"

"New policy." His gaze shifted to Becks. "Alice, is it?"

"Yes." Her eyes narrowed. "What policy?"

"We need to see official ID from all employees," he said. "Passport, driving licence…"

"I don't drive and I've never left the country." Oh, *shit.*

"Do you have your birth certificate?"

"Well, no. Who carries their birth certificate around? Besides, I lost it when my house was destroyed two years ago. There's nothing left."

A lie. I'd never had a birth certificate. The notebook I'd arrived in London with listed the 11th March as my date of birth and I assumed it was right, because I had no memories before I was twelve and Cori was five. The only other information the notebook had given me was a guide on how to survive as a dragon shifter in a world that wanted me dead.

"Then apply for a new one," said Old Harwood. "There's a waiting list. Until then, you're not permitted to take on work from this guild. There are too many people out to take the money and scarper. We're running a business here."

A shit one. What had brought this on? Maybe the mages had given them a shakedown for their lax approach to security, but even they should know that most people had lost everything two years ago and were lucky to have their lives, let alone anything else.

"Never mind," I said. "We'll go somewhere else. Can we have the payment for today?"

"As I said." He crossed his arms. "We're only hiring registered individuals."

Damn him. "You said there's a waiting list. And we already did the work. We need the money today."

I wasn't kidding. We were running low on supplies and Will hadn't replenished his stock of witch ingredients enough to consider re-opening his shop, which left this as our only source of income. Yes, the mages had given us a reward after Will had turned in a local criminal—or witch, who'd already turned *us* in to the hunters and kickstarted the current shit show that was our lives—but that had only been enough for us to get by for a few days. That, and Will had given most of it to the other shifters who we'd rescued from the Orion Stronghold, but the thought of not helping them after they'd suffered so badly at the hunters' hands was out of the question.

"Too bad," said old Harwood. "You'll know for next time."

Like hell. "Who ordered this? The Mage Lords?"

Please say yes. The mages weren't fans of shifters, but they didn't want us dead. Unlike the hunters, who'd have very good reason to have everyone on record.

"The authorities," said Old Harwood. "Get out. I have work to do."

"Work like moving those dead faeries?" asked Becks. "Why are there so many at the warehouse? Aren't they supposed to be taken outside the city?"

He loomed over us. "Get out."

"But we did the bloody job!" Becks stood her ground, outrage flashing in her eyes.

"And you're unregistered. If you show up here with ID, you'll get your payment."

"That's such bullshit," she exploded. "You should have told us not to take the job if you didn't plan to pay us. We nearly got killed."

"You know what you signed up for."

"Leave it," I muttered to Becks. "It's not worth it." Anything we did to draw attention to ourselves would make things worse for us later. We'd deliberately picked this outpost of the city's mercenaries because it was as far from our previous haunts as possible. Applying for official ID documents was out of the question. I could think of a few people who would be delighted to find a database listing everyone who was supernatural. I didn't need to make the League's job easier.

Becks huffed but followed me outside. A few drops of rain fell, and I groaned at the thought of the long walk home. No way would we fork out for bus fare when the only cash we had was the tenner the woman had given us.

"Bullshit," Becks growled to herself as we walked. "Who the hell makes those regulations?"

"It's gotta be the Mage Lords," I said, burying my hands in my pockets. "They can trace their ancestry back for a thousand years or more. They assume all supernaturals are the same and have nothing to hide."

"They've never had to live in hiding. I haven't seen a mage in weeks, and they're meant to be cleaning up this." She waved a hand at the street, which resembled the others in the area in that half of it was in ruins and the other half pristine. The wrecked shops had been cleared of broken glass, the holes in the road filled in, but few people had returned to places the faeries had run amok in.

"It really doesn't make sense," I said. "They've got to know half or more of their recruits are supernaturals. Most humans wouldn't sign up to go on monster-catching duty except out of desperation."

"Yeah. What are they doing, creating a supernatural registry?"

"Bloody hope not." Rain fell, soaking my hair and sliding down the back of my neck. I growled in annoyance.

"What I wouldn't give to be underground," Becks said.

"Me too." We'd rarely used our tunnels in recent weeks. Though the hunters hadn't so much as stirred, the memories were too fresh and the knowledge that they knew all our best hiding places made me reluctant to take the risk. For all I knew, they were the ones hiding underground now. *Yeah, right. They found it easy to blend in.*

Anger churned inside me, the helpless sort I'd come accustomed to in recent weeks. I'd been counting on today's payment to put towards trying another potion to wake Cori. I'd thought she was just exhausted or drugged when we'd first brought her home, but it had been weeks and she hadn't so much as opened an eye. We depended on spells to keep her alive, spells which wouldn't last much longer if we didn't get more cash to buy them. If not for Will's connections with other witches, we'd be screwed.

All this because the Orion League had decided all supernaturals, especially shifters, deserved to be wiped off the face of the earth. Why they hated dragons in particular was a total mystery to me, and not only due to my lost memories either. It just plain made no sense to hate someone you'd never met, like most hunters did.

Except two people had met me. Malkin, the deranged head of the Orion League, and Astor, who… well, the less I thought about him the better.

"What now?" Becks said dismally. "We can't go back there. We'll also have to come up with new names, and I've had enough of keeping track of aliases as it is."

"Yeah, I'll have to look at the local job centre."

"We said no local stuff."

"We probably won't be sticking around," I said. "The

neighbours are already starting to ask questions. I'm sure they know about our other guest, too."

The guest in question was a half-faerie named Kit who spent half his time shrieking at the wall and the other half muttering to himself in languages none of us knew. He'd been held captive and tortured in the Stronghold for an unknown amount of time and had barely spoken a coherent word to us since we'd got him out.

A shadow flickered in the corner of my eye, while a dark reflection passed through the nearest window.

"Becks," I whispered. "I think we're being followed."

"You're shitting me."

I jerked my head towards the window of the shop we'd just passed. A crack split the glass in two, but the blurred image of a figure clad in black was unmistakeable.

Great. Looks like we're getting into another unpaid fight after all.

My claws itched to come out, but I rested a hand on the knife at my belt instead. The figure disappeared from sight as soon as I tried to get a closer look at his reflection in the glass. He was male—I thought—but a hunter would have attacked openly. Right?

"Who's there?" I called out.

No reply. A suspicion latched onto me. I pushed sodden hair out of my eyes, anger burning brighter than ever. Dragons didn't like water, and the curtains of rain masking my vision only served to make me more pissed off at the world in general. I wasn't about to play peekaboo in the pouring rain with a possible adversary, so I began walking again, at speed.

"What're you doing?" Becks asked. "I bet we can corner that guy."

"I can't be arsed, frankly."

I surreptitiously peeked over my shoulder. He must know we were onto him by now, but he kept his distance.

Why the hell is he *following us?*

Or rather, why not just talk to me openly? It wasn't like we'd parted on bad terms. At least, I hadn't thought so. It was anyone's guess as to what was going on in *his* head.

"He's still following us," Becks muttered as we picked up the pace again.

"I know."

"Why not ask what he wants?"

"Clearly he's in assassin mode again and doesn't want to talk in public."

He also shouldn't easily be able to keep pace with a pair of shifters, but a certain branch of hunters—the Elites—had been given upgrades which made them slightly more than human. That revelation had been one of many we'd faced in the Stronghold, and to say he hadn't taken it well was an understatement. I could only assume that was why I hadn't seen him since.

I unlocked the door, my wet hands fumbling the key, and footsteps sounded behind me.

I spun around to see Astor—the man who'd tried to kill me, saved my life more times than I could count, literally taken a bullet for me—and then, after sharing a bone-melting kiss, had vanished off the face of the earth.

I expected… I didn't know what I expected. An apology, maybe. A 'nice to see you'.

What he said instead was, "I know how to wake your sister."

ABOUT THE AUTHOR

Emma is the New York Times and USA Today Bestselling author of the Changeling Chronicles urban fantasy series.

Emma spent her childhood creating imaginary worlds to compensate for a disappointingly average reality, so it was probably inevitable that she ended up writing fantasy novels. When she's not immersed in her own fictional universes, Emma can be found with her head in a book or wandering around the world in search of adventure.

Find out more about Emma's books at
www.emmaladams.com.